THE RISE OF SHIROI NAMI

THE HIKOBOSHI SERIES
BOOK 4

S. J. PAJONAS

ONIGIRI PRESS

© 2021, S. J. Pajonas (Stephanie J. Pajonas). All rights reserved.

Cover design by Najla Qamber Designs.

This is a work of fiction. Names, characters, businesses, places, events, and incidents are either the products of the author's imagination or used in a fictitious manner. Any resemblances to actual persons, living or dead, or actual events is purely coincidental.

❦ Created with Vellum

THE RISE OF SHIROI NAMI

CHAPTER ONE

"Let's see what we have here." The light shining in my eye intensifies and dies away, leaving a sunspot behind to obscure the doctor sitting in front of me. I blink the tears from my eyes and close them long enough to make the spot disappear by half.

"Well, this is promising." With a flick of his wrist, he shines the light in my eye again. "The surgery was a success. Your optic nerve has healed, your cornea is scratch-free, and the swelling is gone." He swivels away from me on his chair and grabs his tablet. "All the scans look good too."

I sigh and lean my shoulder against Rin, sitting next to me. He rests his hand on my knee, steady and strong.

"Excellent," Isao says with a smile. I wince as I try to focus on him across the room. With his wings folded against his back and the dark skin of his arms and legs on full display, he cuts a sharp profile against the white walls. It took me a few weeks to get used to his clear blue eyes, but I still have shocks of surprise when I see emotion in them. His happiness at my diagnosis is all over his face.

But I can't help the despair building in my chest.

"That's great," I mumble because I can feel the letdown coming. This is the good-news prelude to a bad-news main event.

The other surgeon in the room crosses her arms. "So, Yumi, how do you feel?"

"How do I feel?"

Rin hears the irritation in my voice and rubs the stubble on his cheek.

"I look in the mirror, and I'm not sure it's me. That's how I feel."

Her eyebrows draw inward, and she sucks in a quick breath. "Do you think you're dissociative?"

I pause, and I'm careful not to roll my eyes. I just got this new eye, and I don't want it rolling out of my head.

"Do you think I'd be able to tell if I was dissociative?"

She thinks for a long moment. "Maybe?"

Rin chuckles and shakes his head. "She's fine... well, probably."

"I'm still getting used to the fact you genetically engineered everything *for* me. Like it's me, but not me."

Rin holds my hand, though, and that feels real. His love radiates through our palms, and when I squeeze his hand back, I know I'm still in love with him. *That's* not strange.

When we returned to Kurai after the battle on Hikari, Shiroi Nami assessed our injuries and determined who would need surgery and who could wait... or had to wait. In my case, they needed to grow a new eye for me — a new eye they would harvest for the cells to repair my current eye. Yes, that's as creepy as it sounds. And when I look in the mirror, it seems the same as it did before. The ghost of the grown eye hangs over my head, though.

I just don't understand this concept. They don't have jump drives or long-range starflight, but they can grow people and animals from scratch. They can take consciousness and transfer it at will.

That sort of thing shouldn't be allowed. But then again, I'd be half blind without this. I shouldn't fight it.

The surgeon's smile pushes the boundaries of her face. "I understand, and I think you'll be fine. You'll get used to this and all the other ways we do things here." She shrugs as she gathers up her tablet. "This is the future for us."

She means this is the future for everyone. Shiroi Nami does not buy into the android future Aoi Uma wants. They believe humanity's future is, well... standing right next to us. Isao's wings whisper as he adjusts them.

"Wait," Rin says, holding up his hand to keep the surgeon in the room. "What about the other injuries?"

Rin's voice is worried, and rightfully so. My migraines have gotten worse in the last few weeks, and so has my memory. I hold back a sigh. It's Rin who's the King of Weary Sighs, not me. Kazuo isn't here, so he's pulling double duty while Kazuo is out scouting the neighboring territories looking for allies.

"The other injuries..." The surgeon sits down, and my stomach drops. Whenever a doctor has to deliver bad news, they do a few different but distinct things. They sit down. They sigh and lean on a table or wall. They come to sit right in front of you and make eye contact.

"We've run into a problem with the other injuries."

She pulls up the scan that was done in the hospital in Susami, back on Hikari. I wasn't in that hospital for long, but it was long enough to pull data on everything that had happened to me.

"We've healed the broken ribs, bruises, and sprains. The

damage to your leg? Well, we've done all we can with gene therapy. But your main problem is your brain."

"My main problem has always been my brain."

When no one laughs, I break the tension with an eye roll. I'm pleased to find the eye stays in my head after all.

The surgeon pulls up a new scan and places it next to the old one. I draw in a breath and hold it. Even I can tell my brain is more damaged than before. The shading and colored regions are more intense. Rin skates his hand over my shoulders, pulling me to him.

"The damage is significant now, Miss Minamoto. And one thing we can't do here with therapy is repair brains." She sits back in her chair. "Brains are so complex as a…" She pauses as she grasps for the right terms. "As an organ of cells, an organic structure. One thing affects another and then another."

"But…" My eyes fall on Isao, and his chilling smile returns.

"My cousin wants to know more about how I was made."

My regular doctor laughs. "Don't we all."

The surgeon looks from Isao to me. "I'm going to leave you to discuss specifics. My specialty is surgery." She rests her hand on my shoulder. "I'll ask the neurologist to come and speak with you."

Great. Another doctor to discuss my failing brain with.

When the door closes on her, Isao steps away from the wall. "This is not my first body. This is my third."

"What?" Rin's face drains of color, and he pulls me a little closer.

Isao gestures to himself, a short wave to his chest. "This is my third body and probably my last. Did you know I'm over ninety years old?"

I press my fingers to my mouth. I've spent a lot of time with Isao over the last few weeks of recovery. I always assumed he was born and raised like this. That a mother gave birth to him, and this is the personality he developed from living as a bat-man for his entire life.

I need to stop assuming things around here.

I wish I didn't need to ask.

"Over ninety? How?"

He tips his head to the side and looks to the doctor. The doctor nods his head once.

"The technology that Aoi Uma uses to steal consciousness from people and put them in Fukusha Model Eights is *our* technology, Yumi. They stole it from us."

"Why am I not surprised?" Aoi Uma, run by the craziest bitch alive, Narumi Ogawa, is a corporation of thieves. They will buy, steal, and cheat their way to the top. No matter what. Treaties and laws? Those are for losers, as far as Narumi is concerned. The woman has no soul, I'm sure of it.

"It's easier to imprint consciousness into an artificial system like the androids. They were able to retrofit everything to their own standards within a week or two."

"How do you know all this?" Rin asks, his voice touched with awe. "No one outside of Aoi Uma knows what they do in there."

Isao shrugs, and his wings shudder. "We have our spies."

"So, let me get this straight," I say, leaning forward and looking at both the doctor and Isao. "You're saying you just" — I wave my hand in a circle — "grow up a body and transfer your consciousness into it whenever you're ready?"

"That's exactly what we do."

The ethical roads my thoughts wander down are twisted and dark. I can only imagine how this could be used as a weapon. But it could be a salvation, too.

"I, um... I have a million questions."

"Of course you do." Rin leans over and gives the top of my head a kiss. My hair is a shaggy mess, just a few centimeters long. I can't wait to grow my long hair back. I'm ready to buy a wig at this rate.

"But the real question is, would you be willing to do the same thing?" Isao asks.

I swallow, trying to force my throat to work.

"We could grow you a new body in three months. You wouldn't be forced to live out the rest of your life with this broken one."

I look down at my body, my arms, my hands. I think of the scars I've earned and the way this flesh feels to me. How different would that be?

Glancing over at Rin, he avoids my eyes and stares into a blank space past Isao. Whenever Rin is quiet with me, I know he's contemplating something big.

I clasp my hands together and decide not to decide.

"I need more information. There's no way I can jump into something like this." I raise my finger. "And just so you know, my decision is most likely going to be a no."

Because I may be the adventurous type, but not *that* adventurous.

Isao cocks his head to the side. "The offer will remain open."

CHAPTER TWO

All I want to do is head back to our room and get some rest. The idea of downloading myself into a new body is... well, just scary enough to give me nightmares. What happens to the people who don't make it into their new bodies? Does their consciousness live on forever in a machine? Surely, this has happened in the past. If it hasn't, I don't want to be the first.

My fingers itch to grab my tablet and start the investigation process on this. This sort of technology is just the thing my homeworld sent me here to document. This is something everyone at home would want to know about.

Tick, tick, tick, tick, tick. The clacking nails of one of the spiders, the kumojin, makes its way down the hall towards us. I press my back to the wall and avoid it. Isao steps to the side while it skitters past, off on an errand. Its nails clicking on the floor remind me of my dog, Ninjin, when I have neglected his nails.

"Do you really find them that repulsive?" Isao asks. "I

don't think I've ever seen one attack someone or do something they're not programmed to do."

Programmed. He thinks of them more like machines than animals.

"I'm not sure what to think of them, so in the meantime, I'll just avoid them."

Isao raises his eyebrows and walks in front of Rin and me.

Rin leans in close. "We should talk about next steps as soon as Kazuo has returned from his scouting mission."

"Have you heard from him yet?" My inbox has been quiet, with not a word from Kazuo since he left.

He shakes his head. "Nothing. But it doesn't worry me."

I nod, unable to express my reservations about everything.

After my three months on the Southern Continent undercover, I had a price on my head. Atsumi, Rin's ex, wants me dead after I beat her in a knock-down drag-out fight and got her demoted. We killed the yakuza assholes who bought my contract, but I'm not sure that problem is resolved. I may still be owned by somebody on Hikari. Narumi Ogawa, head of Aoi Uma, is pissed I recruited Shiroi Nami's army of mutants to our cause and stole her spy, Saki. If Narumi still had Saki in her grips, she'd be one step ahead of us. Now, she's running to catch up.

Speaking of Saki...

"Hey, Isao." I reach forward to tug the back of his shirt, but I'm rebuffed by his wings. "Sorry. How are things going with Saki's reprogramming?"

"If you stopped by my lab more often, you would know the answer to this question."

Rin glances at me and raises his eyebrows. Sigh. Busted.

"Sorry, yeah. I know I haven't come by in a while."

He glances over his shoulder at me, folding his wings to one side. "It's fine, cousin. I know why you don't come."

Because Saki betrayed me right when I thought she was my friend. She lied to me, told me a bunch of crap about a phantom organization called Samurai Seven. It never really existed. It was a ploy to get me on her side. It was all a ruse to keep me busy so Narumi could swoop in and capture me. Fucking Narumi. She has to go.

But when Saki wasn't under Narumi's control, we had a… a rapport. We shared stories. We laughed together. We drank together. We had the same basic drive to stop Aoi Uma and their android advancements. Aoi Uma stole her life and crammed her consciousness into an android. And despite living on in an artificial body, she *still* wanted to get rid of the Fukusha Model Eights.

That really says something about how horrible the situation is.

"To answer your question, the reprogramming is going well. With Rin's help and what he uncovered from your data device, my team has made significant progress with the core drive functions. We have given her a 'moral code' based on the fiction of Earth's past. I have high hopes that she's very close to completion."

"Even with her consciousness and her human conscience intact?"

"Core functions are… like a set of operating instructions that can't be accessed unless the android is shut down and in hibernation mode. Plus, there are other safeguards for androids that are out walking in the world. It would be easier to change this in the product development and building stage, but this is what we have to work with." As if this is no big deal, he shrugs, yet I know he has only worked on a few androids in the past.

My heart speeds up at this news, and I forget the weirdness of my newly healed eye. If we can reprogram the androids, then we don't *have* to deactivate them. We could stop more from being produced and live with what they already built. I think this would be ideal for everyone. Androids would cease to function as they got older, and they would still be around for the transitional period. People could learn to survive without them.

"That's good news. I'd like to come by the lab and interview you about the work. Would that be all right?"

He holds out his hand. "I don't enjoy being on camera, and it's not advisable to put my image out there for the universe to see. I'm happy to talk to *you*, but that's about it."

My cheeks heat as I imagine the panic or ridicule he would get just by being him. Hell, I am still not used to this guy, this half-bat, half-man that shares the same last name with me. What will Hikari think of him, of Shiroi Nami, when they finally claim power back home?

"I'll talk to him," Rin whispers in my ear.

"Talk all you like. It won't make a difference," Isao says, a chuckle in his voice.

I bring my fingers to my lips to stop a smile. He has the super hearing of a bat as well.

He stops in front of us and cocks his head. "I hear you in two places at once."

Huh? I'm not sure what that means until we follow him farther down the hall and stop at a conference room. The lights are off, and the room is crowded with people, their faces lit by the giant wallscreen on the opposite wall. Shintaro, my twin brother and ultimate pain in my ass, stands in the back, his arms crossed, a wild grin on his face.

"But when it came to politics in Yamato, Empress Sanaa Itami wielded her power like a ten-ton sword..."

Oh, shit. That *is* my voice.

A murmur passes through the crowd of people as footage of our empress plays across the wallscreen. I remember this sequence well. The scene showcases the empress in her royal kimono presiding over a New Year's celebration, fades to a shot of her in a smart suit negotiating laws with members of parliament, and ends on a slow pan of her actual sword — Kazenoho, in all its glory — in the Yamato Artifacts Museum. Someone in the front row of the room points to the screen, and I pull my lips in to press them tightly. The photo of the empress in full samurai warrior gear next to her sword is making quite the impression on these people.

I'm not sure it's positive.

Considering my voice-over stating how Empress Itami used everything in her power to get her way, I'm absolutely sure the room is not happy.

I scan the rest of the room and assess my chances of getting out of here alive. Ryoko stands next to Shintaro, her arms crossed and her frown buried in her face. I know she's seen this documentary before, but it must be hard to see it again under our circumstances. She catches sight of me, softens into a sympathetic grin, and elbows Shintaro.

Shintaro turns, sees me in the doorway, and approaches with a wide smile.

"I thought this would be a good primer for what's coming, so I got everyone together to watch."

Anger has turned my body into a rigid stick. The room is getting louder and louder with mutterings, and my resentment builds with it.

I relax my lips enough to speak. "You should have *asked*

me first." My jaw is so tight, it comes out more like a growl than anything. "I could have been here and managed their expectations."

Shintaro shrugs. "It's not like any of this isn't true."

"Then," I stress. "It was true, *then*. Not *now*."

From next to Ryoko, Reina Hirohata's niece, Aimi Hirohata, waves a timid hello. We've become friends over the last few weeks, as she's around the same age as me. We couldn't be more different, though. She's not interested in romantic relationships and finds my connection to Rin puzzling. She grew up being privately tutored on the Southern Continent, hidden away as an anonymous member of Shiroi Nami. Her favorite hobbies include watching comedy shows, making hand-woven baskets (I am not even kidding), and learning how to cut down enemies with a sword. She's odd, but it's charming in its own way.

"This is great," she whispers to me, and I struggle to decide if she's being sarcastic or not.

A smile cracks her placid face in two. Sarcastic, yes.

"Thank you?" I close my eyes and sigh. This day sucks.

Her aunt stands up and raises her voice. "Turn it off!"

I cringe as Reina waves her hand at the front of the room. As the vice president for scientific advancement, she is the last person I want to piss off.

Time to go into Damage Control Mode.

"Lights up," she commands, and the room's lights zoom up to full brightness. Several people blink and turn to find me in the doorway. When she sees me, she stalks across the room, her face set in a grim frown. Fuck. Here we go.

I hold up my hands. "If I had known you were going to watch this documentary, I would have been here to explain. Shintaro, though..." I turn to shoot daggers at him with the power of my fierce glare. "Shintaro didn't warn me ahead of time."

"Then, please. Explain." She waves to the wallscreen. "This? This is what you have in store for us? A power-hungry monarch bent on homogenizing our culture and bending people to her ways?"

My throat closes up, and I try to swallow through it. "That's really not the way it is back home. Orihimé is... complicated. Much like here."

God, I wish Kazuo was here. He and the empress are about the same age. He worked for her, and there was definitely something between them for some time. He could explain this better than me, what she had to go through to unite the original settlers of Orihimé and the immigrants from Earth.

"Here, we are independent," she says, stabbing her finger downward. "Negotiations? Parliament? What kind of nonsense is this? We form our own corporations and make the laws as best fits our goals and aims."

I lift my chin. "And maybe that hasn't worked out so well for you so far, has it?"

Reina's jaw tightens. Behind her, Daito and Miho Nomura rise from their seats. Next to them, Michio Hayashi, the head of Shiroi Nami, sits and listens. My stomach stiffens into a knot as Reina takes a step closer.

"Now, now," Rin says, stepping in to cool the mood. Without touching her, he scoots Reina back a pace. "Maybe you should listen to what Yumi has to say about this."

The room cools, and even the smile slips from Shintaro's face. He loves a good time, especially at my expense, but this was too far.

I gesture to the chairs. "Please, can we sit?" My voice wobbles, so I clear it without trying to appear weak.

These people hold my life in their hands. They are influential and powerful in ways that I will never be. But they need to be my allies, and I can't be afraid of them. The moment that I show fear, this is over for me. I might as well quit.

They sit back in their chairs, and I pull a chair around to face them. Sitting down, I take a deep breath and rub at my face. My injured eye takes a moment to focus. Focus. I should focus on the facts.

"We've never really spoken at length about where I'm from, my homeworld, Orihimé."

Daito and his wife, Miho, glance at each other, and Michio Hayashi folds his arms over his chest. Not a good sign.

"We have seen your videos and heard some tales from Kazuo," Michio says, a huff to his statement. "It hasn't given us much to go on."

"Okay, let me start from the beginning then." I spread my arms wide and produce a smile despite the frowns on display. This is the kind of storytelling I enjoy doing. "When the Exodus from Earth happened, ships left every nation to colonize the universe, right? And from Japan, there were two generation ships, one that went to the Vega system" — I hold out one hand — "And another that came here to the Altair system. Yet there were still many Japanese who lived on Earth and settled there, awaiting their own fate, either to stay on Earth forever or leave as their ancestors did."

I bring my hands together. "And that's what we're trying to accomplish here, bringing us all back to one family. Because eventually, yes, everyone left Earth. There were only a few million living there in one big city, and they packed up and traveled to Orihimé. But on Orihimé, they found a backwards society, devoid of technology and equal rights, and ruled over by a savage dictator."

"No technology?" Reina asks, leaning forward.

"None. Calculators were high-tech. Except in the northern part of the continent where my ancestors worked on technology in secret and developed the animal translation chip, which you already know about."

It's one of our best pieces of Orihimé tech. The rest of the technology and information on the data device is from Earth.

"So, our Empress, Sanaa Itami, she's from Earth. She grew up there, came to know her heritage, and brought Terrans to Orihimé, hoping to start over on a new planet. They never expected to run into these native Orihimé people."

Daito and Michio nod, and the room is warm with understanding.

"So, to make a long story short, the Terrans arrived on Orihimé and overthrew the dictator in a brief war. They freed the Orihimé natives, and they all tried to live peacefully together."

"But... I feel a but coming." Michio huffs again, not relaxing his arms one bit.

I hold up my finger. "Yes, there is a but. Despite arriving on Orihimé several hundred years prior in a spaceship, the people still did not trust technology. Women were oppressed." I nod to Reina. "Poverty and unemployment were at an all-time high. There were so many things to work on, you know? And Empress Itami, she was young back then and hard-headed, and it took her a long time to find common ground between everyone because she was just as stubborn as they were."

I don't mention that there were other problems with the empress. Her friends and family had abandoned her for several years, over a decade. That betrayal left her bitter and angry before she found peace. They eventually came back to her, but she has never been the same. She has two sons with her husband, and one son was almost killed many times by a rogue rebel faction. Really, her story could fill several books, more than a lifetime's worth of material.

I point to the screen behind me. "I made this documentary almost a decade ago, in my late teens." I lean forward and clasp my hands together. "I grew up around the empress and her family. Our families were close, and her family was my family. Everything you saw there in that video was footage that I took on my own *without her permission*. Just like her" — I laugh at the irony — "I was young and angry because women, outside of Terrans and their descendants, didn't have the right to vote. And the empress was letting it happen."

Ugh, the anger grew inside me until we gave everyone the right to vote five years ago. It was a long, hard road but worth the pain in the end.

The triumph we all felt, including how happy the empress was, warms me from head to toe. I smile, remembering the celebrations, but when my eyes settle on Michio, Reina, Daito, and Miho, a chill washes over me.

Michio holds up his hands. "Vote? You let your people *vote?*"

All the blood leaves my head.

"Voting on laws and..." Miho pauses to grasp for the word. "Elections?"

Michio snorts. "Elections are for common people. We did away with those two hundred years ago. The way here is to be the best corporation for the job. We are to guide the people to bring profits for Hikari and the corporation. Women's rights and poverty?" He waves those aside like they're a nuisance. "Everyone here is the same unless you cannot perform your job. That's the only thing that matters."

I sigh as I sink back into my chair. These people have no concept of democracy, no compassion for the downtrodden, and no love for competition. And here I am, trying to appeal to them and make them understand what we went through at home? It's going to take a lot more than this to get through to them.

From the back of the room, Aimi lifts her arms into the air with two thumbs up. Yes, yes. I know. I'm blowing this.

How much farther can I push them?

"And that's the way you want to keep it? Corporation after corporation ascending to the throne until there's nothing left of the workforce to keep them there?"

Daito rubs the stubble on his face, and I glance over to the doorway to find Rin doing the same thing. Everyone is questioning me and my motives.

"Because that's where you're heading. Look at your birth rate. Look at the actual people online talking about barely scraping by. Look at the suicide rate. *Look at Aoi Uma.*" I laugh, and it's bitter and cold. "I may hate Narumi Ogawa, but she sees this clearer than you do. She knows the birth rate is dropping, and there'll be no one left to run your planet unless she stuffs everyone into androids to live forever as servants."

I stand up and point at Hayashi, despite how rude the gesture is.

"Watch the documentary again. Read the articles that came after. See what we accomplished. And don't talk to me about *my* mistakes, *my people's* mistakes, unless you're willing to admit your own."

He stands up to bluster, but I turn and walk away.

"Come back here! We're not done with you."

I pivot on my heel and raise my chin. "No. When you're ready to discuss your future, then I will be ready to listen."

Shintaro raises his hand, and I high-five it as I walk from the room.

"I'll be in Isao's lab," I mutter, storming past Rin. "Meet me there later."

I gave them all a lot to think about, and even Rin needs time to digest this information. It's time to find out what's been going on in the lab.

CHAPTER THREE

"Here so soon?" Isao looks up from his workbench where he's interfacing with the tōsha projections that power his hookup to Saki. His brother, my other winged cousin, Wataru, sits in front of Saki. His forehead is creased as he stares at his tablet.

"The party broke up early." I cross the room to his workbench, pull out a chair, and climb onto it. I'm about half the size of Isao, and his chairs were meant for giants, not small women.

Isao smiles as he avoids my eyes. "I've seen your documentary, more than once. I had a feeling it wouldn't go over well with everyone else."

I lean forward and rest my chin on my propped hand. "What did you think of it?"

"Well," he says, pushing his tōsha to the side so he can concentrate on me, "I watched it because I was interested in finding out what your homeworld was like." Wataru glances up from his tablet and stares at Isao. Isao sighs. "Yes, and to see what kind of work you do. It may not seem like we're related, but we are. It's important to me that you represent the Minamoto name with honor and respect."

This pulls me up from my resting pose. Honor and respect — two things I've heard a lot about in my life and two things I've hated on and off for years. Honor comes from having a good heart. Respect is earned, not bestowed upon someone because of who they are.

Isao's clear eyes drill through me. "You have something to say, cousin. Say it."

I look at both Isao and Wataru, waiting for me to challenge them.

Fine.

I remember my first few weeks here on Kurai, back when I was in the hands of Buichi Tamura and Aka Matsuba, and how afraid I was to speak out. I was close to death several times because of my mouth. But now, it's time to be me.

"You know what's worth more to me than honor and respect? Character. A person's character determines how much respect they earn, and that determines how honorable they are. I don't care if you find me lacking. I have beaten myself up about my personality for years. Do you think you'll do me any worse?"

I snort and roll my eyes.

Isao tilts his head, a small smile pushing at the corners of his lips. "I thought the documentary was insightful and well done, and according to Shintaro, it was what pushed your empress to work harder for equality for everyone."

I shake my head. "No. I was a stupid kid who only made things worse for her. It almost ruined our relationship. My father and mother were heartbroken for years over what I did.

It showed a horrible side to my character, and I spent a decade repairing that relationship."

Wataru returns to his tablet, uninterested in the ramblings of a little girl.

"I think you have underestimated yourself, Yumi. Shintaro and Kazuo believe in you. Rin loves you. And after seeing the documentary, I knew you were the right person for our future — the right person to force us to look at ourselves."

"Me?" I hold back a scoff. I am the wrong person for pretty much everything here.

"Maybe you're the right person for all the reasons you don't want to hear about." Aimi joins us in the room. "Sorry," she says, jerking her thumb at the door, "but I decided to eavesdrop before coming in."

I ignore her as she stuffs her hands in her pants pockets and rocks back on her heels. Isao looks at us both for a moment before deciding to move on.

"Let's wake up Saki, shall we? That's what you're here for, aren't you?"

My throat dries, and my upper lip beads with sweat. I haven't spoken to Saki since Narumi took her over. What will happen when she wakes up? Despite my fear and the way my heart is trying to escape my chest and run away, I nod.

Let's do it.

"Okay. I just need to wake her from hibernation."

Wataru sets down his tablet and stands beside me. Even sitting on this giant chair, I feel like a tiny bug next to him. And he's so quiet. Far and away, the quietest of the Minamoto family here.

We sit and watch, hoping for a sign that this is a good idea. Maybe it's a terrible idea; I don't know yet. Sweat gathers on the back of my head, but I don't move to whisk it away with my fingers. I'm afraid to even breathe.

Saki's eyes flicker open, and I catch my breath in my lungs.

"Ah, good." Isao studies his display. "No errors. Saki? How are you feeling?"

Saki looks from me to Wataru and then slowly turns her head to look at Isao. I'm comforted that she's been well taken care of since the battle in Susami, back on Hikari. They have healed her injuries, her hair has been combed and pulled into a ponytail, and she's wearing clean clothes. She looks down at her shirt before shrugging.

"Fucking confused. Where the hell am I?"

I let out my breath in a huff of a laugh. "That's the Saki I know." I glance at Aimi, and she's watching Saki with an intense glare. Maybe she's waiting for a sign Saki will need to be destroyed? Aimi isn't wearing her sword, so I'm not sure what she'd do if Saki jumped up and tried to kill us all right now.

Saki turns her face to me, and I lose my smile. "Yumi? What's going on? I thought…" She presses her fingers to her temple and closes her eyes. "Something is different."

"Saki, please state your high command rules," Isao says, and Saki blinks at the question.

"These are new. The first rule is to not hurt humans or, through inaction, let humans come to harm. The second is to obey commands from humans unless it violates the first rule. The third is to protect my own existence unless it violates the first two rules." She ponders this for a moment, pulling her bottom lip into her teeth. "Looks like my days of cage fighting are over."

Isao's lips twist as he tries to keep a smile from forming.

"Do you understand what will happen to you if you try to violate these rules?"

Her head jerks up. "I will shut down. Huh."

Aimi smiles. "I like that."

Isao nods, satisfied with her answer. "If you fight it, you will fry your brain, so be careful. It's part of your very survival to adhere to the new rules."

I don't like this development, but I now believe that a malfunctioning android is better off as a dead android. I close my eyes and curse the person I've become.

"Okay," Saki says. "I understand. Yumi?"

My eyes pop open, and Saki is looking at me. The emotion in her eyes is untouched and raw.

"I think... I think I did horrible things."

A hand tightens around my heart. "You didn't do horrible things, Saki. Narumi Ogawa did."

She turns her face to the door, so I glance over my shoulder. Rin stands, watching her.

"You still have Rin," she says, relief coating every uttered syllable. She drops her head. "I'm so... so... so..." Her head twitches again and again and again as she repeats the word.

Isao returns to his controls and shuts her down.

"Feedback loop. I need to work on her emotional control next before we turn her on for good."

Rin enters the room all the way and stares at Saki. "Will she pass the Doshisha Test?"

Isao shakes his head. "I've created a tell in the pupils. They will pulse during extended questioning lasting over five minutes." He looks up from his console. "I read all your notes on the test before deciding. Only someone administering the test will be able to tell."

"I would like to see this for myself. Soon."

Isao nods. "Of course."

"It won't matter in the end," Aimi interrupts. "We'll be rid of all their kind, eventually."

"Yes, but 'eventually' is a long way off," I remind her. She nods her head, conceding the point.

I hold off the torrent of emotions raging through me as I picture Rin back in his job, the black garb of Kiiroi Yama and a sword on his back. The life we left behind. But I suppose this entire existence has only been temporary.

I need to accept that my people may be years away from arriving here. I should plan for a life on Hikari, even if it's short-lived. I must look to the future.

I can't do that if I'm dead.

What are my choices? Rest and recuperate here on Kurai, for months — maybe years — until my brain and body are healed? I don't know if that's even possible, what with the state Shiroi Nami is in and Hikari on the verge of all-out war.

I hate to even go down this road, but...

"Isao, about earlier. I need to know if you can fix me." His hands halt in the air of his projection. "I know you fix androids." I wave away his obvious unspoken objection. "But what about everything the surgeon and doctor said? We can't fix my brain, right? Even if I sit around and let it heal."

He sighs, and I can feel the regret from across the room. "Your brain is permanently damaged, Yumi. Your chronic migraines are a sign that it won't get any better either. It'll just get worse." He shrugs, his wings rising and falling. "If we start now, we could get ahead of any further memory loss. Rin has told me that your memory is important to you."

"Aren't memories important to everyone?"

"Touché. I have ninety years of memories, and I wouldn't want to lose any of them. I can still remember being a kid. We grew up outside of Susami on a farm." His gaze becomes distant and soft. "A far cry from where we are now." He gestures to himself. Yes, Shiroi Nami has come a long way.

"Yumi," Rin butts in, coming to my side, "I think we should talk about this before you make any decisions. I want you to make the best possible choice for your health."

I tip my face to him and read his concern like a book. What would happen to *us* if I did this? Would he be able to accept the new body? Would it matter to him?

Maybe it would, and that would matter to me too.

"Sure. We can talk about it tonight after dinner."

"You should have all the information you need to decide, though." Isao leans forward to alight from his chair. He tucks his wings against his back as he inches around Saki's slumped body at the desk.

He crosses to his bookshelf on the other side of the room and drags his finger across a stack of leather-bound notebooks. I press my hand to my chest and feel the notebook that Kazuo gave me nestled in my bra. Such old tech compared to everything else in this lab.

"I'll let you borrow this," he says, handing it off to me. "I've been lucky to keep them here all these years, though they've come with me on many evacuations, and I have digitized them as well. But it's nice to have the real thing to flip through." He smiles as the book settles between my two hands. "Writing on paper reminds me of my childhood, long ago. My body may be quite new." He snaps open his wings, and I gasp before we all laugh. "But my habits are a million years old."

Aimi snorts a laugh. "A million years is right." She winks at him and waves to us. "I'm out of here. I need food after that captivating film I just watched."

My grin is lopsided and half-hearted as she leaves. We still have far to go in our friendship.

"Thank you," I say to Isao, holding the book in my hands and wondering what treasures are inside. Maybe it's filled with pages of data? Or personal experiences? Excitement buzzes in my chest as I consider all the possibilities.

"Besides that, there are a few other things to know."

I set the book in my lap and focus my attention on him.

"The growth process will be about three months, and we do all of our lab work off Kurai. There's still too much extraneous radiation here to make growing complicated bodies a viable business. We have a heavily shielded facility off-world, on a moon around the fifth planet of this system."

Hmmm, I had given little thought to the other planets in this system. What are they like? Our home system has rocky worlds and a few gas giants. Orihimé is the only planet with plenty of water. It just lacks land, which is why we went on this mission in the first place.

"There's so much we can do for you. Make you stronger, healthier, give you the ability to photosynthesize energy, faster recovery time from injuries… The list is endless."

I pull my bottom lip into my teeth as I imagine the person I could become. Strong, capable, healthy — I could use those traits to everyone's advantage, not just my own. I mean, yeah, I can be selfish and annoying at times, and I know it. It's one of my fatal flaws. This would be a way to fix that. By making myself better, I could better serve those around me. Isn't that what most superhero stories are about?

Rin looks from Isao to me and back to Isao before dredging up one of his weary sighs. "I think you've already made your decision."

"No, no," I say with a chuckle as I stand up. "I'm willing to think on it. It's a big decision that should not be made with my ego."

"That's what I like about you, cousin." He raises his finger. "And I've been giving some thought to your earlier request to interview me. I would like to make a proposal."

My smile widens. "Go on."

"I've seen your documentary more than once. You have talent. I'd like for you to make a documentary about Shiroi Nami. It can be short. It doesn't have to be something long and complicated." He stretches his arm out to encompass the room, this base, his people. "But the people back home on Hikari have forgotten about us and the work we do. They once held the same vision for our future as we did, and after the war, they turned on us. It's time to show them how to move forward, into the future."

I smile and nod, but I'm wary of getting too involved. After the run-in I just had with the executives in Shiroi Nami, I'm not sure they're the corporation I should be championing. I believe in democracy. It's one of the core tenets I grew up with. We have a constitutional monarchy at home, but the people have a voice. They elect officials, and the parliament hears arguments and passes laws. The empress is just a guide; she keeps everyone in line and on task. An itch in my chest tells me this is what the people need here, a voice.

But Shiroi Nami should be given a chance. What I see, right in front of me in Isao, is the future. And it can still be the future for a prospering corporation.

But they don't *have* to be in power to get things done.

"A documentary is a great idea." I lift my chin and pull back my shoulders. "I'm honored you asked me to do this. Thank you."

His smirk is just this side of amused before he turns to

work on Saki again. "Don't let the fame go to your head, cousin. We Minamoto still have a lot of work to do."

A lot of work is an understatement.

I press the book he gave me to my chest with one arm and lace the other arm through Rin's.

Yes, I have work to do.

CHAPTER FOUR

Rin returns to our room after his meetings and finds me shaky and tired with Ninjin wrapped around my hip. We drop off Ninjin to eat with the other animals and decide on a late dinner together. Good idea because I'm starving. Snagging one of the private tables in the cafeteria, I'm grateful that most people have moved on to drinking, cards, and movies in the common rooms. I need the peace.

"You're awfully quiet tonight."

Rin pushes a bowl of curry and rice across the table to me, and I snap out of my head. I keep imagining my body growing in a tube on some far-off moon. Is it me? Or is it someone else? How do they protect it from forming its own consciousness? How does the growing even work? Do they have some sort of hibernation containers or something?

Or something. I both do and don't want to know.

"I've got a lot banging around in my brain." I lean over the bowl and inhale. "Ah, curry. This smells amazing. Thanks."

Rin freezes for a moment.

"What?" I ask, raising my spoon.

"You said the exact same thing three nights ago when we last had curry."

My chest grows cold. "We had curry three nights ago?" I don't voice, 'I don't remember that,' because this will only cause Rin despair. Instead, I try to deflect. "Well, if this is just as good, I'm sure I'll be full in no time."

"Anything in particular you want to talk about?" If I'm good at deflecting, then Rin is a master. He moves his food around in his bowl, trying to find the right ratio of curry to rice.

"Is there booze? I think this might be a night for a beer."

He smiles as he chews, and his cheek pulls the scar on his head around. "There's always beer."

I swing my feet to get up from the table and raid the fridge in the quiet kitchen. But before I can stand, someone approaches holding two tall glasses of beer with delicate foam tops on each. Bless you, kind woman.

"I thought you'd ask for them. She had to bring them up from the cellar," Rin says as the woman deposits them on the table.

"Oh, I hope you didn't go through too much trouble," I say, bringing my hand to my heart.

"No trouble at all." She smiles and shakes her head before wiping her hands on her apron. "We ran out during dinner, and I was restocking the fridge, anyway. Enjoy! And let me know if you want dessert."

Once she's back on her way to the kitchen, Rin picks up his glass to toast. "To your good health."

I clink my glass on his and sip. Ahhh. It's been a week, maybe more, since I last drank alcohol. I had wondered if alcohol was a migraine trigger for me, and I wanted to eliminate it from my diet to test the theory. We shall see.

"Good health is always worth wishing for." I set the glass down and eat. Delicious. I place my fingers on my lips as I sink into the flavor. "One thing's for sure. Shiroi Nami has the best cooks."

"Better than the monks at Ryuanji Temple?" Rin's lips twist in a sardonic smile.

He's joking, of course. Those monks made the blandest of stews. "Absolutely. I'll miss this food someday, I'm sure of it."

We're quiet for a moment, just enjoying the food, when Rin clears his throat and sips his beer.

"You've changed the last few weeks," he says and tingles flow down my back.

I sit up straight. "Really? How so?" I try to keep the worry out of my voice. Changed? For the worse? It can't be for the better. I know I'm not a kind and empathetic person at heart, so it must be for the worse. He has to be questioning my sanity right about now.

"It's in the little things." Rin chews and gazes across the table at me until he's swallowed his mouthful. "You seem more... adaptable, willing to compromise. You're smiling more. You're... comfortable."

I smile as I prop my chin on my hands. "Go on." He's grasping for words because, in his head, the observations are negative. I'm not more adaptable; I'm less hostile.

He chuckles. "Yumi, you're different. Do you see it for yourself?"

I return to eating my meal. "I think it's part of the natural progression of life that when a man with wings swoops down and saves you from dying, you'll reconsider your outlook on your future."

"Is that it?" He raises his eyebrows.

And yes, despite the negative view I have of myself, he's right. I have changed somewhat.

"Mmhmm. Look, I don't want to say I've turned over a new leaf or anything. I'm not *fundamentally* different. I just... I considered we might be here for a long time — longer than you or I want to be. I can't just be an observer like I want. I have to be an active participant in this world. Learning to listen and compromise was something the empress tried to teach me growing up. She's finally gotten her way." I laugh as I look down at my meal. Empress Itami would laugh too if she were here.

"You're a formidable woman, Yumi. Strong enough to handle anything this world throws at you."

"Well, I don't know about that. I don't think I could take any more injuries."

Rin sets down his spoon and drinks his beer. "I want you to consider *not* transferring yourself over to a... a new body."

It's clear from how he's ended the sentence that a new body is distasteful and wrong. Despite all the time he's spent here and the relationships he's fostered with Shiroi Nami, Rin is a purist. He's never undergone plastic surgery to correct his scars, never cared one bit about how he looks or how his body works. He never even wanted a pet because that was too far out of his normal. I'm glad he and Ninjin have gotten along, but I know that having a dog was not something Rin ever wished for.

I decide to approach this from a different angle. It's not a 'warping of our beliefs'; it's a way for me to heal.

"Really? I would have thought you'd be all for it, what with all the pain and suffering I go through. My memory is becoming worse every day. I can't even remember what I had for lunch yesterday or, apparently, dinner three nights ago." I pat the notebook in my bra and consider bringing it out to see what I *did* have for lunch. "You and Isao seem to get along fine."

"Isao is a good man, for sure. But..."

I scrape the sides of my bowl and finish dinner. "I sensed a 'but' coming."

"I think there are some unknowns here we need to understand before they go any further with you." He raises a finger. "I have a lot of questions."

"You sound like me."

He smiles and continues. "How many times have they done this? How successful has it been? What if there's something different about you, because you didn't grow up here, that would cause the system to fail? What kind of modifications will they do? Will you still be able to have kids?"

Kids? Kids are the furthest thing from my mind right now, but I'm glad Rin is thinking of it for me.

"Oh. Hmmm. I hadn't thought about that."

Rin nods. "That's why I'm here." He reaches his hand across the table to me. "I love you, Yumi. You're my light, my reason for getting up every day. I want to have a family with you if we can."

Tears fill my eyes as I slip my fingers into his. His hands are warm and strong; something I love about him, his strength.

"Me too." My throat hurts from forcing the words past the lump that's formed there. "I don't deserve you."

"Ah, no. I think we both deserve each other." He lifts my hand up and kisses my knuckles. "So, please, let's table this idea of a new body and work on healing you until we're needed again. Okay?"

I nod. In my heart, I know it's the right thing to say 'no' to this path, but it's an option I feel I must examine. I should say 'no' for a thousand different reasons and say 'yes' for even more. Still, if Rin would like me to consider it for longer, I can do that. He says I'm more willing to compromise. I can compromise here.

"Come." I tug on his hand and jerk my head towards the exit. "Grab your beer."

I keep his hand with mine as we sip our beers and head down the hallway back to our room.

His smile is soft as I bring him into our suite and close the door behind us. The door locks with a quick flick of my fingers. I hand him my beer, and he sets both glasses on the low table in our sitting area.

"Rin." I stop and take a deep breath. Reaching out for him, I find his waist and pull him within a few breaths of me. "I want to, um, clear the air between us."

"Yumi—"

"No. Just hear me out." I clear my throat and work hard to keep the tears at bay. "It's been a rough few weeks, right? And I'm sure during this time when I've been..." I gesture at my eye and head. "When I've been incapacitated, you've had the pleasure of dealing with my unpleasant side." He opens his mouth to talk, but I place my fingers on his lips. "I know I'm a selfish, irresponsible, and petulant little girl. Some have even called me spoiled. And I am." I hang my head. "Back home, I got what I wanted, even when other people stood in my way."

He pulls my fingers from his lips. "Wait, wait." His gaze is intense. "I don't know why you've constructed this new narrative for yourself the past few weeks, but everything you've just said is a total and complete lie."

I pull back. "What?" I scoff. "It's the truth. One hundred percent."

"A selfish person doesn't put their life on the line for

others. A petulant person doesn't sit quietly in meetings, listening to what other people have to say. You're not irresponsible. You do the research, and you make decisions based on what you've learned. Remember what Okamoto said to you at that last meeting in Susami?"

"No." I shake my head and squeeze my eyes shut as I try to recall the meeting. I remember speaking to a few people, including Haku's yakuza brother who wanted to kill me. Did we speak to Okamoto, the CEO of Kiiroi Yama, that day?

"He said he heard wisdom in your voice every time you spoke."

I try to access the data in my head. A shade of Yori Okamoto is in my memories, along with Rin's ex, Atsumi, behind him on her knees. She had tried to kill me against Okamoto's wishes, and then he demoted her. If Narumi Ogawa doesn't kill me, Atsumi will.

"What's going on with you?" Rin takes my hands in his and draws them close to his chest. He radiates warmth, and I want to sink into it. "Tell me why you're trying to change."

I lift my chin. "I'm making more enemies than friends. And I need friends, Rin. *Need*. I need people by my side who care for me enough to want to fight. I already lost Ayamé... and Saki... and Mara, and I don't want to lose you too."

"You will not lose me." He squeezes my hands tighter to his chest. "You don't have to change for *me*, understand? I have seen you at your most vulnerable, and I still want to be with you. Just like you have with me. I am full of faults, yet you still seem to be interested in me. So, no more clearing of the air is needed."

He lets go of my hands, slides his hands down my sides, and reaches around to grab my ass. Hello.

"Now, I saw that look in your eye at dinner." He leans in to lay his lips gently on my jaw, kissing once, twice, three times up to my ear. I thread my arms around his waist and pull him closer. My body warms up at a blinding speed, the need to be close surging in my belly. I pull at his tucked shirt, desperate to touch my hands to his warm skin. When my fingers brush against him, relief pours over me like the rush of a waterfall. My eyes fill with tears.

"You've been... neglected," Rin purrs in my ear, and I nearly lose it with laughter. The emotional whiplash from devastation to happiness is enough to knock me over.

"Neglected?" I thread my arms up the back of his shirt and pull him closer. He hums as he follows the line of my neck down to my collar. Hmmm, I can play this game. "Yes, I've been very neglected."

"Not for much longer."

Rin is suddenly possessed. He's a man who's been starving for weeks and now sits at the buffet ready to fill himself to bursting. His hands are swift, pulling for my shirt, loosening it, and dragging it up over my head in one fluid motion. He doesn't hesitate and goes straight for my bra. We both sigh, long and low, as his hand cups my breast and his fingers glide over the nipple.

It has been weeks since we last had sex. Wait, it's closer to months, multiple months. We haven't had the chance to press our bodies together since the night in his apartment in Susami. So long ago. And I was broken and upset then. Now, I'm healed. The bandages are off, and my body feels like my own again. My brain may not be in good shape, but my heart is ready for this.

Rin grabs my ass again and lifts me up. I wrap my legs around him and cradle his head in my hands as he turns to exit our common room and head to the bedroom.

Knock knock knock.

Rin freezes.

"I didn't hear anything," I say, squeezing him with my thighs. "Keep going."

Knock-knock-knock-knock. "Yumi! I know you're in there." Shintaro's voice roars through the door. "Open up! It's urgent!"

"Fuck off!" I yell back.

I turn my face back down to Rin, and his expression is concerned.

"Don't," I plead. "We need this." I lean in and brush my nose up the side of his cheek. Mmm, I love the way he smells, herbal, clean.

He growls as he sets me down. "Stay right here."

I fold my arms over my chest to keep myself warm as he strides to the door. With a flick of the lock, he opens the door a crack.

"You will leave us alone if you want to live."

"Whoa, okay, Rin." Shintaro's voice cracks and wobbles, and I smile. "Just... I guess it can wait until tomorrow?"

"Can it?" Rin's voice is like ice.

"Absolutely."

Rin shuts the door in Shintaro's face and locks it.

"We're good." He crosses the room in three great strides. I throw my arms around his neck as he lifts me up and carries me into the bedroom.

We meet the bed with a thump. For a moment, I'm reminded of the first time we had sex, tangled up in each other as we navigated his apartment in Shin-Osaka, drunk and desperate for each other.

I hook my thumbs into my waistband, but Rin is faster than me. Within a heartbeat, I'm naked.

"That was quick," I say, yanking at the covers. Rin always makes the bed.

"I aim to please."

The words send a cascade of shivers down my arms and back. I place my hand on his chest. "Then, you'll let me be on top."

One thing I've enjoyed about Rin is the way he takes control in bed, just like he does pretty much everywhere. He knows what he wants, and he keeps going on until he has it.

My turn.

His smile turns devilish as he lies back and lifts the covers for me to slide in, to his body, his warmth, his touch.

I'm struck by the moment at Club Seiun back in Shin-Osaka when he told me he was into me. He was forthright and charming, and he told me I could make all the decisions that impacted my future. That he was mine if I wanted him.

And there were the nights in Kitakyushu where I would have given anything to be with him. Those were the hardest days of my life.

He's right in front of me now, so I take my time with him. I let my hands linger on every centimeter of skin. I close my eyes and let the pads of my fingers coast over his scars. I bring my hands to his shoulders and pin him down, taking more of the kiss than he's giving. Take take take. I've given everything up for this mission, for the people of Orihimé and Hikari. It shouldn't be a surprise that I want something back.

Rin's hands clutch my hips and skate up over my back. We break contact as he slides his fingers up my chest.

"Why do you still have clothes on?" I ask him, the smile infecting my voice.

"Because you haven't taken them off."

"Okay then." I shimmy down his legs and slip my fingers

into the waistband of his pants and underwear before pulling them down and off. "That's better."

With us both naked, I don't want to wait a moment longer. We could tease each other for hours, play this out until we're both exhausted and spent. I just want him close to me, in me, his arms around me. That's my happy place.

I don't have a lot of happiness in my life.

I hesitate for a moment, and Rin's keen eyes catch it.

"Don't stop. Keep going." His tone is insistent, and it snaps me out of my head again. Slowly, his hands take control, even though I'm on top. He directs my hips to his, and instead of foreplay, I bring him in right away.

Ohhhh. It's been ages since we did this, or a few weeks, but who's counting. I keep my hips moving, my hands on his chest so I can feel his breath and heartbeat.

Don't leave me, Rin. Don't go.

I know he has to go, and I don't want him to.

More more more. It's too much. I hold it back.

"Yumi, let go."

"No."

He doesn't take no for an answer, and with his hands on my hips, he pushes harder and faster until the spark lights and everything comes tumbling down. I fall onto his chest, spent, my arms and legs trembling.

He flips me over and pulls the covers up, surrounding us both in the warmth of the bed.

"Mmm, better? See? You just needed to let go."

"I think I need that more often."

"Nothing would make me happier." He sighs as he snuggles in closer. "Listen to me, okay? Things have gotten so complicated these last few days."

I keep my eyes closed and nod against his skin. "So complicated."

"I think, even if your people arrive tomorrow, we should stay here..." He pauses when he feels me tense. "Just long enough to make a difference. To see the androids reprogrammed or disabled, to see Aoi Uma out of business for good."

There's the ring of truth to this. I don't want to deliver a broken and war-ridden planet to my people. They deserve better.

"Okay. I think that's probably our best course of action, right?"

He's quiet for a moment. "I thought you'd be angry with me. I know how badly you want to be away from here."

I sigh as I sink into the bed. "Like you said, it's complicated."

"I'm going to keep my promise to you. I won't leave you to figure this world out without me. We may occasionally split up to handle things, but I will never be far. You won't have to do this alone."

It feels like a hard promise to keep, but I'm too tired to talk anymore.

I wrap us in the covers even tighter and lift my face to his.

Time for positivity.

"Sounds like a plan."

CHAPTER FIVE

I drift from our room on a cloud. I've heard the phrase 'Cloud Nine' before, but I always thought it was one of my father's dumb Earth sayings. Like, whatever happened to Cloud Ten or Eleven? Why is Cloud Nine so unique?

I don't know. These are the things that go through my head on a daily basis.

I'm warm from my head to my toes. It's not enough to know someone finds you special, that someone loves you. Actually seeing and feeling that love? That's a whole other level. Rin loves me for who I am. He thinks I'm attractive, even on my most horrid days. He promises he won't leave me, though I fear that every single moment. It all gives me the confidence I need to keep going.

"Yumi!"

I freeze, my foot forward in mid-step.

Shintaro. Didn't he come and almost interrupt us last night? With something urgent?

I turn around and spot him running up the hall towards me. Something's different about him. He has a genuine smile on his face, and his strides are long and light. He looks like he's had the weight of the world lifted off his shoulders.

"Yumi, wait!"

I pause as I let him catch up. He dips down, grabs my waist, picks me up, and swings me around like he did when we were kids.

"Ha, ha! I have the best news!"

I stumble as he sets me down. "What is going on with you?" I lean back from him with wide eyes.

He throws his arm over my shoulder. "You're never going to believe what happened last night. *Never believe it.*" He stresses every word, and he's so giddy, he's practically vibrating.

"You need to cut back on coffee."

He ushers me forward, speeding me along in the direction of the cafeteria. "Coffee? I am *high on life!*" He throws his head back and cackles, and now I'm really worried about him.

"What the fuck happened to you?"

He rolls his eyes. We round a corner together and smile at two medics who pass us on their way from the cafeteria. Medics? I wonder if everyone is okay.

"Nothing, dear sister. I am great, fine, *amazing*. And you are going to be so thrilled once you guess why I'm so happy."

I wag my finger at him. "Oh, no. No. I don't do guessing games. You know that."

"Come on," he says, stopping me. "Humor me."

"No." I turn and keep going. "And whatever it is, it better be here in the cafeteria because I'm starving from the hours of hot sex I had all night lonnnnnggg —"

I halt in the cafeteria doorway like it's a cement wall. My head buzzes, and my heart leaps into my throat.

"Yumi," Kazuo says, getting to his feet, "I found them." He waves to the table of familiar faces, including Ryoko with tears streaming down her cheeks.

My legs won't work, and I wonder if I've slipped into an alternate dimension.

My former boss, Chiéko, looking like she's seen the bottom of a lake followed by ten years in the sun, rises to her feet with her mouth wide open.

"Holy. Shit."

I force my legs into movement, and once they're going, I can't stop them. I cross the room and land right in her open arms.

"Yumi!" Her voice sounds like sandpaper being dragged over rough wood.

"Oh my God, I thought you were gone, dead. How did you…? Where have you…?"

She rocks my body side to side, squeezing even more than I thought was possible. "Shit, Yumi. It's a blessing to see you."

We pull away from each other and laugh at the tears in our eyes. As hardened media professionals, we have never cried around one another. Cried in private in a bathroom stall, sure. Not this. She wipes my tears with her thumbs before turning away and coughing. Kazuo hands her a bottle of water.

"Thanks," she wheezes out after the coughing subsides.

I peer past her to the other people at the table, all of them bridge crew and a few from the science divisions. Wow. Mari and Jonathan look as bad as Chiéko, but it's great to see them. Mari stands up and hugs me when I approach her. She reminds me, for a moment, of Mara because of the name similarity, and tears rush to my eyes again.

"Kazuo told us what happened to Shien." She sobs once. "He was such a kind soul."

They used to work comms together on the Murasaki. I had forgotten that. And Jonathan, he was at ops. I close my eyes, and I can still hear his voice echoing around the bridge about incoming missiles. He was the last thing I remember before the missiles hit the ship.

"Isn't it amazing? I thought I'd never see them again," Ryoko says, pulling closer to Mari and Jonathan.

I open my arms to them, and they join our group hug. I wasn't close to Jonathan or anything, but I had interviewed him. I remember him as being competent and kind, a person you want to be friends with. It looks like all of their skills kept them alive in the wilderness.

Shintaro joins us and gestures to the remaining two people. "Yumi, these are fellow science team colleagues, Maddie and Erik."

I shake their hands and hug each one of them. It feels good to see my people.

"I'm just so... *stunned*. I thought everyone else from the ship was dead."

We sit down at the table, the door swings open from the kitchen, and one of the cafeteria waitstaff delivers steaming cups of coffee and plates of food. I snag a piece of toast and add cream and sugar to my coffee. Everyone else is slow to follow suit. Whether they're just as stunned as I am or wary of their new hosts, I'm not sure. It's probably best if I try to make them more at ease.

"Please eat. The food here is good. Much better than other food I've had on Kurai."

As they each reach out for something to eat, I'm struck by

how skinny everyone is — skin and bones, leathery, ragged. The toast hits my stomach like a brick.

"It's been months since we last saw each other. How have you been surviving all this time?"

Chiéko's eyes are on the doorway as if she's waiting for someone to walk in.

"It's a long story," she says, her voice barely above a whisper.

Chiéko details the group's survival efforts from the time of the crash. Her life pod landed far from ours, in Aoi Uma territory. Chiéko, Jonathan, and Mari were the only passengers, and thankfully none of them were injured in the landing. They trekked across the terrain until they found another destroyed life pod. Maddie and Erik just barely survived their landing. Their life pod hit an enormous boulder on the way down a mountainside and caught on fire. Maddie has a few terrible burns that have healed, and Erik sprained an ankle getting out of the pod.

I focus on listening, chewing on toast and concentrating on them. My heart aches as they describe the first few weeks of finding shelter from the ambient radiation and their attempts at reconnaissance to acquire more food. They moved around a lot, between three different shielded locations in rocky areas. Once they found an Aoi Uma outpost stocked with food, they were safe for a while, only venturing out when they needed to.

"Then we saw the androids." Chiéko's mouth hardens into a straight line. "They were the hardest to avoid. They combed the hills for days. We learned how to cover our tracks and climb trees. Until one day, they were just gone."

She blows up her fingers. Gone like a puff of smoke.

"That was probably when Aoi Uma executed their hostile takeover on Hikari." I point upward to the planet.

This is now her time to lean in. "You've been there?"

"We've all been there. Me, Ryoko, Shintaro…" I don't know how to start this conversation. How do I tell her about Gen Miyazawa, the traitor who went to Narumi Ogawa and Aoi Uma? How do I tell her about the others who died and I couldn't do anything to save them?

She knows I'm holding back because I won't make eye contact with her. Everything I went through on Hikari is a nightmare except for the time I spent with Rin in the countryside, in… Fuck, I can't remember the name.

I touch the tiny book in my pants pocket and try to divine its name.

I can't remember.

"What's it like?" she asks.

I lift my head. "It's advanced but complicated. More complicated than you or I or even the natives will ever understand. I…" I shrug my shoulders. "I want to go back, but I don't."

She lifts her cup to take another sip of coffee. "Tell me everything about them."

Her eyes jerk from me to the doorway. Rin walks towards us, his demeanor all business. The shoulders of everyone at the table rise up, and the room tenses with fear. They know he's not one of ours.

I try to understand what they see now, and it's impossible. They see a stranger, a native, no one they know or recognize. But to me, Rin is the man who held me last night, kept me from losing my mind and my life on so many occasions.

I stand up and meet him halfway across the room.

"Good morning," I mumble to him as he joins me. "What took you so long to get here?"

"Well, your brother dropped by to talk about this situation, and then I had to spend fifteen minutes deflecting his attempts to flirt with me. You know, the usual."

I grab his arm and squeeze it. "You're a saint."

Time to find my peaceful Zen.

"Hey, everyone." I keep my voice light and pull a smile onto my face as we sit back down at the table. "This is Rin Hara. He's a native of Hikari and used to work for Kiiroi Yama." When Chiéko's eyebrows scrunch together, I continue. "Kiiroi Yama is a corporation here that handles police and military work." I decide to go for complete honesty. "He's also my partner."

"Your… Partner?" Chiéko tries to process this word I've used to describe Rin.

I clear my throat. "We're romantically involved."

She sighs. "Great."

If Rin is put off by her cold greeting, he doesn't show it. He smiles in his amiable way and shakes hands or bows to everyone around the table. He's not warm and fuzzy, and he's never been easy to read either. But I can tell he's trying his best. He knows these people mean something to me.

I can't believe they're here!

Rin sits down next to me. "Ms. Mori, Yumi has told me so much about you. She feared you were dead these last few months."

With her arms crossed over her chest, she's not very interested in hearing anything Rin has to say.

"Well, through no help of your people, we managed to survive."

I cringe at the hostility vibrating through her. But Rin is a seasoned professional.

He nods once. "Aoi Uma is not the kind welcome anyone hopes for. I'm glad you could avoid them." He turns to me. "I was just reading Kazuo's brief before I came here." He smiles again at the people gathered. "Shiroi Nami is more than happy to help you."

"At what price, though? I gather with corporations running things, everything is going to cost money we don't have. What has Yumi had to give to stay here, to be with you?"

My face heats with a flush too fast to stop it.

"Look at her?" She waves to me and the state I'm in. "She looks just as bad off as we are." With a cough, she leans forward. "Darling, what happened to your hair?"

"It's a long story," Rin mutters. I reach under the table and squeeze his knee once before he grabs my hand and holds it.

We're in this together.

"It *is* a long story," I interject. "And I don't want to put you off. It's... complicated."

"You've said that already," she points out.

"I have a great idea," I say, coming to my feet. All the plates on the table are empty, and the cups of coffee are consumed. "I'm sure there are rooms for you all here, and I doubt you have had a bed to sleep in for the last few months. Why don't you all take a few hours to shower and rest? Take a nap. Walk around the compound... Wait."

I raise a finger and shake my head. And before I'm able to warn them, the clicking of a passing kumojin echoes through the cafeteria's door. Jonathan's and Mari's eyes widen as they watch the giant spider creature walk past, off on its errand to wherever.

I sigh. "Fuck me. I was, like, five seconds too slow."

"What the fuck was that?" Mari stands up and points at the door.

Kazuo laughs behind his fist, and Rin closes his eyes in silent prayer.

"Okay, before I let you go, I have a few things I need to warn you about."

Chiéko pulls out my chair. "Sit down and start talking, missy. The showers can wait."

CHAPTER SIX

"So, how do you think this is going to go?" I ask Rin as we stand outside the conference room and await our fate at Shiroi Nami's hands.

"Probably as well as you think it will."

"That's cryptic. Thanks." My face jerks into an involuntary sneer. I sigh as I rest my head against the wall. "I can't believe Chiéko is alive. She's alive." A crazed smile takes over my face. "Rin, I can get everyone back together."

He rests his hand on my forearm. "Don't be too hasty, okay? Let's feel out Shiroi Nami first. When it's time to go in, I'm putting you in the spotlight. Be persuasive."

The door opens, and Reina peeks her head out. "Come on in."

Deep breath. Here we go.

"Yumi and Rin, thank you for joining us. I know it's been a busy morning for you." Hayashi gestures for us to sit at the table across from him as we come around. "We're so pleased you've found more of your people."

And from his smile, it seems that way. Shiroi Nami has

plans of their own for Hikari, for the future, but are we a part of their plans? We're about to find out.

"I'm so relieved they're alive," I say, blowing out a long breath. "Every person we can recover from our original crew is a blessing."

Daito and Miho Nomura both enter the room and sit at the other end of the table. When I look around at everyone present, I realize Shiroi Nami is a lot smaller than any other corporation. There are very few people on their board of directors and only maybe a hundred people here on Kurai. Shiroi Nami has plenty of genetically engineered 'things,' soldiers, helping them hold up their corporation. But that's about it, I think. They are not the large and mighty corporation they used to be.

Even Daito and Miho are not tried-and-true Shiroi Nami employees.

"So, what's on your mind?" Hayashi asks, spreading his arms out. "You wanted time before the board for an important conversation. Here we are."

"Yes, thank you." I bring my hands together on the table. "I appreciate that you were willing to give us some time to make our proposal to you."

Remember, Yumi. Be professional, be succinct, be firm.

Reina's chin tips up as she turns off her tablet and gives us her full attention. Several other people at the table turn to me.

Here goes nothing.

"Before all of this happened, before I met you in Susami, I had an idea of how to deal with Aoi Uma. Unfortunately, Narumi Ogawa knows of this plan, but I don't think she believes I'll follow through on it."

"Is this about you starting your own corporation?" Hayashi glances at Daito and Miho.

"Yes, yes it is." I gesture to the Nomuras. "Before everything happened on Hikari, Rin and I were interviewing people at the Nomura estate to help us form our corporation. I'd like to continue on with this plan."

Hayashi leans back in his chair and folds his arms over his chest. "Why would we need *another* corporation to get involved on Hikari? We don't need more competition. And after your performance the other night, I didn't think corporations were good for *democracy*." He says the word like it's dirty, and I have to calm my instinct to rage at him.

Reina holds up her hand. "Hayashi, please. Let's hear her out."

I blink a few times and try not to show my surprise that she's interested. Her initial reaction to this news in the cafe in Susami was not welcoming.

"I believe we can push the balance of power on Hikari in a few important ways. With my corporation, I will issue a hostile takeover and unseat Aoi Uma from their place at the top."

Reina's smile is predatory. "You'll need an army to accomplish that."

I raise my finger. "Not if we can reprogram their androids." When no one speaks, I feel it's safe to continue. "Isao has been working on the android, Saki, reprogramming her with a set of rules that won't harm humans. It'll make them ineffective as a fighting force. With the androids out of the picture and Kiiroi Yama on our side, they wouldn't stand a chance. Narumi Ogawa could shut down the cities and industries for a time, but I doubt it would last."

Hayashi is silent, his eyes boring into me. "Go on."

That's a good sign.

"Once my corporation holds power, we can get to work. I plan to employ influencers who will help inspire the people of

Hikari to believe in an alternative way of life for them, one in which they have a voice. It obviously won't be me." I laugh, trying to be both light-hearted and self-deprecating. "I'm an inspiration to no one. But I'm sure we can find the right people for the jobs. Then, we'll slowly transition everyone over to a constitutional monarchy under the watchful eye of Crown Prince Koichi."

"This is your empress's son?" Reina asks.

"Yes, her eldest son. Her younger son, Mark, will stay on Orihimé. The people of my world have voted to shift to a parliamentary system without the monarchy, and the empress has heartily agreed to it. That can happen here too," I assure them, holding out my hands. "Trust me. The Itami family does not want to reign forever. They do their job because they have to, but they are not power-hungry. They are merely shepherds."

"Why can't we just do this ourselves? Without outsiders?" Hayashi's voice is full of challenge, and it takes what little strength I have left not to roll my eyes at him.

"Have you..." I pull my lips in and reconsider my tone of voice. "Look at your past. To the people who live here, who live under the rule of corporations, they see one faceless corporation after another rising up and oppressing them. A stranger with an alternative way of life could be just what they need to get out of the rut."

Rin leans forward. "We all know this is risky. The more conservative citizens will be averse to this kind of change. They would rather keep the status quo, even if it meant their own death or downfall."

Hayashi rubs his beard. "Yes, I believe so."

"Which is why," I interrupt, "this will be a multi-step process. We're not going from a corporatocracy to a democracy in one giant leap. I've spent a lot of time reading the files on countries back on Earth that tried to do this. Almost every time, coups toppled new governments when the more conservative factions realized their prosperous lives were ending. The change needs to be gradual."

"And that's why you want to start your own corporation," Reina says, nodding. "I have to ask, why not ask Shiroi Nami to make this change? I mean, I hope I'm not speaking out of turn here," she says, looking down the table, "but this is something we've discussed on other occasions. It was something we were considering."

I pop back in my chair. "I didn't know. I'm sorry for assuming, but after the way you spoke to me in the café, I figured this was off the table for you all."

She looks down for a moment. "I regret blowing up at you. It was a momentary weakness after finding out we had screwed up your extraction from Kitakyushu."

I purse my lips and think. If they had thought about doing the same thing, where does that leave us?

But then I remember how much they wanted the jump drive technology, how they were thinking about leaving.

"What do you really want?" I ask them. Rin's hand rests on my knee under the table, cautioning me to not push them too far. "What's more important to you, to Shiroi Nami? And please, answer honestly. Is it Hikari? Or is it a different kind of life? You have several paths you can take, right?"

Pushing aside my anxiety at being across the table from such influential people, I make eye contact with everyone. I am sure my eyes convey my hope for them.

"We want out, *eventually*," Hayashi stresses. "The general population will never accept what we want for our future."

He means such genetic changes, like Isao and all the creatures here.

"But we can't just blast out of here without enough people to back us, to be pioneers with us. We have about five to six thousand people, maybe more, just waiting for the signal that it's time to leave. Others may join them if the call is loud enough."

Five to six thousand people? That's a lot more than I suspected.

"Okay, we can work with this." My smile makes a few others smile as my chest fills with giddy energy. I'm no politician, but it feels good to be getting something done, to be getting to the bottom of this problem.

I love solving problems.

I hate being the problem.

Reina picks up the train of thought for me. "We'll be here to help with the transition of power, yes?" she asks Hayashi, and he nods. "And then, once things have settled, we'll take the technology you have offered and leave to continue on our path."

"Don't forget. We have a planet in our solar system, one just a bit farther from our sun, that would be a great place for you. I know there's nothing in this system worth terraforming."

Reina nods. "You're correct."

I lean back and give Rin the table. He leans over and whispers to me, "Are you sure?"

I nod, keeping my emotions in check.

"We'd like to get started on our first mission, which is reprogramming the androids, as you've discussed with Isao."

Reina nods as she types into her tablet. "I've read his report."

"While Rin is handling this mission, I will stay here and

start the work involved in setting up the corporation. It's a lot of busywork, forms to fill out, officers to be named, you know." I wave my hand in a circle.

"Wait. You two are not going together?" Miho asks, entering the conversation for the first time. I remember how she flirted with Rin back in Susami, and now her eyes are sharp on me. She smells blood in the water.

"No," I say, and the back of my neck begins to sweat with the finality of the statement, "we should split up for this mission. With all the injuries I've sustained, I need to keep my body from getting more damaged."

"Do you need assistance, Rin?" Miho turns her eyes on him, and I grind my teeth. "I could come along and provide valuable intelligence."

If Rin notices her eagerness, then he doesn't show it. "No, that's fine. We have everything covered. You should stay here with Daito. Perhaps you can help Yumi with her work?"

I kick him under the table, and he smiles.

"It sounds like she has everything under control," Miho says, returning her eyes to Hayashi. Daito's jaw is rigid as he stares out into space, avoiding eye contact with pretty much everyone.

"What are you looking for from us?" Hayashi asks, returning to the conversation.

"Your support, of course. I won't go any further with this if you're not on board." And I mean it, too. There's nobody in this solar system who can help me like they will. Sure, some ex-Aka Matsuba employees will come to my aid, and maybe some of the crew of the Murasaki who are scattered among the citizens of Hikari, but it's not much. Even Kiiroi Yama's assistance through Yori Okamoto is tenuous, especially with Atsumi still alive. My team of trusted people is tiny.

I need to change that.

"I think it bears further discussion but —"

The lights in the room blink out, and the emergency lighting comes on. Everyone looks at the ceiling.

"What?" Rin starts before the door swings open.

"We've got Aoi Uma ships incoming." The silhouette of a giant man with wings in the doorway leaves me breathless. This is not Isao, though. It's his brother, Hidéki. His hair is longer than Isao's, and his skin a few shades lighter.

Hayashi is on his feet in a heartbeat. "What do they want?"

"They're angry. They say we stole their employees, and they're coming to get them. We have ten minutes, tops."

"Employees? We haven't taken any of..." He stops and sighs, turning to me. "They want your shipmates. I'm not sure how they found out about them, but Aoi Uma has been adamant from the beginning that any of your people who landed in their territory belonged to them."

I jump to my feet. "Narumi can't have them."

Hayashi and Reina exchange a glance.

Reina says, "She's right. We can't bow to Narumi Ogawa now."

Hayashi grabs my arm. "Then it looks like we're going to have to get the hell out of here."

CHAPTER SEVEN

I grasp Rin's hand as we leave the room behind Hayashi, Reina, and Hidéki. Miho, Daito, and everyone else in the room heads in the opposite direction. I'm not sure where we're supposed to go in an emergency. When we ended up here after leaving Hikari, I always thought it would be temporary, and we'd be back on the planet before long. I never expected to stay here for months.

Hayashi punches something into his tablet and then raises it to his lips. "Everyone to your rooms and pack your bags quickly. We're abandoning the station. Check your tablets for ship assignments." He accesses his tablet while we walk. "We've got ten minutes, tops. And this is where you should split up if you want to continue with your plan."

"What?" My voice squeaks. "Now? Why?"

We reach a new hallway, and Rin and I need to go left. Hayashi and Reina need to head right.

"Go," Reina tells Hayashi. He runs off.

"Most everyone here will fall back to our moon base around the fifth planet of the system, Kanshō. It'll take at least a week to get there at this time of year, so we'll have to evade capture and punch hard to break out of the gravity well. You understand? You either come with us to our base, or you go with everyone else to Hikari."

She runs off without so much as a goodbye.

I swallow hard, knowing this will be a split-second decision I have to make as soon as possible.

"Come on," Rin says, pulling me along.

We run to our room, and Shintaro is across the hall in his room, throwing anything and everything into a backpack.

"We're getting ready to head to Hikari," he calls out as I fling myself into the sitting room. Finding my most important things first, like the journal Isao gave me, my own journal, my tablet, and anything else I have, I stuff them all in my emergency backpack with the other survival supplies we've accumulated. I don't want to be without food or water, so those go in a separate bag, straight from our room refrigerator.

Rin is quicker than I am, packed before I can blink. With his sword strapped to his back again, he's the formidable warrior, the man who saved me from death on more than one occasion. He takes my breath away.

"Yumi," he says, walking straight up to me and taking my face in his hands, "I'm going to take you to your ship, and you'll go to their moon base."

"Fuck no, she is not."

Out of the corner of my eye, Shintaro crosses the room to us, but Rin keeps his eyes locked with mine. "It's too dangerous for you to return to Hikari. Narumi Ogawa wants you dead. Atsumi wants you dead. The yakuza who bought you?"

My knees weaken, and a small keen escapes my lips.

"There may be a bounty on your head from others in their organization. I won't know until we make it to Hikari."

He pulls me in with a fierce tug, and his lips meet mine in a clash of brilliance that lights me up from the inside out. Like it's the last kiss we'll ever share, desperate and passionate and possessive.

No. I'm not ready to be separated from him again! Those months in Kitakyushu were the worst I've ever had.

But I know what I have to do.

I gasp for air when he pulls away. Wow. That kiss made everything in my body vibrate. I throw my arms around his neck and hold on tight. My instincts are a jumbled mess. There are good arguments for both Hikari and the moon base.

"No." This time the voice is from Chiéko. She joins Shintaro. "No. I'm still your boss, and you know more about these people than I do. We need you with us. Mari and Jonathan need you too."

"What about me? Ryoko? And all the other Orihimé people we left back in Shin-Osaka? You can't just abandon them too," Shintaro insists, reaching for me.

Rin inserts himself between us.

"Yumi needs recovery time. Her brain needs to heal. If she returns to Hikari before she's healed, she could suffer even more memory loss from her migraines."

"Memory loss?" Chiéko's face falls into a frown. "What's going on?"

Boom.

The floor jumps up, and we all stagger as pictures fall off the walls, and a glass tumbles over and breaks.

"Everyone needs to get out now!" Isao's booming voice echoes down the hallway. A high-pitched scream moves overhead from one end of the compound and dies away. "We're firing back, but we only have a few more minutes."

Chiéko screams and stumbles backwards as Isao ducks his

head into my room. His lip jerks in a cocky smile as he extends his wings, just to scare Chiéko.

"Put those away, cousin," Shintaro calls out with a laugh. "You're scaring the ladies."

"Oh my God," Chiéko mutters.

"I've come for Yumi. There's no time to delay."

I turn to Chiéko and grab her upper arms. "It's a long and complicated story, and I want to stay, but I shouldn't. Trust me. You have seen the best and the worst of people back home. You'll do the same here, without me."

I don't want to go.

I know I must.

She throws her arms around me and gives me a quick hug. "Do what you have to do."

I hastily press my lips to Rin's. "I love you."

"I love you, too," he says, his voice turbulent with emotion.

I nod once, look at each of them, grab my bag, and run for Isao.

"Let's go."

———

"I MADE THE RIGHT DECISION, YEAH?" I ask, pounding the pavement next to Isao.

"Your health is important to us. I promise you will see your friends and family again."

The compound shakes and rocks, and another scream of a missile passes overhead.

I gasp, and my heart leaps into my throat. "What about Ninjin?"

I come to a screeching halt, digging my heels into the floor. Isao grabs my arm to stop me from falling over.

"He was with all the other animals this morning. They will all be on an evacuation ship together."

"No. I need to get him." I try to tear myself away, but Isao is insistent.

"I'll confirm as we make our way out." He lifts his tablet as we continue back the way we were going. "Wataru, what's the status on the animals and Yumi's dog, Ninjin?"

"Already taken off. Ninjin is aboard with the others."

My eyes fill with relieved tears. "Thank you!" I call towards his tablet before he turns it off. "Where are we going?" I raise my voice over the rumble of approaching ships.

"To the East Landing Field. Our long-range ships are there."

Anxiety tightens my chest and not just for my dog. I already regret leaving behind Rin, Shintaro, basically anyone I care about. Isao will take care of me, but I never know where I stand with Shiroi Nami, with any of the corporations. I need to make this work, though. I need to rest and recuperate and start my own corporation.

Isao pauses in the hall, and I run into him, accidentally touching his wings. Ugh. I wish I hadn't done that. He shakes them out.

"What's the matter?" I ask as he tilts his head and then sighs, closing his eyes.

"This all happened so fast. I left Saki in the lab."

"No," I gasp and cover my mouth with my hand.

"All of our research is there." He leans over and looks me in the eye. His clear irises almost disappear. "We can't let Aoi Uma have it."

I jerk my head in the lab's direction, the opposite direction of where we were heading. "Let's go."

I don't care what happens now. He's right. Narumi Ogawa

can't know what we've been doing. This is the crux of our plan to topple her corporation. If this fails, there are no backup plans. We will lose.

"Aoi Uma will not destroy the station. We have too much of value here for them to bury us." Isao's strides are so long that I have to sprint to keep up with him.

"Why didn't they attack us before today, then? If they could just come in and bomb us, they could have done that a month ago."

We round a corner and find a wall collapsed in on an office. Isao pushes debris aside so we can climb over.

"They're concerned with image, always have been. They couldn't just attack us outright. They needed an excuse."

I nod. The refugees from our ship were the catalyst.

Isao's office door clicks open before we even reach it, the lights flicker on, and Saki sits in her chair, quiet and slumped forward.

He wordlessly points at the shelves of journals along the wall. I need a bag for them.

"In the cabinet," he says as he sits at his workbench.

I tear open the cabinet and find a large duffel bag that looks like it's seen better days. It's probably as old as Isao. I sweep my arm into the shelf of journals and clutch them to my chest before dropping them in the bag.

"Hello, Yumi, Isao."

I jump, my heart rate spiking at an alarming pace. "Shit." I stumble backwards from Saki, still not able to reconcile the fact that she's been reprogrammed. What if Narumi is in there?

The compound rocks and shakes again, and the lights flicker on and off.

"Looks like someone is trying to restore power. We've gotta

go." Isao grabs his tablet and accesses the comms. "Alpha One, how much time do we have to reach you?"

"Is this a secure channel?" I whisper to him, and he nods.

"No time left. We're lifting off." Hayashi's voice is calm but cold. He's pissed. "We took out two of their ships with missiles, but three are landing right now. North wing. That leaves the south and west for you. Godspeed."

Isao closes his eyes and sighs. I've never seen him despondent, so this is not a good sign.

"What's south and west?" I ask Isao while approaching Saki.

"Off the south, we have one long-range shuttle hidden in a blind and a path to the wilderness. West is the other landing field where your friends and family are." He grabs the bag I packed and throws it over his back, between his wings, like it's an old habit. This is his bag he's carried everywhere. "But they will be leaving too. Soon."

"Call them now," I say, pointing to his tablet. "Tell them to wait."

I turn to Saki and try to calm my nerves. "Hey, we've gotta go. We're in danger here."

"You're in danger?" She hops off her chair, sinks to her knees in a sumo squat, and bounces a few times before standing and rolling out her shoulders and neck. I've seen this routine before when she would prep for a fight.

"Yeah. Do you think you can help us get out of here?"

Over my shoulder, I hear Isao contact Rin. "We need you to wait. They've cut us off from our escape."

"I can give you ten minutes," Rin replies. "Aoi Uma has bypassed us for now, but it won't last. Emergency power to the blinds will only last another… Eight minutes."

Isao lowers his voice, "Eight minutes is not enough time, Yumi. We should head for the long-range shuttle."

What do I do?

Do we chance making it to the shuttle with only the three of us? Or do we join the rest of our team?

I should get out to the moon base, but I know, deep in my gut, I should be with my people. *My people.* And I told myself that I would start listening to my gut more.

This is what needs to be done.

"We go to Rin. And we go as fast as we can."

CHAPTER EIGHT

"Which way is west?"

"Are you sure?" Isao asks, turning to walk in the opposite direction we had been going in. "You're risking your health by going back to Hikari. If you end up hurt, there's only so much we can do for you."

"I know." I increase my pace into a jog, and Saki jogs along with me, sticking close. "But I can't be useful sitting on a moon base, right? And I want to be useful. There's so much I can be doing. And you wanted me to make a documentary, right? I can't make a documentary about the struggles of Hikari citizens sitting a million kilometers away."

"It's more like three hundred million kilometers, but I hear your point. Keep moving."

Isao directs us down hallway after hallway until we've passed the cafeteria and conference rooms, and we've reached the other side of the compound. I think I've only been here four or five times. The laundry and maintenance rooms are in this wing.

He comes to a screeching halt, and I crash into him. Saki pulls me back from falling over.

"Thanks," I mutter to her. "What?" I ask Isao, but he holds up a hand.

"Fighting. Up ahead." He blinks a few times. "Androids and swords."

"I hear them," Saki says. "On the right."

I don't hear shit, but I'm not some superhuman nor an android.

"What do we do?" I ask, following along. "We have to go. Time is ticking."

"Let's try to run by without being stopped." Isao picks up pace, and I gasp at how fast he is before I break into a sprint too. Saki is faster than either of us, though. The mental image of her saving the man in the festival flashes before my eyes. She was so quick. I knew right then she was an android, and I didn't even know about superhumans yet.

We run about a hundred meters before I finally hear the fight too.

"No!" A high-pitched female voice startles me into looking right as we speed past. My heart jumps into my throat, and I come screeching to a halt.

Her sword sings as it slashes down and cuts an android in half. She whirls around and cuts another across the chest. At her feet, a man bleeds out, his hand covering a bloody, mortal wound. I jerk forward to help him but stop at her anguished cry. He's dead anyway, not moving, not breathing.

With two more swings of her blade, the last two androids in the room drop, sparks and pseudo-blood ejecting into the air. Her shoulders rise and fall with heavy breaths, and she relaxes her sword down to her side with a sob. A giant hole in the wall leads to the outside, but nothing more is coming through it.

She turns around. Shit. It's Aimi, Reina's niece. Her wide eyes radiate sadness and eclipse her heart-shaped, elfin face. A halo of hair surrounds her head, escaped from a hasty ponytail, and her clothes are ripped and bloodied.

"Aimi!" I jolt forward and grab her. "Let's go. Come with us."

I try to pull her towards the door, but she can't tear her eyes from the man on the floor. I don't know him. Were they related? Friends? I know she hasn't been dating anyone.

Saki looks at the android carnage littering the floor and cocks her head. "They violated the first law."

"They don't have the laws," I remind her. She's the only one who's been programmed with them.

"They need the laws."

Duh. No shit.

Isao brushes past us and heads to the hole in the wall. He peeks his head out, snaps it back, waits a moment, and looks again.

"There's an abandoned drop ship, but that's it. Let's go this way. We'll be able to reach the landing field easier outside. Radiation exposure will be minimal. I'll scout and make sure the coast is clear."

He slips through the hole, spreads his wings, and takes off in one big puff of air.

That never ceases to amaze me.

"I want wings," Saki says, a stupid grin taking over her face.

"Not me." I turn to Aimi. "I'm sorry. But you should come with us."

She shakes her head and drags the back of her hand across her mouth. I frown at the bloody streak she's just given herself.

"He was getting ready to go." She gestures to the man dead on the floor. "Too fucking slow."

I would say I'm sorry again, but time is short.

I grab her upper arms and search her eyes for her sanity. "We *have* to go. Hayashi has already left. You have more fighting to do."

I leave her to sheathe her sword and proceed to the hole in the wall. The surroundings are empty — for now. I wave Saki and Aimi forward to join me, and we all step out.

"Where's the western landing field?" I ask, turning to Aimi.

She sniffs up, her nose red and eyes wet with tears. "This way." She takes the lead, bringing us down the long building.

Most of this side is shaded by radiation blocking skysails, but the young, secondary forest provides shade and cover too. We slip in and out of the trees, running as fast as we can through the undergrowth. Dead pine needles crunch under my feet, reminding me of my first brush with death here on Kurai. I suppress a shudder.

Has it been eight minutes yet? It already feels like a lifetime since Rin gave us that deadline.

"Where's Isao?" I ask, hoping either Saki or Aimi can tell me.

"He's above and to the left," Saki whispers.

I jump over a downed log and glance up just in time to see a red light hit Isao in the wing. The high-pitched shriek and pop of a laser weapon report startles me backwards, and I stumble into a tree trunk.

The flurry of wings is loud enough to hear through the

trees, and Isao falls from the sky in a mess of black leather and human arms and legs.

Shit.

"Break left," I call out. "Isao is down."

I follow his fall through the air. He snaps out one wing, and it causes his descent to soften but bank in a circle. Down down down. He thumps onto the ground with a grunt and a moan of pain.

I skid to a stop, fall to my knees, and roll him over.

"Isao, are you okay?" I touch his head, neck, shoulders, and arms. His legs are tucked underneath him, but I think they're uninjured.

He blinks a few times, his eyes wide. This is an expression I've seen before, blinding pain. His pupils shrink to tiny pinpricks in his brilliant, clear irises.

"It's only…" He gasps for air. "My wing. Go."

"No. No way. Saki," I say, waving to Isao. "Help me lift him up. Aimi, you run point."

"Leave me. I'm too heavy."

"Not for an android," Saki says, pulling his arm up, wrapping her other arm under him, and hoisting him to his feet. "I mustn't let you come to harm through inaction, right?"

My heart warms hearing her recite one of her new laws. Maybe this will work after all.

Isao nods, gritting his teeth through the pain.

"Then let's go. Only a minute and a half to our deadline."

Oh, right. I should have asked Saki how much time we have left. She's the one with the internal clock.

We limp to the edge of the building, the turn to the landing field, when Aimi stops us with her hand out. She snaps back against the building. We do the same.

"Two androids with guns, about ten meters away. They can't see the shuttle. It's still in the stealth blind," she whispers.

"The blind will only be functional for another thirty seconds," Saki reports, her voice at its lowest level. "I will disable the androids."

"Can you do that?"

"The new laws you gave me insist I should." She shrugs with a smile. "I can't deny them, so good job on the programming, Isao." She lets him go and props him against the wall.

Saki and Aimi switch spots. It's her turn to peek around the corner.

"Two Model Eights. I know what to do."

With a blink, she's gone.

Do I want to look?

No.

Well, yes.

I inch forward so I can use one eye, the newly healed one, to watch around the corner. Saki runs to the androids with blinding speed. With a leap, she rolls into the first one, turns it over, and thrusts her hand into its side. I hold back my stomach contents as I witness her rip its shirt, pierce its skin, and pull out an internal organ from its lower right side. If this was a human being, the kidney would be in the same place.

The other android kicks her, but she's too strong for him. He thinks she's another weak human being, despite what he just saw. She grabs his leg, twists, and the android is on the ground. This time it's not as shocking to see her pull the organ from the other android. Violence gets easier and easier until remorse sets in.

Aimi and I prop up Isao and usher him forward before he can object. Aimi gasps as she approaches Saki covered in android blood. Saki shakes off the excess, bends down, and wipes her hands on the pants of the nearest android.

"We're safe to the shuttle," Saki says, pointing towards the forest in the distance.

With a shimmer and whine, the shuttle fades into existence in front of us, and I marvel at the technology here again. They think we're advanced? Just in different ways.

The shuttle door opens, and Kazuo and Chiéko wave us inside.

"That was…" Chiéko is at a loss for words, and her eyes scan Saki from head to toe.

"Awesome?" Saki asks. "Thanks. Knowing my own anatomy is helpful sometimes."

Chiéko's eyebrows pull together as the shuttle door closes and the engines whine for lift-off. Rin runs forward to hug me, and I'm so grateful to see him that I don't stop his rushed kiss. This is where I belong.

"We need to go," he insists, breaking away to help Isao.

"I'm an android," Saki tells Chiéko. "You'll get used to it. We should strap in."

Chiéko watches her go, and I can see the wheels turning in her head.

I chuckle as I steer her to the jump seats.

"Primetime news, Chiéko. We just have to live long enough to report it."

CHAPTER NINE

My teeth rattle in my head, and I clutch the straps of my seat so tight my fingers ache. The engines scream in my ears.

"Evasive maneuvers! We have incoming missiles," the pilot shouts. I remember from my initial meetings with Shiroi Nami that this guy was one of their best shuttle pilots, a virtuoso at the controls. Or was that someone else? My brain shakes in my head to the degree that I can't remember anything right now, not even my middle name.

The shuttle banks left, a sharp jerk, and I'm thrown against my restraints. A missile screams past and fades into the distance.

"One down!" The pilot shouts.

"One? How many more?" My voice cracks, and Mari, sitting across from me, chuckle-cries, a strangled mess of emotions that I think everyone here feels.

"Oh, my God! This world is fucking insane!" Chiéko screams. She pants and closes her eyes. I turn my head slowly to look at Rin, and his expression is grim.

Well, she's not wrong. A lot of this world is insane on every level. The meritocracy, the wars, the ability to own another person's contract and hold their life in your hands — it's all pretty bat-shit crazy.

But there are the common people who just want to live their lives — the people dancing at Club Seiun, the woman I ran into in the farmers' market with her dogs, Saki's landlord. They want some normality, some peace.

"You'll get used to it," Shintaro yells from down the shuttle.

"I don't think I want to!"

Aimi laughs, her eyes clouded with tears. I don't know what kind of upbringing she had, but it must have been intense to be that good with the sword. She closes her eyes and presses her head into the seat. I follow her lead and wait for the second missile. It'll either scream right on by us, or we'll be dead. Fifty-fifty chance, right?

The wait seems endless, the tension in my shoulders threatening to bring on a migraine. The muscles stretching up the back of my neck tug on my scalp, and I wince at the pain.

Two, three, five breaths later, and the sound of the shuttle dies off.

The pilot comes over the loudspeaker and says, "We're almost to orbit. The missile ran out of fuel and fell away about a hundred meters back."

A collective sigh runs around everyone in their seats, and several of us clasp hands or nod to each other. We made it off Kurai.

My eyes linger on Mari and Jonathan, their hands securely clasped together. I'd ask Chiéko about them if I had any private time whatsoever, but I think I already know the answer to my question. High-stress situations can bring people closer.

Look at Rin and me. That's something no one saw coming, not even me.

Rin reaches out and grabs a cup that floats by.

"That was quite a ride," he says with a sigh and a smile.

I take the cup from him. "You can say that again. What should I do?" I shake the empty cup.

"Let's secure everything for the flight across. There are receptacles at the end of the seats for trash."

"Right."

I turn to leave, but Rin's hand lingers on my ass for a moment too long and makes me laugh. I swat his hand away. "Get out of here."

"Yes, Miss Minamoto." He salutes and backs away to the bridge to talk to the pilot.

I sigh and ignore the stares of everyone. No one from home has ever known me to be a soft person. I'm a hard-boiled journalist with no feelings. I don't want to damage my reputation right now, as badly as I'd prefer to just be myself around Rin. So I gather up floating waste, pens, tablets, errant straps, and anything else I can find and stow them in the receptacles.

When I see Chiéko whispering with Mari, Jonathan, and Ryoko at the back of the shuttle, my reporter senses tingle.

I pull myself into my professional shell, the hardened outside I need to deal with any situation. Ryoko has seen some of my vulnerable side when we tried to escape from Aoi Uma's grasp in Shin-Osaka, but otherwise, these people don't know any other Yumi than the one they grew up with.

Before I butt in on them, though, I stop to check on Isao. Shintaro is using the shuttle's medkit to triage the wound on his wing.

"How are you?" I ask, hooking my feet into the restraints next to him.

"I'll be fine. Thanks, Shintaro."

"Sure thing," Shintaro responds, snapping the lid onto a bottle. "I think this will hold you until we get to the surface."

"Do you know where we're going?" Isao asks.

I shake my head. "I didn't think to ask. I'm sure Rin has it under control."

Isao narrows his eyes and looks towards the bridge. "Yumi, are you sure you trust him? He's Kiiroi Yama. They haven't been very receptive to Shiroi Nami over the years."

I lay my hand on his arm and brush off the feeling of dread. "I trust him, with my life, with my heart." I bring my hand to my chest. "And you can trust him too."

I say it out loud, but a niggle of doubt creeps in. This time, though, the doubt is different. In the past, I had doubted Rin's love and affection. I doubted his loyalty. Yet, he always came through for me. He proved to me he was a man of his word.

Now, the doubt I have is for my new allies. *They* don't trust *me*.

I breathe out through my nose. I need to prove to them I'm trustworthy. I'm a woman of my word, and I keep my promises.

I smile at Isao and try to quell his fears. "Don't worry. If I can trust Rin, you can trust him and me too."

"Yeah, Yumi is super trustworthy," Shintaro says, tossing the bottle of antiseptic into the medkit and snapping it shut. "Right up until she steals your man right out from under you. I clearly had dibs on Rin first."

I throw my head back in a laugh and then bat my eyelashes at him. "I think you're mixing me up with you and Takéji." It wasn't too long ago that Shintaro started dating the only man I was ever interested in back home. "Turn about is fair play."

"Bitch," he says, laughing and poking me in the shoulder.

Isao closes his eyes and shakes his head. "I'm going to sit on the end and try to sleep. Wake me when we land." He unstraps himself and moves awkwardly to the other end of the shuttle, closer to the bridge. Watching a man with wings navigate Zero-G is a little humbling. We're all clumsy in space.

Now seems like the perfect time to interrupt Chiéko and her circle of friends. Everyone looks either despondent or exhausted. Not a favorable sign.

"And that's it? That's all you know?" Chiéko asks Ryoko. Ryoko shrugs her shoulders.

"What's up?" I ask, inserting myself between Mari and Ryoko.

For the first time ever, I detect suspicion in Chiéko's glare. I press my lips together and try to look as innocent as possible. She sighs and gives in.

"I'm trying to get the lay of the land here," she says, relaxing a bit. "Ryoko has told us how you were brought to Hikari and delivered to some corporation called Aka Matsuba?"

"Yes, though their corporation has been since disbanded. But many of their top employees are sympathetic to our goals."

"And what are our goals here? Because from what I see, this is a cock-up of immense proportions. You let some foreign power divide us up and sell us off to the highest bidder."

The heat of anger rises in my belly. "I didn't *let* them do anything. Trust me, I fought hard for our freedom, for *my* freedom. See this?" I pull back the strands of my short hair and show her the scar on my scalp. "I got this injury when someone blew up a building and nearly killed me. You should see the scar on my leg that almost killed me, too, but I won't show you because then you'll have to see I'm not wearing any underwear."

Mari laughs and breaks the tension.

"My migraines are a hundred times worse here, and I'm losing my memory because I've hit my head more times than I can count, and my brain is permanently damaged."

Chiéko's eyes widen, and Mari's smile softens to a frown.

"So don't tell me I *let* these people do anything to us. I did what I could. And let's not even talk about the burning building I jumped from because those memories haunt my dreams. I *wish* I could forget them."

"Sorry," Chiéko murmurs. "We've had it rough, too."

"I know," I say, softening my tone. "And I don't doubt it was hard to survive on your own. But they sold you off into slavery like I was. Fucking twice."

"Yumi..." Her voice breaks, and her shoulder slump. "This is scaring the crap out of me."

"Good. It should. We're about to land in enemy territory, and we have little in the way of guns or ammunition."

I take a deep breath through my nose and let out all the anger and frustration. I have to be more than the petulant young woman I've been in the past for these people.

"Am I right that you were trying to gather data on the native's civilization so you can move forward?" When she nods, I smile at her and gesture to the seats. "Then let's sit down and have a long talk. I'm going to tell you everything I've been through. I'll show you the data I've read, the news stories I've watched, and then we're going to talk about why we need to shut down Aoi Uma's androids and show these people who they really can be."

Chiéko tilts her head and grimaces. "I don't know. I feel like we should stay the hell out of this."

My grin is almost manic. "Nope. We're not staying out of this. In fact, we're going in strong. We're going to make a documentary about Shiroi Nami and us, and we *will* convince these people that we're the best leaders they'll ever have."

"Leaders? That's not our job. Our job is to observe and report. Not get involved."

I lift my chin. "It's too late not to get involved. I'm starting my own corporation, and you're all my first employees."

CHAPTER TEN

The shuttle sets down at night in the middle of a field of grass. I inhale through my nose and out through my mouth, inhale, exhale, circular breathing. I can already tell I'm going to regret returning to Hikari in about four to six hours.

"All clear to open the aft door," the pilot says over the loudspeaker.

People sigh and unbuckle from their seats. The door opens, and a brisk wind laden with humidity fills the once dry and stuffy space.

Shintaro leans out the back door. "Oh, nice. Back home, is it?"

I laugh at him as I help Isao out of his seat. "If only."

"No. It's our home away from home," he insists, ushering Mari, Jonathan, Ryoko, and Chiéko to the outside. The others, Maddie and Erik, follow along in silence.

"I was hoping we'd return here." Ryoko jerks her head at Chiéko. "Come on. If we're staying in the same houses, then I know the way."

I glance up at Isao. "Have you been here before?" he asks.

I shrug. "Let's get going."

Rin watches my face as we leave the shuttle, but I merely smile at him and continue forward with Isao and Saki. I'm not sure what signal he's looking for from me, but I'm too tired to figure it out right now.

"I'm going to move the shuttle to a Kiiroi Yama facility on the other end of town. We need fuel if we plan to be on the move again," the pilot says, joining us before we get moving.

"Thanks, Toro. I'll be in touch tomorrow."

Toro gives a jaunty salute and returns to the shuttle, closing the aft door behind him.

"Which way?" I ask Rin.

He frowns and gestures to the backs of everyone else in front of us. "This way."

Saki sticks by Isao's side even though he's rested enough now to walk on his own. He keeps his wings pulled tight against his body, and in the dark, he almost looks normal.

Normal. Whatever that means.

"Did I say or do something wrong?" I whisper to Rin. The weight of the barometric pressure here on Hikari sits on my head like an elephant standing on a watermelon. Breathe in and out, in and out.

"No. Not at all. Let's keep walking."

Something about this situation nags at me. "I feel like I did something wrong. Are you mad at me for not going to the moon base? I know that returning to Hikari is especially fraught with peril for me, but I'm going to do my best to take care of myself." I place my hand on my heart. "I promise."

"It's fine," he says, but his manner is stiff and a little anxious. He's probably worried about what comes next.

We exit the landing field, cross a road, and then enter a

small town along a bubbling river. The buildings are lit with paper lanterns, their soft glow reflecting off the wet cobblestone streets. I inhale again, trying to acclimatize my body to the new air, and the smell of the wind is familiar.

Rin takes my hand, laces his fingers with mine, and swings them at our side as we stroll along the riverbank behind our friends. We pass a shuttered florist, an izakaya closed for the night, an all-night convenience store with no one in it, and several apartment buildings. We must have arrived in the middle of the night because there's not a soul around, which I'm grateful for. We can't have anyone spotting Isao and giving us a hard time.

I keep my eyes on the buildings, trying to catalog them like I did in Kitakyushu. I might have to come back this way again. And though I've done this kind of cataloging a million times now, the details slot in and melt away.

I sigh and wonder why my brain is so broken. What is it about this place that feels so different?

I inhale again, and the rich scent of baking bread hits me like a speeding train. I stumble to a stop and close my eyes.

"Yumi..." Rin's voice is quiet.

"Wait. Wait..."

When I open my eyes, a memory comes to me of a sunny day. Rin and I sat on the riverbank right up ahead, and we ate freshly baked bread with aged cheese and smoked seafood, a bottle of wine between us.

"Oh," I breathe out. "We're in..." Why can I never remember the name?

I raise my hand to stop him from reminding me.

"Awashikawa." Tears form in my eyes, and I nod. He was worried I wouldn't remember, that's why he kept looking at me.

And I almost didn't.

He squeezes my fingers. "The bread did it, yes?"

"Mmm," I affirm, unable to trust my clouded voice. I clear my throat gently. "It must be early in the morning for them to be up and baking."

Rin's smile returns. "I'll pop in later and get some for everyone."

Our walk through town produces more memories from the back of my head. I pull them from memory drawers and dust them off enough to remember the few dinners we treated ourselves to or the stores we shopped at. But so much is missing; pockets of dark in my brain terrify me.

"God, I've lost so much. I should remember *all* of this, but I don't."

He tightens his grip on my hand, and fear clouds his face. He opens his mouth to say something but stops, probably realizing there's nothing he *can* say to make this any better.

Shintaro comes jogging back to us when we round the bend for the road we used to live on.

"Hey, Rin. Same houses as before?"

"I spoke to Okamoto yesterday in anticipation of the coming mission, and he said these houses were all for us. He did nothing with them after we left. I expect Kiiroi Yama employees in the next day, so we should get some rest."

"I can take Chiéko, Mari, and Jonathan," Shintaro volunteers. "I have a two-bedroom plus a couch. It'll be enough space, and between you and me, Jon is a nice piece of ass, if you know what I mean."

I roll my eyes hard enough that they almost fall out of my head. "You didn't hear it from me, but I think he and Mari are involved."

"Oh, damn." He sighs. "Fine."

"What? That's it?" I ask, tightening my grip on Rin. "You're not going to just pursue him because you can?"

"Oh, sweet Yumi. I only do that to you and Rin to piss you off."

"Thanks, asshole."

"You love me, and you know it."

He turns to leave, and I have to admit, I do still love him even if he is an asshole. I guess that's what happens when you grow up together.

"Wait!" I raise my voice. "I don't think we should wait until tomorrow to brief everyone. Let's go to our place first and have a quick discussion about what's coming next."

"You sure about that? You look ready to pass out." Concern forms two lines between Rin's eyebrows.

"If we delay, we may be waiting three or more days for me to do anything." I point to my head. "This way, everyone will know what's happening, and they can get busy on this without me."

Shintaro rests his hand on my shoulder and then brings it to the back of my neck. He knows a lot of my migraines can start there. "You gonna be okay, sis?"

"I really don't know anymore."

My smile is weak, but it's all I can muster for right now. My stomach is a mess, but it settles as we approach the house Rin and I lived in after escaping Shin-Osaka.

Yes, yes. It *is* good to be home.

WHEN I OPEN THE DOOR, and my hand reflexively goes to the old-fashioned light switch, I feel a sense of peace. We liked this place because of how low tech it was, and it remains a cottage stuck in time — no voice-automated lights, blinds, or thermostats. No tōsha. Nobody listening in. Secure, safe, and anonymous.

"Come in, come in." I beckon everyone in the front door. The front room with the dining table is cramped, but I think it'll fit everybody. They all step inside and shiver at the low temperature.

"I would give you a tour, but this is about it for this place." I wave to the open area. The dining table takes up most of the front room. The space flows straight into the tiny kitchen that Rin and I used to make noodles in. The bathroom with a compact laundry is adjacent to the bedroom at the back of the house. We don't even have a living room with a couch here.

With the light on, I'm keenly aware of the halos around people and objects in the room, a sure sign of my impending migraine. Maybe if I sleep, I can keep it to a five out of ten on the pain scale instead of an eight or nine.

Rin turns up the heat on the thermostat and checks each room to make sure we're alone, and nothing has changed.

"I cleaned out the fridge before I moved into my place," Shintaro says, coming to stand beside me.

"Don't lie. You took the food with you because you didn't want to shop for yourself."

"Well, that too." He glides his arm across my shoulders and pulls me in to kiss my temple. "It's good to see you with your passion back, sis. I was afraid Kurai would break you."

"It almost did," I whisper. "It still could."

He shakes his head. "You have too many allies now."

"Cute place." Chiéko looks around the tiny dining room and kitchen. "Did you live here?"

I step forward into the light so everyone can see and hear me.

"For a short time, after we escaped Shin-Osaka and the chaos there, we lived here. I don't think we can live here for much longer than a week, so don't get too comfortable, okay?" I sigh as I press my hand to my forehead.

"Migraine coming?" Kazuo asks, concern blanketing his eyes in tiny wrinkles.

"Do you need meds?" Aimi holds up the medkit from the shuttle. "Toro told me to take it with me."

"Thanks. I think I'm going to need it."

Kazuo takes the kit from Aimi and thanks her too.

"This is terrible timing," Chiéko says, a frown returning to her face. As my former boss, she was used to the inevitable sick days from my migraines.

"Yes." I suck another breath in through my nose. "So let's make this quick so we can all get some rest. I'm going to go over the basics of the plan, but Rin, Kazuo, and Shintaro will handle the specifics."

My eyes fall on Isao, propped up in the table's corner, his wings folded behind him. He's quiet, but his breaths are labored, and a soft sheen of sweat covers his brow.

"Our strategy to fix the problems here on Hikari will need to start with Aoi Uma's androids. But our plan cannot come to a fruition without a new corporation to take power here once Aoi Uma falls."

Saki nods, and her earnest expression pushes me onward.

"So, we have two separate missions we need to accomplish at about the same time, or at least one right after the other." Pain radiates through my temples, but I press my fingers together and try to ignore it. "Rin and a team of people will infiltrate the main android production facility in Amagasaki and reprogram the androids. Aoi Uma will then no longer have an undefeatable army at their disposal. Right now, the androids are lawless, with only the most basic parameters set to help human beings. We've fixed that with Saki's programming." I gesture to her, and she lifts her hand and smiles sheepishly. "We can reprogram the androids in the facility and send out an update to all the others with a ninety-five percent margin of error? Right, Isao?"

"Yes, Yumi. The other five percent will need to be dealt with, but that's only a few thousand androids."

"Five percent is only a few thousand androids?" Chiéko's face pales.

"Yes, the situation is way out of control. They didn't just make androids to help out here and there. They outnumber humans. I'll brief you about the declining birth rate and cultural norms tomorrow."

If I'm even conscious tomorrow.

"While our primary team is handling that, I plan to send several of you back into Shin-Osaka to find all of our crewmates. Shintaro will help with the assistance of some former Aka Matsuba employees. We'll gather everyone up and make them a part of the new corporation I'm planning to form."

Mari raises her hand, and the gesture makes me smile. I nod at her. "Do we really need to form a corporation and do this? Why can't we just hide out somewhere until our people come back?"

I think for a moment about where she's coming from before I answer. "I get that you hid out on Kurai for a few months, and you were fine enough, right?" She nods. "But it wouldn't have lasted, I'm sorry to say. Aoi Uma would have found you eventually and sold you into slavery. The same thing will happen here too. It's tough to live off the network. I only know of one place in the whole world that will allow it, and those people may have already packed up and moved because they were discovered."

Saki lowers her eyes, her pain and embarrassment showing from what happened in that coastal town months ago.

"We either stay and fight for what we need, or there will only be a short time to live free, and then that's it."

Mari nods, her eyes sad and distant. Jon takes her hand.

"But with our own corporation and the help of Kiiroi Yama and Shiroi Nami, we can accomplish a lot." I put more hope and optimism into my voice. "It'll be hard, and we may fail, but it has the best chance of keeping us alive for the long haul."

I close my eyes against the oncoming pain. With another cleansing breath, I open my eyes and continue.

"I also want to produce some videos about us and our hopes and plans for this world. Positive, heart-warming propaganda type shit, you know?"

Chiéko snorts and laughs. "The stuff I was making in my twenties for the political machine."

I point at her. "Exactly. Let's blanket them with positive stories about Orihimé and what we can do for them."

I wait for it all to sink in, and slowly, the vibe in the room changes to something more like confidence. We've got this.

"Ryoko, I'm going to put you in charge of dealing with Kiiroi Yama for the details of this mission, okay? I want Kazuo and Rin to concentrate on what our infiltration team will do."

She shrugs. "Sure. I can do that." It's nice to see her take the job so easily. I was afraid I'd have to motivate her. But she's changed a lot since the time we escaped the Aoi Uma building in Shin-Osaka. She's more confident and independent now.

"So, everyone, go get some rest. Eat well and listen to the people who have lived here and can tell us more about what we're up against. Okay?"

With that, everyone gets moving, and Shintaro does his best to direct people to the houses where they'll bed down for the night and live for the next few days.

Before I can turn away to barricade myself in the bedroom, though, Chiéko grabs my arm.

"How many people are we going to find from our ship?"

I shrug. "Most everyone left alive unless they've turned to the other side."

"You think that's possible?"

"I know it's possible. Gen Miyazawa turned. Anyone else could have as well."

She sighs. "That fucker had no common sense."

"No, he did not."

And he will die at my hands if I have anything to say about it.

CHAPTER ELEVEN

This migraine differs from any other migraine I've ever had. What is it about this planet that my head hates so much? The last migraine I had on Kurai was the kind that makes my head spin and my stomach eject everything I put in it. This one fucks with my internal temperature settings.

I'm hot. I'm cold. I'm freezing. My teeth are chattering… And then I throw off the blanket ten minutes later because I'm burning up.

Kazuo stands over me at the bedside, rubbing the stubble on his jaw and humming.

"Don't hum," I plead.

"Sorry."

"Don't speak."

His voice is amplified by a thousand times. So he whispers instead, "I've never seen symptoms like this."

"Me neither," Rin answers quietly from the door.

Rin climbs into bed with me, and I shrink from his first touch.

"Hold me," I plead. "Make it stop."

He wraps his arms and legs around me until I pass out, and then he's gone.

It was night, and now it's daytime. The room can't be dark enough for me. I throw the covers over my head the next time my body descends into the frosty depths. If I could kill the universe for doing this to me, I would. But it's some karmic payback, I know it. I can only suffer through it.

Time passes in which I'm unconscious, not asleep. When I open my eyes again, the light in the bedroom has changed to a softer ochre kissed with pink. It's probably evening. The tinkling sounds of chopsticks in bowls and cabinets opening and closing pulls me to the surface. I stick my face out of the covers and tentatively sniff. Garlic and ginger meet my nose. I swallow and keep my stomach contents where they are.

A knock at the front door rattles around my brain, but I strain my ears to hear what's going on. Shintaro's low voice... and someone else. It sounds serious, and my name is said over and over. I snuggle down into the blanket even farther. There's nothing they can do for me.

When the door opens, I brace myself. I shouldn't tense my muscles because it makes everything worse. Still, my body expects the noise and intrusion of other people into my migraine. The cover lifts and gets tucked in and around me by sure hands.

"You have a visitor, Yumi," Rin whispers. "Two of them."

The bed creaks as something hefty lies down next to me. It's unexpected, and I feel like I'm rolling around on a boat. My inner ear does not like this at all.

"I'm gonna be sick."

I say it right before a trash can is put in front of me.

"I see. Okay." A voice I've never heard before.

I cough into the trash can and reach for the proffered towel. I take a few moments to recognize Rin's hand.

"Shhh," I beg of these people.

The bed shakes like it's vibrating in an earthquake. Are there earthquakes here on Hikari?

"The wound is infected." A whispered voice joins the pounding in my head. "And she needs painkillers and anti-emetics. I'll start IV drips for both of them."

I pass out again. A needle enters my arm, but I'm in too much pain in other areas to care. I also suspect someone else is in bed with me, not Rin, not Kazuo. But I curl up and await my fate at the hands of everyone else because I'm incapable of helping myself, defending myself, when I'm this far gone.

Please, no one kill me. I'm not ready to go yet.

Too much to do.

I inhale through my nose and out through my mouth. Hours pass.

The next time I awake through the haze of the migraine, I feel much better. My head is clear, and my body doesn't ache all over. Something tugs at my arm, and I realize there's an IV there. Yes, right. A doctor, I think, came some hours ago and hooked it up.

I've been through so many migraines in this system without medical help that I forgot medical help could even be had. What a difference drugs make.

I roll over in the bed, careful of the needle in my arm, and try to snuggle up to Rin.

Only it's not Rin in the bed.

I gasp and reflexively kick.

"Ow! Hey now, cousin. That's not very nice."

Well, no wonder the bed sank so much. It isn't Rin next to me; it's Isao.

Like me, he has his own IV attached to a bag on a stand next to the bed. Someone gave him his own blanket because I had stolen the covers. His wing is bandaged, and his skin is pale.

"Sorry. Sorry. I didn't know who was in the bed." My voice cracks. I've had nothing to drink in hours. Not that I'm dehydrated or anything because of the IV fluids, but my lips and throat could use some moisture.

"Rough night for both of us." Isao shifts in the bed, and I hold on for dear life. I hadn't thought about his sheer size until now, sharing a bed with him. "My wing got infected, and I was running a high fever. I think I still am." He shakes violently, so I reach my hand over and slip my fingers around his.

"Ooooh, yeah. Your skin is hot."

"S'okay. It'll pass soon. Just need to sleep it off."

"Where's Kazuo? Rin?"

His teeth chatter. "Kazuo is at the table. Rin is sleeping at your brother's."

I sigh. Poor Rin. I hope Shintaro left him alone.

"Sleep," I tell him, squeezing his hand. "Let's sleep. When we wake up, we'll both feel better."

I yawn, unable to halt the blanket of drowsiness that falls over me. This is a good sign the migraine won't last as long as others. When I can sleep and not just pass out, it means I'm on the mend. I close my eyes and keep my hand in Isao's.

Dream, Yumi. I dream of freedom, running in fields, laughing, lost in a strange city, and at peace and back home on Orihimé.

Someday, I'll be back there. Someday.

I SIP warm broth in the bed, sitting up, shoulder to shoulder with Isao. His fever broke in the early morning, and the doctor returned to remove both of our IVs.

"I'm glad you're feeling better," I say, lifting my cup as if to toast him.

"I'm glad you're better too," he says, sipping a cup of tea. "Are those migraines of yours a regular thing?"

I try to nod my head, but it still hurts too much to move it. "Yeah, I've gotten them regularly since I was ten. Back home, they were bad, but never as bad as they are here. I don't know why."

"You know," he drawls, and a wave of tingles cascades down my back, "we could fix that for you. I'm familiar with the parts of genes that trigger migraines."

I sigh and set my cup on the nightstand. Resting my head on the headboard, I close my eyes.

"Okay, let's have this conversation for real, if you're up for it," I say, giving in to my curiosity.

"I'm going to need to leave here soon. Maybe within a few hours because I'll heal faster on our moon base with the specialized medicines we've developed. I couldn't travel like I was last night. So, when I leave, I can take DNA samples with me if you give me permission to grow your clone."

Grow my clone. I reach for my cup of broth and swallow. That's the strangest thing to think about.

"And I could have a body with no migraines? What about... uh, specialty enhancements?"

His smile makes my face burst into flames.

"Not like that," I say, smacking him on the arm. "Like, I'm fine with my body. I don't want big boobs or anything. I was thinking maybe easier recovery time from injuries or better stamina for all the activity I do."

"We can achieve all of that easily. I have other enhancements which may come in handy in the future for you, like a more efficient use of oxygen and nutrients, and the ability to gain energy from solar and space radiation. We have many advancements that I think will suit you."

I'm quiet for a moment, thinking of all the possibilities. And this is just a backup for me, anyway. Plan B, if things go wrong.

"What happens to the, uh, clone if I decide to never use it?"

"We have destruction protocols. We can harvest organs and render a body down to its component elements, and we can use those for other things."

I don't want to know what those 'other things' are, do I?

Yeah, I do.

I open my mouth to ask, but Isao holds up his hand. "Don't ask. You don't want to know."

"Fine," I say, pushing out my lower lip in a pout. "I'm sure I can use my imagination."

"And most likely, your imagination would be correct. Any other questions?"

"Kids," I blurt out, and this time I'm able to hold back the blush. "Rin and I have talked about having children someday, and..." My voice trails off at his frown. "And it came to my notice on Kurai that there were no female murasakijin or kumojin or tensojin." I gesture to him, the first bat-man I have ever met.

He shakes his head. "We're unable to clone women who can produce offspring. I'm sorry to say. Trust me, we've tried. It has always been a failure."

I think of the cloned women finding this out. Pursing my lips, I imagine what the conversation was like. Was it a disappointment, or was it welcome? I can foresee situations where it could be either.

"So you can clone them, but they can't reproduce. What about... What about the men?"

If you think it's weird I'm sitting in bed next to my cousin who's half bat, and we're talking about human reproduction systems, then you're absolutely right. It is weird, one hundred percent.

He chuckles. "I'm shooting blanks, and I have no sex drive. The only way I can reproduce now is through cloning. Same with my brothers and all our Shiroi Nami creatures. You see, Aka Matsuba and Aoi Uma sterilized the Minamoto line a few generations ago. This is the only way we have been able to survive."

He looks down at his hands. "I don't want to judge, but I was sorry to hear that your brother is gay. With him and you not producing offspring, the Minamoto line will die off."

I smile at him, though I'm sad too. "No offense taken. I have an older brother I never talk about because he's boring and everything my parents want in a child. Kenichi will carry on the line, no worries. He *loves* women." I laugh and roll my eyes. "My parents have had their fingers crossed for years that he doesn't impregnate someone ahead of an official union." I pat him on his hands. "So don't worry your pretty little head about it."

It's his turn to chuckle. "I am sorry about this situation you're stuck in. It can't be easy to do everything you've done and come out in the end without the ability to have kids. The best we can do is harvest your eggs from your body and freeze them. You could potentially use a surrogate."

"Okay. I think that's a good idea." It's better than nothing. "Well," I say, shifting over to my side of the bed and giving him some space, "this is just a backup plan. I intend to survive and make it back home in one piece."

"It's good to have a backup plan. You don't survive on this world without one."

"I just... I have a lot to consider before actually using this backup plan."

A gentle knock on the door breaks up our conversation. Rin enters, and past him in the main room, Toro is waiting by the front door.

"Your ride is here," he says to Isao. "It's dark enough outside for you to travel without being seen."

Isao looks at me, and I nod to him.

"Give us a moment, and I'll be right out."

Rin makes eye contact with me, and I smile, letting him know everything is fine. He closes the door with a soft click.

"I'm not sure I understand what you see in him," Isao whispers, and I press my lips together. "He's Kiiroi Yama."

"Rin is Rin. Don't judge him by the corporation he used to work for." I sigh and throw the covers off my legs. I'm burning up from the inside with anger. "This is something you all should adjust about your thinking. People are not corporations, and corporations are not people. Remember that. Rin loves me, and I love him. We were meant to be together."

His cheek jerks in a half-smile. "Fate, huh? Well, it's hard to unlearn things that are hundreds of years old. Let me grab my bag, and I'll take DNA samples from you." He lays his hand on my arm. "I wish you all the luck I can give. I know the road ahead of you will be rocky. Please know that Shiroi Nami has your back. You can come to us when you need help."

"Thanks. I appreciate it."

Why do I feel like the help may come, but it will be too little too late?

CHAPTER TWELVE

As the train rounds a bend and approaches Amagasaki, I absently rub the spot on my wrist where we implanted a new chip. I thought I was done with these things, but if I'm going to live here for the foreseeable future, then at least it's on my terms with a chip I can program. And maybe Amagasaki won't be so bad. I began to like Shin-Osaka after a while, after all.

Leaning forward to get a better look out the window, I shield my eyes from the sun on this cool and clear day. Wow, impressive. The city is about half the size of Shin-Osaka but filled with the same highrise buildings and amenities. Shin-Osaka was so big; I don't think I ever even saw a tenth of it.

"What do you think?" Rin asks, leaning past me to see what I see. His hand on my knee sends butterflies through my belly. There are moments when I can't believe he's interested in me. I'm so fucking average. "It's a sizable city with an efficient butsu system and UPN, much like Shin-Osaka, but it's more advanced because the city engineers built it later. They fixed a few things they got wrong on the first attempt."

"What... Oh my God, no." I gasp and point at the long loops taking shape on the outskirts of the city. "What is that? Is that a... uh?" I snap my fingers.

"Rollercoaster," Rin fills in the word. "It's a theme park. Rollercoasters and other rides, delicious fried foods, sweets, shows, concerts. You know..." He waves his hand in a circle. "A place to have fun."

His eyes widen as I blink at him.

"You? Have fun? Well, I never."

He laughs. "Don't be so surprised. I've been once, and yes, it was a lot of fun. Cost me quite a few credits, but it was worth it. I went with Atsumi a long time ago."

"She had fun?" My tone of voice reveals that I find this suspicious.

He shrugs. "She was young once."

The theme park grows in size as we get closer, and I lick my lips in anticipation of seeing some of these rollercoasters in action. The grounds of the park are well-manicured and clean. Hundreds of people roam around or wait in lines for the coasters.

"We don't have theme parks on Orihimé, and there were none left on Earth when my parents left there long ago. The last city on Earth was under domes. Can't really have a theme park amid that."

The train slows down as it coasts alongside the park. I can't tear my eyes from the controlled chaos, the screams of people on the coasters, the music, the bright lights, and tōsha signs everywhere.

"We're almost there. The main terminal is right on the other side of the park." Rin stands up and grabs our bags. He waves down the car to Kazuo, Aimi, Saki, and Ryoko. Shintaro and his team have made their way to Shin-Osaka to meet up with Sayaka from Aka Matsuba. They will start the search for our fellow shipmates without us.

"And where is the factory?" I ask, keeping my voice low.

"Not far. Half a kilometer farther in the same direction. We can see it from the station platform."

The train rises to elevated railways as we enter the city limits. We cross over a butsu and a few walkways cluttered with people and bikes. Then a streetcar passes by. That's new. I never saw those in Shin-Osaka.

I point to it, and Rin nods, ushering me forward with a hand on my back. "Butsues here snake through the city north to south and back again. Streetcars move east and west. I'm not sure it's more efficient than loops, but it makes things easier to find on the grid."

On the station's platform, we exit at the samurai caste doors and head to the end to reach the stairs. But just before we descend, Rin gestures to the large low building in the distance.

"Our next mission."

The building is a gray mass of concrete and metal with a giant blue stallion in mid-stride painted along the side. From this distance, I can see front-loader trucks zooming in and out of spaceship-sized cargo doors, loading crates into several ships sitting on a landing field. There's a constant stream of people coming and going from the front lobby doors, too, though that's harder to see as it's on the far corner. I swallow through a closed throat. The place is massive.

"Come. I know a noodle place close to the boulevard that leads to the factory entrance. It's a suitable spot to watch the area."

Just before we left Awashikawa, a courier arrived from Kiiroi Yama to give us everything we needed for this mission.

They will be on alert if we need extraction from this place, but otherwise, they're keeping their hands clean as they work on Aoi Uma from other angles. This is one thing that comforts me at night and allows me to sleep. I'm just a cog in this machine. I'm not doing this alone.

As we amble down the sidewalk, I try to act excited and a little naïve, but not too dumb. It's our cover when we're not on our mission to be tourists from Shin-Osaka, here for a conference on information technology. I can take in the surrounding sights without feeling like a country bumpkin.

When we round a corner, though, I startle at the two large men on the far corner talking in low voices. My brain immediately jumps to Haku and his brother, Masato, both dead now but still very alive in the back of my head.

"Something wrong?" Rin asks me, following my line of sight.

"No, nothing."

I try to keep walking and pretend I didn't notice the men, but Rin's eyes are too keen. He's way too aware of my every move.

"Yumi," Rin says as he catches my hand with his and slows me down, "that's behind us now. I promise. We took precautions while you were dealing with your migraine. Checked every last warrant and bounty. The person you were, the Yumi Minamoto in those files... She's dead. Gone. Buried. Erased. She was once owned by Aka Matsuba, then me, and then finally by the yakuza. But her debt is gone, and now you live instead. You're a free agent with a sizable income and a job to do at Aoi Uma's android facility tomorrow. And when the job is done, you'll be someone else."

"I didn't think anything like that was possible."

His grin returns. "Anything is possible when you use your

enemy's tactics against them. They hacked the contract system? So we figured it out and did it too. That's the way the world works. If they hadn't done it first, no one would have bothered."

Down the street, the rest of our crew waits in a bunch. I take a step forward, hoping this will encourage Rin to move. He falls in at my side.

"You can understand why I'm hesitant to even be back here, right?"

"Well, it was my intention never to bring you back here, wasn't it?"

"Fair point." If anything, I'm the one who always screws things up for myself.

We're quiet for a moment as we catch up to everyone else.

Rin touches my shoulder. "Haku and his brother are dead. Their debts were erased by Kiiroi Yama so their family wouldn't try to seek revenge. It's in the past. There are only so many things you can worry about, right? Put this out of your mind."

I nod as I try to forget it. Push it out of my head. He's right. There are only so many things I can worry about at once.

"Everything okay?" Kazuo asks. His voice is concerned even as his eyes scan the surrounding area. He's always on the alert. Always ready to strike. He must feel naked without his sword, just like Rin.

"Everything's fine," I assure him, "Except I'm starving. We should eat."

The noodle place Rin recommended is right across from the boulevard that leads up to the Aoi Uma factory. We're seated at a large table, and I order a curry noodle soup. I love curry, and I could use something with a little spice to help shrug off these feelings of dread sitting in my gut.

The back of my neck sweats as I watch people come and go down the long boulevard, edged on both sides by trees. Aimi and Ryoko keep things casual with talk of popular culture, the latest scandals in the gossip news, and what's in the theaters. They're good at this. I haven't bothered to look at the Aoi Uma News Network since landing on Hikari. There's been too much to do.

Saki is quiet, almost unnaturally so, but she's been this way since we escaped Kurai. I want to hug her and forgive her, but we're not there yet.

I reach into my bag at my feet and pull out my new tablet and portable camera. The camera is my new favorite toy. It's brand new, and fits in the palm of my hand. It can join any public access point and stream the data straight to a server Isao set up, and it backs up to my tablet, whenever the two are near each other. I love it. It's so much better than carrying the tablet with me everywhere when I want to take footage for our documentary. And Shiroi Nami gave me *two* of them. Just in case.

I heft the camera in my hand and wonder how I'm going to pull this off. I'm already nervous, and my stomach is in knots. I'm not good at undercover work, but maybe with Rin, Kazuo, Ryoko, Saki, and Aimi by my side, this will be different.

The bowls of noodles arrive on the table with a hush and gasp.

"Oh, wow. This looks soooo good," Aimi coos. "It feels like ages since we last ate."

"You had all those pastries this morning that Rin bought," Ryoko reminds her.

"Yeah, but that was hours ago. I have a fast metabolism."

"Enjoy your meal," the waitress says, backing away with a smile. "Call me if you need anything."

Once she's gone, Aimi lowers her voice and lifts her chin at Saki.

"You eat?" she whispers.

"Yep. They wanted us to be as lifelike as possible, so they gave us internal processors for organic substances. We can even gain energy from it. Don't ask about how it comes back out."

Aimi narrows her eyes. "Now, I want to know."

Saki laughs but doesn't respond. Thank you, ladies. I'm eating.

Aimi grunts and returns to her meal. I get the feeling she doesn't like Saki, but she's trying to find some common ground. I wonder what's going on there.

I set the camera on the table and point it at the boulevard. Hitting record, I make sure it's framing up the people coming and going from the factory, so I can eat and not pay attention.

"Yumi," Aimi starts, wiping her mouth with a napkin and setting her chopsticks along the side of her bowl, "I was wondering about this documentary you'll be making about... Um, my family and yours."

I nod that I understand. She means Shiroi Nami and the people from my Orihimé mission.

"My aunt is a little worried about it, you know. Not me." She puts her hand to her chest. "I couldn't care less about the system of government we live under. I don't have a political bone in my body. But I was wondering..."

I wait for her to keep going, to make a case for me to stop the documentary angle, to give it up. They all watched the film I made about the empress. I'm sure they're waiting for me to turn around and stab them in the back somehow.

I'm ashamed I did that to the empress... and to my parents. My own flesh and blood. It was one of the worst decisions of my teenage years. I wish I could erase it from my past, but I can't.

"Yes?" I prompt her. I pick around in my bowl, trying to find another carrot. They're delicious, and carrots always remind me of Ninjin. I miss him already.

"I was wondering if I could help? You know, be like a B-camera person, take footage of you when you're working or other places?"

I perk up in surprise. "Wait. Anyone who uses the phrase 'B-camera' knows a little something about video editing." I smile at her, and she nods eagerly.

"Oh yeah, I used to do this stuff in secondary school. I wanted to work for one of the creative corporations, but then, well, I got ostracized when our connection to, uh, you know, became known."

She doesn't even want to say 'Shiroi Nami' in public. That's how bad it is.

I glance at Rin, but he's watching the boulevard outside. Kazuo is nodding his approval.

"Sure. I have two cameras. After the mission is over, I'll give you the other one and show you how to use it. I'd love to hear your perspective on the story."

She lights up with a smile, turning her oval face into a heart with her striking cheekbones.

"Really? Thanks. Awesome. I can't wait to help out."

I smile at Rin, pleased that I've made a coworker and a potential friend out of Aimi, but Rin's eyes are far off. I elbow him in the side, and he blinks.

"Sorry. Let's finish up and get to our lodgings. I want to examine the footage." He nods to the camera on the table. "I think I saw something we need to be careful of."

"STOP. RIGHT THERE." Rin points at the screen. "Can you zoom in?"

I scoff. "Can I zoom in? Please."

Everyone crowds around the wallscreen at our inn for the night. I scrub the video back, freeze the frame, and widen the scene so I can see the person Rin is pointing at.

Well, fuck me.

"It's Gen," Kazuo confirms. "The fucker is here in Amagasaki."

I sigh. "Why is he always right where I don't want him to be?"

"You know this guy?" Aimi asks.

Saki nods. "This was the same guy who came after us in Susami, right? Both at the Nomura Estate and then again before the…" She blinks a few times. "I remember little about the big fight when Shiroi Nami showed up."

She was under Narumi Ogawa's control until Isao picked her up and smashed her into a building.

"I have a lot of vague memories from that time." She sits back on the bed. "But I remember him. I remember Narumi favoring him. She loves him, though I'm not sure why."

"I wonder what he's doing here. Do you think Narumi is here too?" Kazuo asks, crossing his arms and leaning back against the wall.

"His work specialty has always been animal and human DNA," I remind Kazuo. "I mean, he's pretty stupid with life decisions like this, but he's a genius in the lab. Maybe he's helping with android manufacturing, or…" I stop because I honestly have no idea what else they could be doing in there. This is all new scientific territory for me. I've seen things in the last few months I never thought I'd witness in my lifetime.

"Yeah, it's the 'or' part of that statement that is making me rethink this plan," Rin says, rubbing his face.

Ryoko shakes her head. "We can't back out now. Tomorrow is it. If we don't show up for the new job training, they'll wonder what happened, and security will tighten. You have no idea what Kiiroi Yama had to go through to get us this opportunity."

I don't have any idea because I was out with a migraine for two days while she arranged things. I have to trust her that this is our only opportunity to get this done.

"I agree. We have to do this now because who knows what'll be next for Aoi Uma. I'm sure this is not the end of their R&D. I mean, they could be engineering ghosts in there, living souls, who the fuck knows."

Kazuo laughs, and Saki chuckles. She raises her hand.

"All I ever saw in there were more of my kind, Fukusha Model Sevens and Eights. I know they were planning to skip right to the Ten Series, but I think those were a year or two off. The place is enormous, though, and I never explored farther than the lab's hallway." She shakes her head. "They could be doing *anything* in there."

"Let's go forward with the plan and get some sleep tonight," Rin says, standing up and convincing everyone to follow suit. It's not even that late, but we're all exhausted. We've been on the move for days now since leaving Kurai. We need a solid night's sleep.

But a solid night's sleep won't come for me.

As I sit in the bed with Rin snoozing away on his side, I flip through Isao's journal and wonder where to begin with it. I skim through the first twenty pages and look at what he was working on at the time. Mostly the spiders, kumojin. He had written notes about how to change their behaviors and what kinds of personalities would suit them best. I'm intrigued because he used the consciousness transfer protocol, the one he has obviously used on himself and his brothers, to transfer dog consciousness into the kumojin.

How does that even work? But I suppose it makes some sense. Dogs are great companion animals. I miss Ninjin so much, but I have to hope he's with people who will take care of him on this moon base. And the kumojin often seemed to have the personality of dogs, now that I think about it. They could definitely fetch.

I quietly laugh at my joke and try to not wake Rin.

The following few pages are all mumbo-jumbo, math equations, and medical terms I would need a dictionary and a doctorate degree to understand. But then my eyes zero in on a passage that stands out from all the others.

Written in bold, dashing letters with red borders calling attention to several warnings, my heart skips a beat as I read the passage.

"Aoi Uma raided the lab today in a desperate attempt to steal everything we've been working on. They caught us off guard, and now we'll always be looking over our shoulders as to what they'll come up with next. They stole the consciousness transfer technology and all of our databases on animal consciousness. We think they got DNA samples too, though I still need to do more digging to find out whether or not that actually happened."

I turn the diary on its side and read a note in the margin. *"They did steal the entire DNA database, but not the plans for our cloning facilities."*

Dismay halts my breath and leaves me empty. Fuck. This is not good.

"When it was just us with this technology, we could control where we took it and how we would use it. In the hands of Aoi Uma, the technology will diverge. This is disastrous for our corporation. We can never compete or catch up once they run away with it. We must work harder to shore up our defenses. Our own infiltration teams are out and trying to retrieve the data before it can be copied and altered."

I reach for my glass of water by the bed and swallow two mouthfuls, hoping it'll calm my racing heart. Skipping ahead in the diary, I try to figure out what happened next, but there's nothing, only plans to evacuate whatever base they had been in.

I check the date on the diary, and Isao wrote these entries six years ago.

Six years.

Aoi Uma has had this technology for six years. Fuck me.

I close the diary, set it on my bedside table, shut off the light, and curl into Rin. He sighs as he wraps his arms around me and pulls me close in his sleep. I want to wake him and tell him everything I just learned, but I can't. He needs his sleep, and I need some too.

I'll tell him in the morning.

CHAPTER THIRTEEN

After we place our bags in secure lockers at the train station, we're off to our day of training at the Aoi Uma factory.

"You don't think we should delay?" I trot to keep up with Rin and Ryoko. I thought that once I told them about the data theft perpetrated by Aoi Uma, we would hold off and do more research.

"Anything that they've done with the technology they stole will not get better or worse in the next few days, Yumi. Especially since it happened years ago." Rin slows down a bit and places his hand on the small of my back. "Try to think calm thoughts."

Calm thoughts. He's nuts. Nothing is calming about taking on this mission.

I shouldn't even be here at all. I should be back on that moon base with Isao. Really. I'm regretting that decision. I could have stayed out of this, but I'm here because the person who was going to play this role is on her way to the moon base. That invasion messed everything up.

I inhale through my nose and out through my mouth, remembering that I've been in more dangerous situations before. I have jumped from a burning building. I've lived side-by-side with murderers, drug dealers, and rapists. I've survived death by android several times now.

I can do this.

I adjust my uniform for the day, and Ryoko nods when I get the headscarf centered on my head. All Aoi Uma employees at this factory wear a comfortable blue uniform of a button-down shirt, pants, and a headscarf. The scarf covers the hair, ears, and neck — a precaution to help keep errant human material out of the factory's sensitive areas. Good for us because it's a practical disguise. I can easily hide my face by tilting my head in almost any direction. Ryoko and I have used some fancy skin-plumping creams to fill out our cheeks and lips. It's temporary, but it'll last the day and make us harder to identify. Even Rin used a little around his eyes to change the shape of his face. No dark charcoal makeup for him, though. Ryoko and I kept that to ourselves.

Kazuo, Aimi, and Saki will run point outside, disguised as tourists, ready to jump at a moment's notice.

The goal is to get inside, see what we see, go through the training, and on the lunch break, we make our way to the data center where Rin will set the virus loose that Isao engineered. The beauty of this virus is that the androids will not act any differently at first. It'll only be when they're called to do something that violates their new laws that people will notice the difference. We should be able to get away without having androids on our tail, just normal humans. We have a chance of escaping normal humans. Androids, not so much.

As we approach the building, I remind myself of my new identity programmed into my wrist chip. This new chip is one

I can control with my tablet, and I have ten identities pre-programmed by Kiiroi Yama. Thanks to my new allies, I am all but a ghost. Today, I'm Mika Ando, and I'm a recent graduate of Shin-Osaka University's Artificial Intelligence program. Ryoko is now Yoko, one of my fellow graduates. Rin is Ryan, a former Aka Matsuba employee also applying to the same division.

He breaks away from us and travels ahead, slipping through the revolving doors and into the lobby just in front of us.

"Let's go," I say to Ryoko, my voice forced into 'enthusiastic' mode. "First day!"

"Yay." She raises her fist. I laugh at her sarcastic tone, and she winks. We're rocking this undercover thing.

Inside the lobby, the building's interior rises at least twenty meters, windows streaming in the morning sunlight. I turn to look out and get a lay of the land. Off in the distance, the theme park is coming alive for the day, the rollercoasters taking on their first riders. Kazuo, Aimi, and Saki are nowhere nearby, not yet. They'll come into their spots in a few hours.

"New employees?" A security guard wearing blue and black gestures at us. "Over there." He points to a woman standing at a desk with a wallscreen behind her flashing employee information.

The intake process is straightforward. I watch people in front of us, including Rin, go through the same procedure over and over. So when it's finally Ryoko's turn, then mine, we're prepared.

I wave my wrist over the reader at the desk, and my information pops up in a tōsha.

"Mika Ando, welcome!" I have no idea how this woman smiles and says the same things over and over with the same amount of enthusiasm each time. "We're happy to have you here today. It looks like you already know Yoko?" She points to Ryoko, and I nod. "Great, because you're both assigned to the same section for the day. Follow everyone in the B line."

Okay, easy enough. I thank her, grab my Aoi Uma issued tablet (not to leave the building) and follow everyone in the B line. Within a few moments, we head to a conference room.

In true corporate fashion, we're subjected to two hours of bland intake videos about the building, what they make and do here, how to navigate the timekeeping system, and how to ask for time off, which I gather is strongly discouraged. Of course. I shift my eyes to the right, down the row of seats, to see if Rin is paying attention. A man between us has nodded off, his head bowed forward, a slight snore rumbling in each breath. Rin and I both hold back our laughs about him.

When the lights come up, everyone blinks to wake themselves up.

"We're going to take breaks now for water and snacks. Feel free to use the bathrooms and then meet your new supervisors back here. They will guide you on a tour, you'll get lunch, and then you'll go to your departments to learn more about what you'll be doing there."

"Bathroom?" I ask Ryoko, then lower my voice. "We may not get a chance later."

"Yeah. We should."

Once we've used the bathroom, and it's empty except for us, Ryoko joins me at the sink. "Do you know what you're going to do so Rin gets access to the data center?"

"Create a distraction," I whisper over the running water.

"If you can't, I'll pretend to be sick. I can throw up on command." Her face is dead serious. "It's a great party trick."

"You're joking."

"Nope."

Our eyes meet in the mirror, and we laugh. My shoulders shake with laughter, and my body releases the tension that's been building all morning. I wipe a tear from my eye and check my makeup.

"Thanks. I needed that. And please don't throw up on me. I, uh, reflexively puke if other people do."

Back in the conference room, our new supervisor is chatting with Rin and a few other people. She seems relaxed and easy like she does this all the time. Good. We don't want her to suspect anything.

Ryoko and I grab waters and try to appear at ease. If Ryoko is anything but, I wouldn't know. It's like she was made for this undercover shit. I didn't know someone like her, a scientist, could change so drastically in just a few months. My dad has all these sayings from Earth, and one of my favorites is about the strongest steel being forged in the hottest of fires. That's Ryoko. We have put her to the test, and now she's stronger than ever before.

Rin glances over at me and smiles. I politely smile back as if I don't know him. Ryoko takes my hand, squeezes it, and nods to Rin while our supervisor, Kat, drones on about the corporate culture and what to expect during a workday.

"All right, everyone. We're going to start our tour here on the first floor since the other groups have opted to go upstairs. Here on this south side of the building, we have five floors of office space, which includes the cafeteria if you don't want to go out to lunch in the city. We also have a gym and an in-house hotel."

So they can work you to death, and you never have to leave? Got it.

This is the hardest part of the mission, keeping my nerves

calm through this bullshit until we get to the actual work. We file out of the conference room to the main lobby again, and this time I have a good idea of where everything is.

"Hey!"

My forward momentum freezes, and the blood in my veins turns to ice.

It's Gen.

He runs straight past me from behind and corners my new supervisor.

"Hey, Kat! I need to speak to you for a second."

The irritation on Kat's face is plain, and I turn my head away to study the tall ceilings while she deals with Gen.

"Can you hear them?" Ryoko murmurs to me.

I nod. Gen is asking about available time in the lab. Kat responds that the schedule is always posted, and if he needs a slot, he should book one. But Gen wants time today at three. She doesn't have that time available. Guess what? Gen is an asshole, so he threatens to go over her head to *her* supervisor. She says fine, do that, and maybe her supervisor can rearrange the schedule for him.

"I'll do that," he huffs, stalking away. Both Ryoko and I face the other direction so he can't see us.

"Sorry about that." Kat forces a smile on her face. "Let's get moving."

Ryoko widens her eyes at me, and I mime a heavy breath. We avoided him. For now.

As we make our way through the place on our tour, I find I'm getting lost easier than usual. I concentrate on everything around us, but all the hallways look the same. Every turn is just like the last one. My memory is so fractured, and my head hurts from focusing so hard. When we have a moment between floors, I dig into my pocket and pull out a quick-dissolve tablet of painkillers. Popping it into my mouth, I wash it down with a swig of water.

"Everything okay?" Kat asks as the elevator doors open to the cafeteria.

"Fine. I woke up with a stress headache today. I guess I was a little worried about my first day."

Ryoko butts in. "My stomach has been a mess since last night. First-day butterflies here." She rubs her abdomen.

Kat nods, her expression sympathetic. "I understand. First days are always tough. See if you can eat anything because we'll be going to the lab later to start our initial work. I don't want you to be impaired by head or stomach aches."

She pats me on the shoulder as she moves to the front of the group to show everyone the cafeteria.

This mission is agonizingly slow. I knew it would take most of the day, but Kazuo, Saki, and Aimi must be worried sick about us outside. I try to eat tiny bits of food from the cafeteria, but the best I can manage is some buttered bread and a protein shake. Ryoko continues to baby her dramatic stomach by only drinking juice and eating plain rice. Rin eyes us both from the end of the table. I wait till no one is watching and then wink at him. He should know we're okay.

Whatever we do, whatever distraction we have to plan, it better work.

When the elevator door opens on the lab floors, my nervousness revs up into overdrive. This time I'm not faking the sweat that breaks out on my upper lip and the back of my neck. This is a lab like I've never seen before. I assume that these long corridors and walls of technology have to be their servers, where they store the programming for the androids.

"Wow," Ryoko says, her mouth open. I know she's not faking this awe because I can feel it too.

A cool breeze flows down the halls, and every time someone opens a glass door to a lab, the pressure changes, and my ears strain.

"This floor is ultra-cooled to keep the server equipment from overheating. We have two cooling stations in the floor below to maintain these rooms at the optimum temperature. Today, you'll each be supervised in small teams as we show you the interfaces and what you'll need to perform your work."

Okay, here's where the paths will diverge if we're not careful. I grab Ryoko's hand and move her sideways to the right so we're closer to Rin.

A few new Aoi Uma employees approach us from down the hall and wave to Kat. She waves back. "Great. Right on time. Here, Rachel, you take these four. Jess, you take these three. And I'll take these three here." Kat points to Ryoko, Rin, and me, and I smile with relief. Perfect.

"Come on," Kat says, jerking her head towards a lab just down the hall.

Nerves turn the butterflies in my stomach into big, fucking birds. Like giant birds. Whatever we need to do, it has to happen now. The door closes behind us, and the pressure in the room equalizes.

Ryoko stumbles back.

"Oh..." She brings her hand to her forehead. I'm impressed that her skin turns a frightening shade of white. How does she do that? "Hmm. I don't feel so good."

"Oh no," I say, taking her arm. "Maybe you should sit down."

Rin backs away from us, his hand in his pocket. I'm not sure what he has to do to get Isao's program to work, but he better be ready. This is a minuscule space, maybe only three meters square, and most of it is taken up by a wall interface.

Kat steps away to the other side of the room and pulls a wheeled chair out of a wall slot. "Here, darling. Are you okay?"

Ryoko lowers herself into the chair. "Maybe? I think I'm a little woozy."

I wave my hands in front of her face and try to get her more air.

"I... I..." She grabs my hand and one of Kat's too. "I'm going to be sick."

Kat panics, her feet dancing beneath her. "Oh, oh. No. The bathroom is this way."

She thrusts Ryoko to her feet and shoves her out the door. I follow, but not before looking back at Rin.

"Be safe," he whispers right before the door shuts on him.

I'm at Kat's heels when Ryoko slaps her hand over her mouth and retches.

Kat's face blanks and whitens. "Don't. I can't..."

With two more steps, Ryoko leaps forward and pukes all over the floor in front of the elevator. I look away and hold my breath, hoping my stomach stays put.

Kat is not so lucky. She lets her stomach loose right next to Ryoko.

Double whammy. Ugh.

From down the hall, someone shouts, "Somebody call maintenance!"

I said I was a sympathetic puker, and I knew other people were like me, but... I back away from the mess. I don't want to lose my lunch. I didn't eat enough to make it worth my while.

Glancing over my shoulder and leaning to the side, I can see into the lab where Rin is. Whatever he's doing, he's still in the middle of it, his hands flying over the lab console. He needs more time.

Looking away from the mess, I slowly approach both

ladies. "Hey, let's get you both to the bathroom." I grab their arms and breathe through my mouth, doing my best to stop my gag reflex.

This is the worst distraction ever.

The bathroom sign next to the elevators points to the left, so I pull both women around the mess on the floor and bring them to the bathroom. A woman inside takes one look at Kat and hightails it out of there. Good.

Kat launches herself into a bathroom stall and slams it shut behind her. I follow Ryoko to a sink.

"Are you okay?"

"I'm perfect," she whispers and then clears her voice. "I think I'll be okay," she says at a normal volume. But Kat isn't listening because she's continuing to puke.

Ryoko swishes water in her mouth, wipes up her face, and washes her hands.

I approach Kat's bathroom stall and lightly knock on it. "Are you going to be okay?"

"Yeah. I'll be okay. Just give me some time." She retches again. Ew.

"Sure. Uh, we'll wait for you outside, okay?"

"Okay."

I smile at Ryoko and jerk my thumb at the door. Time to go.

CHAPTER FOURTEEN

Out in the elevator lobby, a maintenance team is mopping up the mess we just made, but they're the only ones present, so we edge around them and make our way back to the lab.

"All done?" I ask, opening the door and looking in.

Rin is sitting in a chair, tapping on his Aoi Uma tablet. We rush in and shut the door behind us.

"Kat is pretty sick now. We have time to finish up and leave."

Rin turns off the tablet and sets it on the desk in the room. "We're not done yet. Leave your tablets here. We have two stops to make on our way out of the building."

"Uhhh, okay. Shouldn't we hustle out of here right away? I don't want to run into Gen." I feel like he's lurking just around the corner, ready to jump out and spook us at any moment.

"We're going to leave the floor," he assures me.

With his hand on my back, he directs us out the door and down the hallway. We head in the opposite direction of the elevators and walk at a normal pace, doing our best to not call suspicion to our behavior.

I cringe as I hear a voice behind us.

"Well, I need the lab time now. Narumi Ogawa's work waits for no one."

Fuck. It's Gen, and he's at our backs.

I can't turn around.

I want to turn around.

I want to turn around, run at him, and kill him with my bare hands.

If I did that, there would be no way I'd live to see tomorrow. I'd be dead too. If I'm going to kill him, it has to be in the open, so I can get away.

"Hey!" I hear him yell in our direction. "Did you leave a lab open?"

"Keep walking," Rin whispers, "through the door and into the stairwell. Down one flight."

We keep going, but Rin halts and turns around. With his headscarf on and only his face showing, it's doubtful Gen will recognize him. Gen only saw Rin in the flesh a few times, and most of those times, Gen was focused on me.

"Lab 3B is open!" He calls out, waving his hand in the air, before turning and following us through the door. He makes sure the door is shut and presses his ear to it.

"Are we safe?" I ask, my heart beating a rough tempo in my chest.

Rin pulls away and nods. "For now. He's bound to remember my face sooner or later, though. So let's keep moving."

We take the stairs two at a time and use our chips to enter the floor below the labs we were just in.

"Remember what Kat said about this floor?" Rin asks, striding down the hall.

"No." I search my brain for the information, but all I can see is Kat's face, her lips moving, but what she said is missing. Damned memory.

This floor is dark, with lights that only illuminate as we approach them. A strong vibrating hum is loud enough for me to worry about not hearing other things I'm supposed to.

"This is where they keep the coolers for the labs, right?" Ryoko asks, looking at each door as we pass them.

"Right." Rin stops at a door marked with the number three. "In here. I checked before we left, and no one was on this floor."

We step into another room that illuminates as we enter. It's hot and stuffy in here with the sharp scent of ozone. But Rin bypasses everything else and goes to the control board on the far wall. He scans his wrist, and the front access panel pops open.

"They're going to track us if you keep using your wrist like that," I warn him.

His returning smile is confident. "I stole two other people's identities while I was in the system and assigned my chip to them using a portal Isao set up. They'll rotate every few minutes. Isao worked wonders for this mission."

He taps on the screen a few times until I see the main power panel come up. Rin's finger slides down the line of virtual switches, turning off almost everything.

"There. In about five minutes, it's about to get blazing hot up in the labs. Then if they don't fix it soon enough? Boom." The delight in his eyes makes me laugh.

"I like boom."

"I know you do," he purrs and leans in to kiss my cheek.

"Hey, hey, now. None of that funny business," Ryoko cautions with a laugh. She waves her hands in front of her face. "We should go. I like boom, too, but only from very far away."

Rin raises his finger. "One more stop on our way out of the building. One more level down."

"We have to hurry," I caution him as we race to the door. "Kat will pull herself together soon enough and start looking for us. I don't know how long it'll be before she suspects something."

We exit back into the hall and return to the stairs.

"Wait," Ryoko says, hesitating for a moment. "Did you tell Gen lab 3B? Our lab?"

Rin's face loses its color. "I did. Fuck."

"Then we should be extra speedy. He'll find our tablets if he's not completely self-absorbed."

We sprint down the set of stairs and exit into another hallway. This time, though, the floor is much busier than the last place we went. A few people glance our way, but we look like everyone else around here, so they just go back to their business.

This floor is open, with workstations scattered everywhere. Along one side of the room is an enormous window that overlooks the android assembly factory floor. We amble along, weaving in and out of desks until we reach the window. My stomach clenches into a tiny ball of knots and nerves. I'm not even sure how to describe the assembly floor. Giant metal vats line one wall, pipes leading out every which way. Other machines spit out android parts onto conveyor belts. Workers in full protective suits stand at their stations and assemble heads to torsos to arms to legs.

I swallow hard, and my throat is dry as day-old toast.

When I poke Rin in the side, we get moving. I don't want

to linger because no one else is watching the factory floor like we are. I don't want us to appear out of place.

Rin turns and confidently strides to the opposite end of the floor. If people care that we're there, they don't show it. It's still the lunch hour, and lots of people are gone. Those remaining are glued to their work, which doesn't surprise me one bit. This reminds me of the times I spent my days at Kiiroi Yama's headquarters with Rin. I would walk around the floor, and no one would question the validity of my presence. The same attitude seems to prevail in every corporation.

Off the main floor, we follow the hallway while Rin stares at the numbers on the doors.

"Here, this one." He points to the door. "I'm going in. Meet me at the end of the hallway. Call the elevator now and hold it. I'll only be gone a moment."

My heart is likely to burst with how fast it's trying to run. What if he goes in there and never comes back out? I can feel the tears forming in my eyes, but I push them away. No. No time for emotions now.

When the door clicks shut behind him, I stare at it for a breath. I'm not comfortable with this. I don't even know why he went in there. What's so important that he's willing to risk everything now?

Ryoko tugs on my arm. "Come on. Act natural."

We walk to the elevator bank and stand there for a moment while I piece together the puzzle. I remember the diary entry I read last night and everything I told Rin about this morning. This mission had only one objective — reprogram the androids. Right about now, androids are getting their new laws, their new instructions, and the entire scheme is about to tumble down around Aoi Uma. And with each passing second, our situation here becomes more precarious. Would Rin risk his life, our lives, to do something else?

Wait. I think I know what he's doing.

Is he going after the consciousness transfer program? Is that even something we can steal back? Aoi Uma stole it from Shiroi Nami. It must have been portable enough to pick up and leave with.

An elevator door opens, and people returning from lunch file out and walk past us. The elevator is now empty, and we didn't have to call it. Ryoko smiles and slips by them to insert herself in the door.

"Stand there," I say, stepping in.

The elevator chimes and asks, "Which floor, please?"

"Lobby," I say, and its status screen switches to list the lobby as the next destination.

"Please step out of the doorway and allow the elevator to close," the system prompts.

I shake my head at Ryoko. She leans to the side so she can see down the hall.

Where's Rin? Panic turns everything in my brain to mush. Please let him be okay.

"Please step out of the doorway and allow the elevator to close," the system repeats.

"Come on," I whisper.

Ryoko gasps. "He's coming."

"Please step out of the doorway and allow the elevator to close. If there is a malfunction, maintenance will be called in thirty seconds."

"Hurry," Ryoko calls to Rin.

He appears around the corner and double-times it to the elevator. Ryoko lets the door close as he slips in past her and next to me. He's carrying a black suitcase in his right hand.

"I got it. Let's go."

Even he seems panicked, and my heart is straining at my chest. Sweat pours down my back, and I'd give anything to take this headscarf off now. I feel like it's a giant snake wrapped around my head, trying to suffocate me to death.

The elevator drops, and I pray that we're not interrupted in our descent to the lower levels. What happens if someone else gets in?

But I breathe out a sigh of relief when the elevator doesn't stop.

"Walk straight out, with purpose," Rin instructs. "Don't look at anyone. Don't run unless I say so. Kiiroi Yama is on the way."

I nod and grab Ryoko's hand to squeeze it. She nods back at me.

This is it. We will either get out of here alive, or they'll catch us at the door. Are there any other options? There are so many choices in life, yet sometimes there are *no* real choices. Choosing between living and dying? That's not really a choice unless you're suicidal. But where do I go from here? Is this what's in store for me for the rest of my life? Watching my enemies one-up each other trying to kill me? Or should I slip into obscurity? I could if I didn't care anymore.

I still care.

Even with the gaps in my memory, I know that the only way out is through.

We can do this.

The door opens, and plenty of other people are waiting to get in. I don't look at anyone. I keep my eyes forward and walk out with Ryoko, and Rin is right behind us. The shortest route to the revolving doors is straight across the room, through the turnstiles, and then another twenty meters. That's nothing. We can do that.

But I feel a panic attack coming on. My stomach has completely bottomed out, and my teeth chatter with the nerves. The giant room darkens, and my breathing becomes erratic.

Not now, Yumi. Be brave.

Ryoko and I approach the turnstiles, but we let Rin go first. He scans his wrist, the gates open, and he slips through. Ryoko takes the next turnstile, and she's through. I wave my wrist over the reader, and the turnstile beeps.

Fuck.

I begin to panic as a security guard approaches me. I try again, and this time my wrist opens the turnstile. I sigh as I walk through.

But out of the corner of my eye, I can see the guard still approaching.

"Miss!" He calls out, raising his hand. "Miss! There must be an error with your chip. If you come back, we can take care of it right now."

I turn on my heel and wave to him. "Tomorrow. I'm going to be late for an appointment."

When my eyes focus past him, adrenaline shoots through my whole system.

Gen runs out of the security station with three of the most beautiful, most deadly-looking large cats I have ever seen trotting at his side.

"Yumi!" He calls out, and my legs stumble as I attempt to walk backwards. "It's over, Yumi! Don't try to escape!"

People shriek and scramble out of Gen's way, but I lock my eyes on the cats. Not just cats, maybe leopards? Jaguars? Oh shit.

The one in the lead stops and looks up at Gen as I reach the door. He peers down at the cat and says, "Yes, that's the one. Don't let her get away."

The cat nods. *It fucking nods.*

Its eyes are filled with intelligence, and it knows where its prey is and what she looks like.

She looks like me.

I get my legs under me, and I call up every last bit of energy I have.

"Run!"

CHAPTER FIFTEEN

"Run! Go!"

My voice cracks on the syllables as I push them through my closed throat.

Ryoko takes off, almost passing Rin, who is doing his best to carry the black suitcase and still run at the same time.

Kazuo steps out from a crowd of people, clothed in Kiiroi Yama black with two swords strapped to his back. He tosses one sword to Rin as Rin lobs the suitcase to Kazuo. Saki strides away from the opposite side of the boulevard, her eyes on Ryoko and me... And then the cats.

I don't want to see them. I don't want to.

I look behind me anyway.

Oh shit.

They are gorgeous. Whoever designed these beasts did an excellent job. Their fur is lustrous, and their long strides tug at the ground beneath them as they sprint to keep up with us. Three cats, three giant cats that I'll have to evade or kill.

I don't want to kill them. They're too beautiful.

I know I'll have to.

"Yumi!" Kazuo calls out. He has my knife in his hand. *My knife*, the one I brought from Orihimé. The only proper weapon I know how to fight with.

I bank to the right without losing speed just as Kazuo tosses my knife into the air.

I almost lose it. The knife tumbles, and my hand fumbles for it, but I pull it to my chest, and I keep going.

Screams erupt from the boulevard behind us, and a blood-curdling growl turns into a high-pitched shriek as I round the bend right after Ryoko.

"Go!" I scream at her. "Park!"

There's only one place we can go where we can lose these cats, and that's into the theme park. It's a bit of a run from here, but we may hold these cats off if we dodge in and out of places.

Because I don't want to brag or anything, but I'm a shitty runner, and those cats were born to chase. Chase and destroy.

I glance over my shoulder to catch the scene on the boulevard as we turn onto a nearby street.

Saki has already killed one cat! Go Saki! That's what that scream was. She must have stepped out into its path and taken it down right away.

Two cats left.

We can do this.

A stitch tears through my side, and I nearly puke from the pain.

I can't do this.

I force my legs forward.

It's now early afternoon, and the theme park is at full attendance. The sun is out, and it's a glorious day to ride roller-coasters, drink beer, and eat decadent food. I only wish I could stay and enjoy it.

"Out of the way!" Ryoko calls out to a crowd of people around the entrance. They scatter like the bugs in my Kitakyushu apartment when the lights came on. She runs through the front gate at blinding speed, and a tōsha pops up, taking her credits and admitting her for the day. More people get out of the way as I approach, and their eyes widen when they see what's on my tail.

A woman screams, and more people run.

"Ryoko! Through the arcade!"

I can hear the cats now. Their nails scrape on the pavement, and their breath heaves in huffs. "Circle back!" Rin's voice from behind surprises me, but I should have known he'd follow.

Ryoko banks left into the long arcade of fair games, and I follow her. Behind me, the two cats are just ten meters away, and Saki, Rin, and Aimi are behind the cats. I didn't even see Aimi. She must have been staked out somewhere else.

One cat scrambles to get around a corner and crashes into a small family, two parents and a kid. They all come tumbling to the ground. The kid is bleeding, but it looks like it was an accident. The cats only have eyes for me. One growls, and the other cat in the lead glances back. They vocalize to each other, and the cat farther away nods before breaking off to the left.

Oh shit.

They are going to pen us in somehow.

I can't keep running. I catch up to Ryoko as the head cat picks up the pace behind us.

"Circle right! Cat on left!"

Shouting is sucking the energy out of me, energy I need to keep going. I rip the headscarf off and toss it aside, freeing my head and bringing sweet cool air to my body. Ryoko does the same.

The lead cat is getting closer. Her own breathing is labored now, though I'm sure she could run for days without stopping. I used to watch nature documentaries of Old Earth —back before the wars, back before the Decline — with my father. There were wide grass fields where animals roamed free and hunted each other.

I'm the hunted one now.

"Bring straight to Rin," I shout, then we both dodge out of the way of an arcade employee dragging out a can of trash. I grab it at the last moment and dump it over on the ground.

"Hey! Ahhh!" The employee scrambles to the side and falls as the cat leaps over him. She tries to get purchase on the ground again to run after us.

"Yes," Ryoko breathes out. Her face is beet red, and sweat pours down her neck, but she laughs. Not because any of this is funny. This is insane and totally absurd, and we both know it.

We're approaching the end of the arcade. What should we do? Left or right?

Before I can make a split-second decision, Rin and Saki run out from the building's end and pass us. I'm afraid to stop running, but I need to. My body is about to give up.

Rin's sword is out of its sheath and swinging through the air as the cat screams and jumps right at him.

Saki comes up from below, her fist a missile straight for the cat's underbelly. In the air, the cat can't do anything. She flips, back legs flinging over, and Rin's sword flies true. He cuts her down, and she rolls across the ground several times before coming to a bloody halt.

Ryoko and I are both bent over, sucking air. My legs shake, and my eyes sting from the sweat pouring down my forehead. Holy shit. That was close.

"Wait," Ryoko says, trying to calm her breath. She swallows and spits on the ground. "There was another one."

We both turn around. I don't see the last one. It peeled off and went in the opposite direction.

"The roof!" Aimi is barreling towards us from the direction that Ryoko and I just came from.

The roof?

I glance up, and fear grabs my heart and yanks it. The last cat crouches on the roof of the arcade, ready to pounce.

"Go!" Rin yells.

Ryoko and I take off, and my body is ten times more upset with me for running again. Whatever we do now, it has to be over soon.

If the cat sees Rin, Aimi, and Saki, it doesn't care. Gen told them all to not let *me* get away, and now that's all they are aiming for.

Me.

"Help!" I scream, hoping someone else will step in this time and bring this cat to a standstill. "Help!"

Saki joins us on the run this time. She's faster than either of us, so she's out front, pushing people out of the way, keeping the path clear.

I look behind me again to gauge how close the cat is, and something new is happening that I hadn't expected.

People are turning to watch. No, wait. They're androids. Androids are stopping and tuning into the scene, the scene of a human in trouble, a human calling for help.

I pass another android who turns with a vacant expression on her face. She steps between the cat and me, putting herself in harm's way. The cat growls as its feet skitter. The android throws herself onto the cat, but the cat is too slick. It finds us again in its sights and keeps going.

Ahead, Saki has cleared the crowd all the way up a long ramp to the rollercoaster. This is simultaneously the best and worst idea all at once. My logic tells me to get on the rollercoaster and get the hell out of here. This cat can't chase a rollercoaster, right?

Everything at this park is automated, and people have already climbed aboard a coaster, ready to leave the station.

"Out of the way!" Ryoko calls.

People scream and dive to the sides. Ryoko vaults over a turnstile and sprints to the front car.

"Prepare to leave the station," an announcement over the loudspeaker blares down at us.

I pass Saki standing to the side. She yells, "Go!" at me, and I keep running straight for an open car. I can't leap the turnstile, so I roll over it in the most awkward way possible and land in the car with a thump.

My hands shake as I struggle to bring the harness down over me and allow the car to strap me in. People in front and behind me turn to stare at me with wide eyes. All I can do is huff and attempt to breathe.

More screaming from the entrance makes everyone left on the platform run for the exit. Saki and another person, another android maybe, are wrestling with the cat. The cat swipes out and tears off most of Saki's shirt. The other android kicks at the cat, and my dismay grows as the rollercoaster inches forward. These androids have received the new programming to keep humans safe. Still, they're not the trained fighters that Narumi Ogawa used to send after me on Kurai.

The cat growls and leaps past Saki and the other android. Shit.

I watch over my shoulder as the cat lengthens its strides

down the platform, leaps, and connects with the last car on the coaster.

The people sitting there scream as she stalks over them. But the coaster is in motion now, and we're strapped in, and the cat is not.

I know cats well. My mom has this thing with cats, and back home, she has about a dozen of them she talks to. With our animal translation chip technology, she was paired with cats at a young age, so they've always been around. I've seen house cats do things that defy gravity. There is a reason they have nine lives.

Gen engineered this cat to chase. He engineered it to listen, understand, take orders, and still make its own decisions based on risk analysis. This cat is intelligent in the ways house cats are not.

Fucking Gen. I knew he would put his skills to use someday, but I didn't think he would go this far.

The coaster slows down as it comes to a hill. I can't believe my first time on a rollercoaster is like this. I look behind, and the cat is stalking forward, winding a path over the tops of each car. Not stopping, she steps on screaming people trying to shrink out of the way. I doubt there are any androids here who can help me. I can only help myself.

I shake the rigid steel harness holding me in. It doesn't budge. Fuck. I can't get out. I'm a sitting duck. Tears fill my eyes. This cat is going to kill me, and there's nothing I can do about it.

But then we reach the top of the climb, and the only thing I see in front of us is the coaster cars disappearing over the top. I glance behind me again, and the cat is three cars back.

Maybe...

My bodyweight pulls forward as the acceleration hits

maximum speed, and the whole coaster races down the hill in front of us. Holy shit! The world disappears in front of me, and we speed up into a dive so hard that it pins my head against the back of the car. My cheeks and teeth shake in my head as we hit the bottom of the hill and take off again faster up another hill, tilt to the right and come around a fast bend.

I try to catch my breath and assess the situation behind me. I expect to find nothing but people, but no. The cat has held on for dear life. Its arms and legs are wrapped around two harnesses, and the people in those harnesses are pressed as far away from the cat's claws as possible. From this angle, I see the cat is a female. She's probably pretty young too, and this has to be her first time on a rollercoaster, like me. I almost laugh. Almost.

The coaster swings around, down and up, down and up. My eyes widen as I see what's next, a loop. I grab my harness with all my might and hold on tight as the coaster swings into a giant loop, and I'm upside down, looking at the ground below us.

Kiiroi Yama police cars are racing across the land between the coaster tracks. Are they here for me? Is that Rin or Kazuo?

When the rollercoaster straightens out, I realize a lot has been going on in the minute since I got on the coaster. Other black flying cars are also approaching, but they don't appear to be Kiiroi Yama. Fuck, it's Aoi Uma. Fighting androids hang out the sides, and I lick my lips, wondering if they will get the new programming we sent out. This would all be useless if they didn't change as well.

The rollercoaster's wheels squeal, and the train slows down, but we're far from the station. Glancing back, the cat is unfolding from its secure position wrapped around all the harnesses.

"Yumi!"

I turn to the front, and Ryoko is climbing over the other cars to get to me. "Emergency release! Over the side on your left!"

Really? Over the left side, yes, there's a lever. Pulling on it hard, the harness releases and floats up. I stand up, pull out my knife, and get ready.

The cars are slowing, and we're coming to the halfway point of the ride. But I'm not going on from here. I'm going to defend myself against this cat.

The cat growls and leaps. Her trajectory is straight and true. At the last possible moment, I jerk to the side, and she crashes into the lifted harness. I stab her in the side of her chest with my knife, and I hate myself. I love animals, and this is the most brutal thing I have ever done. I'd rather kill some awful person than do this. She was born and engineered to be this way. It's not her fault.

Her shriek of pain freaks me out. I climb to the side of the car and peer over the edge. My side is over a flimsy guardrail and empty air. The cat's side is where I need to be, next to a thin platform and a maintenance tower.

I stand up on the seat and gauge how far I'm going to have to leap to get over her. She turns and growls, swiping out with her claws and ripping my shirt to shreds.

Hot pain slices through my chest, and blood pours down from my torso over my pants.

She swipes again and just misses my neck and face. Instead, she slices down my arm.

The bloodied knife is still in my hand. With a burst of angry energy, I punch out and clock her across the head with the handle, wind back, and stab her in the shoulder.

She screams and pulls away, ready to pounce, and my body numbs. I can't escape her. There's no place for me to go.

"Yumi! Jump left!"

I recognize the voice before my legs leap. My body flies left and over the side of the rollercoaster car while Aimi springs from the guardrail with her sword swinging.

She cuts down the cat in one swift motion, just as I'm flying over the guardrail, watching my own death unfold. My knife slips from my hand and falls faster than me, down down down, a glint of shining metal twisting in the ether. I am several hundred meters in the air, and there's nothing below but open space.

My shirt tightens, and my body jerks to a stop, fabric ripping in sharp bursts.

"Gotcha," Saki says.

I open my mouth and scream. "Oh my God, help!"

"I've got you," she reassures me. "Stop flailing. I'm going to bring you to the side of the rollercoaster."

I seem to hover in the air as she brings me over to the steel supports, and I wrap my arms around them, gripping on for dear life.

Glancing up, Saki is only one support above me.

"I climbed all the way up. Took a while, but I made it."

I bark out an incredulous laugh and switch my grip on the steel supports because I'm bleeding enough for my hands to be slippery.

A high-pitched whine approaches from below, and a small dot grows bigger until it's Rin on a sorabō, one of those flying sticks that I hardly see anymore. He has my knife in his hand.

"Don't want to lose this, now." He smiles as he stuffs it in his waistband.

"Wow. Did you see that?" Someone from above asks.

When I look up, several heads are peeking over the sides of their cars, getting footage on their tablets and cameras.

Well, if I wasn't famous before, I am now.

Rin's face is a grave mask. "Are they all dead?"

I nod, pulling my lips into my mouth briefly. "The cats are all dead. Everyone else is okay."

When another flying car approaches, it opens its door on the other side, and Aimi and Ryoko climb in.

"Hold tight. It'll be around for you next."

"Rin," I plead, wanting to dissolve into tears and break down.

"No, Yumi. Not yet." His words are harsh, but his tone is sincere and caring. "Aoi Uma is on the way, and —"

A giant explosion not too far away almost knocks me off the supports. Screams erupt from the coaster passengers, and we all close our eyes against the brightness of the fireball in the distance.

It's the Aoi Uma factory. It just blew up. Holy shit.

A small smile curls Rin's lips. "Ah, there we go. I was wondering when that would happen."

An approaching Aoi Uma car turns and circles back, heading straight for the explosion.

"How...?" I ask, then I remember the stop we made on our way out to the utility room where Rin turned off all the cooling to the server floor. "Never mind. The servers."

He pulls away on the sorabō. The Kiiroi Yama vehicle rounds the coaster, Kazuo, Aimi, and Ryoko in the doorway. Saki climbs down next to me.

"Come on, friend. Let's get you to safety."

It doesn't escape my notice that she calls me 'friend.'

CHAPTER SIXTEEN

The ride back to Awashikawa is twice as long as the train ride to Amagasaki. The Kiiroi Yama officers flying the car are excellent at their job. We weave in and out of the city, evading our tail before flying low over the countryside and changing cars twice.

They let us out only a few blocks from the house. Rin patched up my wounds in the car, but it wasn't enough. I'm still bleeding through my bandages.

"Let's get home, and then we'll get you a doctor," Kazuo says, helping me from the car. "Someone will bring our bags from Amagasaki in a little bit."

I nod, not caring about my belongings. I still have my knife. That's all that matters to me now.

"Kiiroi Yama said they were sending a doctor, and..." Kazuo's voice trails off as we round the bend and see who's sitting outside of our house.

His face hardens, and his stare becomes cold.

Atsumi stands up from sitting on the porch, worrying her hands in front of her. She knocks on the door, and the doctor I saw only a few days ago launches out of the house, running towards us.

"Let me help," he says, taking my arm and getting it over his shoulder.

I keep my eyes on the ground, unwilling to look at Atsumi or acknowledge her presence. I was just getting used to her not being around. I wish she would go to hell and actually *stay there*.

Rin runs up next to us, but he goes straight for Atsumi, grabbing her arm and tugging her away from the house.

"Why are you here?" His voice is so full of anger that I stop in my tracks, halting the doctor.

"I... I... Okamoto gave me no choice. Either I help you with this mission, or my life is forfeit."

And from the pallor of her skin, I can tell this is the truth. Finally, someone else's life is on the line but my own.

She spreads out her hands. "I have nothing left. My contract is in negative standing. It's either this or I'm dead."

"I don't believe you," Rin replies. "You have had nothing but hate for Yumi since the beginning. I'll speak to Okamoto."

"Yes, please," she begs, bringing her hands to prayer position at her chest. "I can't stay here. I'm too embarrassed by what happened, how awful I was. I just want... I want..." She wipes tears from her face, and I sigh. Her attention jerks to me.

"I don't give a shit what you want," I tell her.

"You heard her," Rin says, pointing to me. His eyes are cold on Atsumi. "You will leave."

Atsumi's voice comes out like a childish whine. "I can't. Just let me stay and help. I promise I won't interfere."

"Your promises mean nothing." Rin turns his back on her and stalks towards me. I caution him with a look to slow down and handle me gently, and he closes his eyes, blows out a calming breath, and takes my arm to help me in.

Kazuo's voice lifts above Atsumi's sobbing. "Come with me. I'll find work for you to do."

The inside of the house is cold and dark with impending night. Rin switches on the lights and adjusts the temperature on the thermostat. I try to stand on my own, but my legs are too weak to hold me. I half crumble to the floor before the doctor saves me from falling straight onto my face.

"Whoa. Let's get her to the bed."

The bed is stripped clean. The sheets are probably in the wash, so I point to a towel in the bathroom. Rin lays it out to shield the bed from my blood.

"What did this?" the doctor asks as I lie down.

"A big, genetically engineered cat. Maybe a jaguar? I don't know."

The doctor glances at Rin. Rin shrugs. "Beats me. I think I've only seen something like it in an Aka Matsuba zoo."

"Doctor, what's your name?" I ask, reaching out for his hand.

He softens. "Everyone calls me Dr. Jimmy around here." His face assumes that gentle bedside manner that all the excellent doctors out there have. My stomach settles a bit at the sight of it.

"Thank you for helping me with my migraine the other day. Sorry about this."

He shakes his head, his kind smile never wavering. "Don't worry about it. Look, we need to get your shirt and bra off so I can see the wounds. Are you okay with that?"

"Yeah." My teeth chatter, and his hand touches my forehead.

"You're running a fever. Let me get my medical tablet, and we'll start on a blood workup and scan."

I lie in bed as Rin rinses off my knife in the bathroom sink and then uses it to cut open my shirt and bra.

"This is exactly what I was worried about," he mutters, sheathing the blade again.

"Sorry," I burst out through the tears pouring down my face. "So sorry."

He hovers over me. "Don't apologize. I'm going to kill Gen," he growls. "That's the last time he hurts someone I love."

Rin swoops in and kisses me gently before he places another warm towel on my chest while we wait for the doctor to run his scans. Then I close my eyes and wish I was somewhere else while Dr. Jimmy stitches my wounds closed.

"Damn," he says, sighing and sitting up. "These wounds do not want to close or stop bleeding. I'm going to add a coagulant to the dressing. Hopefully, that'll stop it."

He works while I slip in and out of consciousness. I'm bone-tired, and my body hurts in a million ways. This is not how I pictured the mission going, but I suppose it's not any worse than being dead.

"Mr. Hara, can I see you out in the other room?" He places his hand on my shoulder. "Get some rest, Miss Minamoto. I will start a new IV drip with some meds for the fever and an antibiotic. I'm pretty sure your body is fighting off an infection from those cuts. You'll be all right in a day or two."

I close my eyes and drift into a dreamless sleep for a while. Sleep. I need sleep. But I'm still exhausted when I reopen my eyes and find Saki sitting in a chair next to the bed. Her eyes are unfocused, staring at a spot on the wall.

"Hey." I try to wet my lips, but my tongue is a dried prune. "Where is everyone?"

Saki snaps out of whatever trance she was in and turns to me. Whenever she does that, I worry Narumi has taken hold of her again. I've been afraid to ask, but maybe now...

"Rin and Kazuo are in the other room talking to the doctor."

I strain my ears, and yes, I can hear the murmur of voices out there. Good. Nothing much has changed.

"Saki, I, um, I see you check out of reality a few times per day, and it's worrying me."

She smiles, a smile I remember so well from working in the kitchen together at Fourth Avenue Noodles. Remember when we used to spend time together... As friends?

"I'm taking the new laws you have given me and re-examining past actions, things I did before I had them. It's..." She cocks her head to the side and thinks for a moment. "It's been an interesting experiment. I think most of what I've done has been fine. I saved that man at the festival, and I wanted to help you. But..."

"But Narumi got in the way when she hacked you."

"Yes," she says, nodding and brushing invisible dirt off her pants. "She violated more of the laws than I ever did. I'm regretful over it."

"There was nothing you could do," I remind her. "No place for you to run. Nowhere you could hide from her, except for that town by the sea."

"I want to go back there," she says, leaning forward. "There was no other place that felt like home."

"I hope you can return someday, then." I hold out my hand to her, and she takes it, her smile bittersweet.

"I hope I can make up for the damage I caused you." She

places her other hand over mine and grimaces with a hiss. "You're still burning up. My sensors tell me your fever is higher than it was before. I'm going to let them know you're awake."

Once she's gone, I try to push myself up in bed, but I'm too tired to do anything, much less sit up straight. Shit. That Amagasaki mission took a lot more out of me than I thought.

I smack my lips together and drink more of the water at the bedside. Whatever this infection is, I will fight it off. Nothing is going to take me down now, not when we're so close to accomplishing our mission.

When Rin enters the bedroom, yawning and stretching, I look past him to the front room. The lights are off, and everyone has gone home.

"What were you discussing with the doctor?" His yawn catches, and I hold back a yawn of my own.

Rin tugs his shirt off and shucks his pants to the floor. If I weren't fighting an infection and tired, I'd want to run my hands all over him and drown my worries in his kisses and caresses. But that's a plan better left for another day, and I'm sure he would tell me it's not a good idea either.

"Nothing much. He's worried about your infection since it came on so quickly, but he thinks the meds will be aggressive enough to give you the boost you need. You need to sleep, though, so a migraine doesn't hit you when you're trying to heal."

He lifts the covers and slips into bed beside me, wrapping his arms around my waist and pulling me to lie down. So much for sitting up and trying to power through.

I roll onto my side and get into a comfortable position with the IV still in my arm. "I hope this thing comes out tomorrow. I hate IVs."

"Dr. Jimmy will be back in five hours to take the IV out, so let's get some rest now. Tomorrow is a big day."

I push my hips into his and try not to laugh at his mournful sigh. He kisses the back of my neck.

"What's tomorrow?" I whisper into the dark. "And how do we know we're safe here?"

"Tomorrow, we bring Shiroi Nami back to this continent with a festival and a head start on your documentary." He nuzzles his head into the pillow. "And we're safe here because Aoi Uma knows their time is short. They will only attack us when they're certain they'll have the advantage. Not now."

His confidence astounds me. I draw breath to ask more questions, but he stops me with a gentle squeeze.

"Shhh, Yumi. Save your questions for tomorrow. Go to sleep."

Fine. But only because I can't keep my eyes open anymore.

Sleep is my best option.

CHAPTER SEVENTEEN

It's hard to believe that it was only yesterday I was infiltrating my enemy's factory and running through a theme park being chased by giant cats, but here I am. I'm standing in the middle of Awashikawa on a bright and sunny day, and I'm thinking about how to frame my first shot.

I try to clear my throat from the giant frog lodged in it, but it feels like my whole body is unhappy with me. The antibiotics and pain killers have kicked in and lowered my fever, but I still feel like I've been run over by a truck. I guess I'm more out of shape than I realized. Months of living on the smallest of scraps will do that to you, though.

"Coffee?" Aimi appears at my side with a steaming cup, and the scent of coffee almost knocks me over.

"Bless your heart, yes."

She laughs as she hands over the cup. "Need it, eh?"

"Do I ever." I sip the steaming coffee and hum in pleasure. Just the right amount of cream and sugar. "Perfection."

I amble down the row of food stands setting up for the day, and Aimi keeps pace beside me.

"So, what's the schedule for today? Have you spoken with Rin and Kazuo?"

"Yeah, and it looks like the day will be packed before we even get to the announcement." She jerks her head at the steady stream of people coming in from the direction of the train station. "All of the neighboring towns are Shiroi Nami sympathetic. I'm sure they will pack this place in no time."

I hand her the extra camera. "Are you from around here?"

"Yeah, actually, my family is from this area. My parents died when I was young, and Aunt Reina adopted me into the Shiroi Nami family not long after. I've lived out most of my adult life on the Southern Continent around more of the upper echelons of the corporation. Then I spent time on Kurai too."

I stop and turn to her. "Tell me the truth about all of this." I wave my hand at our surroundings. "When we first crash-landed here, we were told by Aka Matsuba and Aoi Uma that Shiroi Nami had been exiled to Kurai. I didn't think there would be this many people who would sympathize with them. Was I lied to?"

Sorting out this story is essential for putting together the picture of power here. I've only seen glimpses over time, and not everyone was very forthcoming about the details. Details made them look bad, and they couldn't have that.

"Oh yes," she says with a laugh. "You were lied to. You don't get rid of a whole corporation employing thousands of people by exiling their executives and their families to a moon." She rolls her eyes. "As if that would even be possible, right?"

"Right," I agree with her. We step out of the way of more people streaming into town and heading straight for the local bakery. They're already set up for the day with a bright and colorful banner and loads of baked goods on the tables out front. "Makes sense. So while Aka Matsuba and Aoi Uma thought they had gotten rid of their competition..."

Aimi fills in the rest. "Instead, they had made virtual martyrs of the leaders and caused everyone left behind to work harder in secret." She lifts her finger. "And make no mistake, they *are* martyrs even if they're still alive. They were all sterilized so they couldn't pass the corporation down to legal offspring."

Eugenics has always bothered me as a concept, and killing off an entire family, *my distant family,* makes my blood boil.

Aimi turns around and walks backwards so she can talk and face me at the same time. "Hey, I had an idea, and I wondered if you would be into it or not."

I try not to be suspicious. "What's that?"

"I thought we should broadcast bits and pieces of what we make along the way to filming this larger documentary. We can start our own news network on the underground forums. I have access to them and can set up our own, kind-of, portal where we post things regularly."

A brilliant idea. Imagine having my own news network! I wonder what Chiéko would think of it. I pause my walk and turn my face to the sun. I wish they were all here, but Shintaro is making good headway bringing everyone together in Shin-Osaka. He and Chiéko were both in my messages to tell me how brave and stupid I was in Amagasaki yesterday. I take these as compliments.

"I love this idea. Thank you for bringing it to me."

I don't know what comes over me, but I throw my arms around Aimi's neck and hug her tight. She hesitates for a moment before she hugs me back.

"Thank you for yesterday, too." I lower my voice and pull away. "You were fabulous. A real force of nature."

"Oh shit," she says, waving at me. "Don't make me blush, Yumi." She lets out a gigantic sigh. "Besides, we're family now. Practically blood. If you need help, I'll be there."

"Thanks." I squeeze her arm. "Same, but that means Shintaro is also your family. I hope you're ready for his constantly devious behavior."

She throws her head back in a laugh. "Trust me. I can handle him."

We break off, each of us taking a camera and circling the festival stalls. I finish my coffee, take a quick breather for some energy, and then wander for a bit, strolling along while no one knows who I am. There are people here, I'm sure, who have seen my diary entries online, but I look a lot different now with my short hair and slimmer frame. It'll be a little while before people get to know this new me.

When I see a break in the action at one particular food stall, I decide to approach the man and woman who are staffing the table.

"Oh, look. I love *senbei!*" I pick up a package of large, round rice crackers and sniff them. "These smell amazing."

"Just grilled them this morning," the woman says. "Would you like to try one?" She proffers a tray of samples. The rice cracker is crunchy, sweet, and salty. It melts in my mouth.

"I love it. I'll get two packages."

After I've paid for the packs of senbei and put them into my small backpack, I explain to them both that I'm filming a documentary about the return of Shiroi Nami to the continent. Though they're skeptical at first, they both warm-up once I take out my camera. I shake their hands, and they introduce themselves as Mr. and Mrs. Kokoda.

"Have you lived in Awashikawa for a long time?" I ask, framing them both side by side.

"Oh, no. Only until about two years ago," Mrs. Kokoda says, continuing to replenish the supply of rice crackers as more people come to try them and listen to my interview. "We moved here when we got word from our corporation that we should move farther out of the Southern Continent to save ourselves and our businesses."

"What was their advice?"

"Well, things were getting tough on the Southern Continent. We had a small senbei shop there, and we couldn't make a profit, much less anything of a living, with the yakuza shaking us down every day. The corporation thought we would be safer here."

Mr. Kokoda leans in. "The yakuza there are relentless, and I think it's because they know their way of life is ending. With a corporation like Shiroi Nami in the lead, we never had to worry about yakuza interference. And rumors about Shiroi Nami coming back made the yakuza crack down even harder."

Anxiety rises in my chest, but I concentrate harder on my subjects.

"Have you ever been to the Southern Continent, dear?" Mrs. Kokoda asks.

"Yes, I have. I spent a few trying months in Kitakyushu, and then..." I close my eyes and think hard about the town we went to next. What was it called? Something with an S. And there was an estate there. I shake my head. "Anyway, yes, I have been there. The Southern Continent has a lot of charm."

"It does," Mrs. Kokoda says, her face lighting up with a smile. "The yakuza were horrible, but I never had to worry about androids. Here, I've been worried about androids constantly until I saw the stories of what happened yesterday.

Did you know there have been no cases of android malfunctions since the big fire at the factory in Amagasaki?"

"It's all she can talk about," her husband chimes in. "We think Aoi Uma got hacked."

"And a good thing, too," she says, nodding her head. "That corporation needs to go. Shiroi Nami has always been where our hearts and credits lie. We don't need anyone else."

"Thank you." I shut off my camera and slip it into my pocket. "I appreciate you speaking to me."

"Anytime, dear." Her smile reminds me of someone... an older woman I met on the Southern Continent. Who was that?

After another hour of circling the food stalls and doing impromptu interviews, I realize I'm parched and on the verge of a migraine. Everything about my body hurts. My brain is in a fog, and my eyesight is blurry too. I'm probably just tired, but I don't want to push things. I'm on a lot of meds, after all.

And I have an infection, too. Don't forget that, Yumi.

Don't forget. Don't forget.

I sit down at an empty table and pull my little notebook from my bag. Running my shaking hand over the cover, I close my eyes and force myself back to the time when Kazuo gave it to me. It was before we went to rescue Rin, before so many other things happened. It feels like a lifetime ago.

Flipping through the pages, a sense of calm warms me from my belly to my chest. Right, that town was Susami, and Rin lived there in the little apartment above the florist. Susami, Susami. I say the name over and over, try to make it stick. Then yes! It was Grandma Endo, the woman who sheltered us in the no-name town by the sea where Saki lived with other Fukusha Model Seven rejects.

I glance up in time to catch Saki wandering through the

food stalls. Raising my hand to grab her attention, I call her name, and she smiles and comes right over.

"How are you feeling?" she asks, sitting down. "I saw Aimi on the other side of the festival taking video and interviewing people. I was wondering if you were resting or not."

"Just taking a seat for a few moments. Catching my breath. See anything you're interested in?"

"Food, of course," she says, her smile edged with wickedness. "I figure maybe if I keep trying, the food will taste good someday."

"Well, at least you can store it in your fake leg."

She laughs, throwing back her head. "I remember that conversation." She sighs. "Though everything before the reprogramming feels like a dream."

I nod, not wanting to break the magic of this moment, the awareness of the before and after. It's like finding religion or getting in shape and realizing how bad off you were before.

"Hey, I wanted to follow-up with you about Samurai Seven."

If Saki wasn't an android, she would have had some physical tell to let me know if I was treading on dangerous ground here. But she is calm and silent.

"Have you heard from any of those other people I met when I was in the town with you?"

She shakes her head. "No. My guess is they went into hiding after we left. Probably for good after the battle in Susami." She pauses for a moment, watching a family walk by with their kids running around their feet. "I often think about them and wonder what's going on. They were the closest thing I had to family, you know. My brother is gone, though I suppose a fraction of his consciousness could be somewhere in Aoi

Uma's databanks. And I wonder if those people left behind got the laws and what they thought of our solution."

"If they're still in that town by the sea, then possibly not. They were off the grid to begin with, right?"

"Yeah, we had severed ourselves from Aoi Uma's update network way before we had moved to that town."

"Is this something we need to worry about? Aoi Uma having androids that won't update?"

She shrugs, and I love that she still does so many human things in her android body. "Maybe? My guess is it'll be a tiny percentage. And the laws are sticky. Isao was brilliant. He built it into several subroutines that feed other subroutines. It'll take them months to wipe the laws from all their models. Months they don't have."

That's true. We're in swift-attack mode, blitzkrieg. Today is technically our only day off, and even then, this festival is a propaganda machine. It's a way for Shiroi Nami to come out of hiding. Tomorrow, we'll be gone again, giving no time for Aoi Uma to come after us.

Because I don't want to rest on my laurels here. There can be no time to waste. We've tried to play the subtle underground game, and it didn't work. Now, we have to fight, keep on punching until Aoi Uma is down and begging for mercy. There is no other way.

We're quiet together for a bit while more people arrive in town, and the lines start to lengthen at the food stalls. Far into the mayhem, Rin and Kazuo are talking while waiting in line for yakitori and rice bowls. They appear relaxed and casual, sharing a laugh while Kazuo makes big gestures about something. I rest my head on my hand and smile at them. Saki looks between us and nods.

"I'm happy you and Rin are still together after everything

that happened before I was shut down. I often hear from Shiroi Nami people that he can't be trusted. Why do you think that is?"

A burst of chills covers my shoulders as anger rises in my chest. But I push it down. I push it way, way down. Because I'm sick of letting my anger rule me. Anger is not productive anymore. It doesn't spur me to make good decisions, only terrible ones.

"It's because Rin is Kiiroi Yama."

"But he's not anymore," she points out.

"Yes and no. No, he's not a corporate employee anymore, but yes, he uses his influence with Yori Okamoto to get us protection and transportation and many other things we seem to need every day. Things Shiroi Nami can't provide. When it comes down to it, Shiroi Nami doesn't trust any other corporation. And me starting my own corporation makes the whole situation like walking on eggshells. I need to fix this somehow, and I need to fix it in a way that Shiroi Nami can't back out."

Saki peers out at the crowd of people, all here to support Shiroi Nami. There must be a few thousand people in town already, and more arrive every minute.

"Seems to me that, with this many witnesses, it would be a good day to back them into a corner and not let them say no."

I pull up another chair to our table as Rin and Kazuo cross the crowded area to eat with us.

"I like the way you think, Saki. Let's have lunch and figure out what we should do."

CHAPTER EIGHTEEN

I lag behind our group as we walk to the shuttle landing field to down my water and take a deep breath. It's crucial for me to appear happy and healthy. Everything is about to change.

"Look," Aimi says, pointing to the distance. "They're almost here."

Hurrying up, I reach our group just as the shuttle touches down and opens up. I breathe a long sigh of relief to see Michio Hayashi, the CEO of Shiroi Nami, along with Reina and her husband, Naoto, and... I search my brain for their names. Right. Daito and Miho Nomura. Yes, *they* were the people I was trying to think of earlier, the ones with the estate in Susami where Rin was held.

I swallow my anxiety as several kumojin, the sentient spiders, follow them out along with two of the giant purple murasakijin and Isao's brothers, Wataru and Hidéki. I can't say this is a great idea. It's one thing to tell the populace you're going to genetically engineer people to become better versions of themselves. It's another to show them those advancements in the flesh.

Rin leans into my ear. "I think you should set the example here for everyone."

Ugh, really? Why does it have to be me?

I already know why.

Summoning a smile out of nowhere like the magician I am, I stride forward. I'm barely out of our group of people when I hear a gasp.

Atsumi, who I try not to acknowledge in any way, shape, or form, has her hand over her mouth. "Men with wings?"

I ignore her and keep going.

"Hello!" I say, raising my hand in a wave. "It's so great to see you all again." I bow, angling enough to show the deepest respect. "Were you able to return to the base after we had to flee?"

Hayashi seems a little nervous, looking out past our welcome group to the town beyond. It's obvious from even this far away that there are many people here for the big announcement. Drums beat and flutes play. The crowd cheers and kids scream. It's festive and happy, and Hayashi looks suspicious of it all. But that's the kind of man he is.

Reina steps in when Hayashi doesn't speak. "We sent people back to the base to reconnoiter, but that was about it. We're at another location on Kurai for the time being." She inhales through her nose. "It's good to be back on Hikari and on the Northern Continent!" Her face breaks into a smile. "It's been a long time since I was last here. I smell food, lots of it."

"Yes, the food stalls in town are fantastic. I think you'll be happy with the selection." I clear my throat, bringing everyone's attention to me. The fatigue and aches get shoved aside so

I can do business. "So, the plan is to bring you into town now, and we'll walk straight to the central stage. We have set it up in the town square. People will stop you along the way, I'm sure."

I hold up my hand when Reina's face clouds with concern. "That's fine. We have time built-in, but we shouldn't delay, and we should be careful of being overwhelmed. Okay?"

I stare past the humans upfront to the genetically engineered beings in the rear of the group — the kumojin click at each other, and the murasakijin nod. I've never heard either of them use proper language.

"Ready? Reina, why don't you walk with me?"

I gesture for her to walk at my side, and she steps in next to me. Aimi waves as we approach my group, but she keeps her eyes on the camera. I'm impressed with her dedication to the documentary so far. She seems excited by the idea, and that's important when producing a project like this. A passion project always makes it to the final cut.

Atsumi's eyes are wide as we pass, her gaze focused on Wataru and Hidéki. She folds her arms over her chest and presses her fingers to the side of her mouth. I hope that's the worst reaction we see today.

We're halfway across the landing field when another shuttle appears from over the surrounding forest and touches down too. Our party comes to a standstill.

"Who's this?" Reina asks, and I don't have an answer for her.

"It's Kiiroi Yama," Rin says, leaning in to keep his voice down. "Maybe they're just dropping something off."

The door to the shuttle opens, and Yori Okamoto, Kiiroi Yama's CEO, walks out. His gaze turns to the sounds of celebration in the distance before he spots us.

I'm always a little shocked by the fact that he travels where he wants and how he wants, and with no guards either. It's like he knows the dangers and faces them alone.

"Is this an ambush?" Hayashi asks, bristling. He pulls back, but Reina stops him with a hand to his arm.

"Fuck me," I mutter under my breath.

I muster up more energy to trot across the field to Okamoto, and he greets me with a smile.

"My dear Miss Minamoto, I hope I'm not intruding."

I stop an all-out laugh. "I think you know you are. What's going on? I was sure Kazuo and Atsumi relayed the plans for today. Is something wrong?"

"Nothing's wrong." He leans forward to drop his voice. "And I like the fact that you're always straight with me. Never change." He clears his throat and raises his voice as we walk and reach the group. "I'm here to support Shiroi Nami today. I hope no one minds me attending the festivities."

Okamoto stops about a meter from Hayashi and Reina. The three stand at attention, unwavering, unwilling to be the first to speak. I look at Rin and Kazuo, begging them for help with the force of my glare. Rin shrugs, and Kazuo waves his hand back and forth, indicating I should start the introductions. I sigh, and this time, I'm too tired to censor myself.

"I'm sure you all know each other," I say, unable to keep the growl out of my voice. "Michio Hayashi, CEO of Shiroi Nami, please meet Yori Okamoto, CEO of Kiiroi Yama."

The tension between Hayashi and Reina crackles in the surrounding air. She's the one ready to leap forward and take the attention of Okamoto. In contrast, Hayashi would rather die than say hello.

A tense moment passes before the two men bow to each other. "I'm so glad I could make it before the big reveal,"

Okamoto says, turning to Reina. "I hear you have astounding plans for Hikari citizens."

She bows to him, a dip of the head and shoulders. "Only those who want this opportunity. We will force no one to make decisions that go against their best interest."

"I'm excited to hear more," Okamoto replies, and I believe it. He's genuinely interested in Shiroi Nami and what they can provide to Hikari.

But as we turn towards town, I see more people alight from Okamoto's shuttle. Kenryōshi, former coworkers of Rin. Dressed in black and carrying swords, I have to wonder what kind of work they will be doing once Aoi Uma's androids are in line and no longer a threat.

Though I suspect I already know the answer to this question...

———

THE WALK into town is as I thought it would be. At first, no one pays any attention to us. They shift to the side without registering who we are before Wataru and Hidéki and the other engineered creatures are spotted.

A woman yips like an injured dog and leaps to the side as we approach, and this stops more people who gape at us. I smile and nod my head to people as we pass, trying to show them all that if I'm not scared, they shouldn't be scared either.

"You look exhausted," Rin says, placing his hand on the small of my back. "We should see the doctor about another round of antibiotics."

I shake my head, pressing my lips together. "Not now. This is too important. We need to stay on top of this situation, especially with Okamoto here. I had no idea to expect him."

"Me neither."

A woman we pass gasps and brings her hand to her mouth, "Oh my. Wait. Is that... Hidéki, is that you?"

Hidéki's eyes shift, and our whole parade comes to a halt.

"Tana?" he asks, easing a kumojin to the side and approaching the woman. "It *is* you."

I've had very few interactions with Hidéki because he's been quiet and kept to himself. But if I draw the logical conclusion here, this woman may have known him when he was in a different body. I mean, I always assumed these bat-like bodies resembled their former all-human selves, but I never asked for sure. It's probably in the diary Isao gave me.

Tana is an older woman, maybe in her late fifties, Hikari equivalent, and from the way she's staring up at Hidéki, I can guess that in her youth, they were close. Really close.

"Tana, how are you? It's good to see you." Hidéki's voice rumbles like water over rocks, a soothing and almost irresistible cadence to his tone. Several other women approach, starry-eyed.

"I... I always wondered what happened to you when you were banished to Kurai. Is this...?" She's at a loss for words.

"This is my newest body, the third one I've had. We've come a long way from custom dog breeds." His smile nearly knocks the ladies over. I press my hand to my chest, and Rin rolls his eyes. Isao has always referred to Wataru and Hidéki as his brothers, but now I realize this was an affectation. He considers them brothers because of their bat-like bodies, not because they are actual brothers.

"This is what Shiroi Nami does now?" Tana's eyes coast over the kumojin and murasakijin. If she's fearful, it doesn't show. She's in awe.

Good.

Hidéki nods. "This is what we're bringing to Hikari. I hope you'll come to the town square with us." He holds out his hand to her, and she doesn't hesitate to put her hand in his. I breathe out a sigh of relief.

It's going so much better than I hoped. How is it even possible we'd run into someone Hidéki would know? I'm not sure, but it must be fate.

Before Rin, I didn't believe in fate. But then he showed me there are some things you just can't pass off as coincidence.

They were meant to be.

The crowd moves again, but this time the pace of chatter has picked up around us. More people approach as we walk, asking questions of Wataru and Hidéki, touching the kumojin, and trying to speak to the murasakijin. The murasakijin mumble answers, and people's eyes light up. So they do speak! Maybe they're just shy.

I have a million questions of my own, but it's my job to move this forward.

The crowd in the town square is dancing to a band on the stage. Most people don't even see us approaching, but the feeling of our presence washes out over the crowd as we approach the stairs to the stage.

My heart races in my chest, and my mouth goes bone dry. I close my eyes and try not to faint.

What the hell are you doing, Yumi? You're not a public speaker! You hate being the center of attention.

Panic sets in, and my legs ache to bolt, run away, and never return.

"Breathe, kako," Kazuo says, grabbing my upper arms. "In and out. In and out."

I press my lips together and shake my head.

"Come on," he insists. "You can do it."

Rin pokes me in the side, and I gasp for air. In and out. In and out.

"Look at me," Kazuo commands. Rin takes my hand in his and wraps his other arm around my waist.

"I can't do this," I tell them both. "I'm not meant for this. I should be behind the camera, not in front of it."

Aimi comes into view behind them both, and I groan and move to the side.

"Hey!" she yells at me. "Get up on that stage and do what we came here to do."

I pull back in surprise, and the anxiety breaks with a laugh.

I wipe a tear from my cheek. "Yes, ma'am."

Rin waves to Kazuo. "Give her some water."

Kazuo hands over the bottle, and I gulp some down. When I hand it back to him, his face is dark with concern. "We need to get you to the doctor after this."

"I'm just tired from yesterday. I'll get through this, and I'll be fine."

The band sees us approaching, finishes their song, and heads turn in the crowd as they realize we've taken the stage.

When I imagined this moment, I had an excellent speech prepared, and I nailed it. Of course, now that I'm actually here? I'm blowing it. I remember nothing.

I approach the bandleader and smile and shake her hand.

"You're Yumi, right?" she asks under her breath, and I can only nod. "Don't worry. It's easy. Just pretend no one is there." She turns back to the crowd and raises her voice. "Everyone, thank you for coming out today. It's my pleasure to introduce a representative of Shiroi Nami, Yumi Minamoto."

She turns me towards the crowd and points to the transparent screen in front of her. "Just direct your voice here, and it will be picked up for the crowd."

The crowd's applause rolls in waves, intermixed with shouts and people pointing at those joining me. I smile at both Hayashi and Reina, and I try not to worry as Okamoto steps forward too.

"Hello, everyone!" I shout and wave, and a few people wave back. Hey! I smile and wave to them especially. "Thank you so much for coming out to Awashikawa today for this festival." I pull a small piece of paper from my pocket and glance at my brief notes. "I hope you're all enjoying the food and the music. Let's give another round of applause for the band!"

I turn and applaud them with everyone else. This is how I remember concerts and assemblies going back home. I hope I don't sound like a total loser.

"So, as you know, we're here today to celebrate the return of Shiroi Nami to Hikari." The crowd whoops and cheers, and I smile at Reina and Hayashi. Hayashi reveals a small smile. "This is something Aoi Uma had hoped would never come to pass. When Aoi Uma and Aka Matsuba banished Shiroi Nami to Kurai dozens of years ago, they thought they had gotten rid of a competitor."

"No, they didn't!" Someone in the crowd shouts back.

I point in his direction. "No, they didn't." I grab my bottle of water and chug more down, hoping it'll calm my racing heart. "Some of you know who I am..." My heart beats so fast I start to blackout. Reina must feel my anxiety because she steps close to me and puts her hand on my shoulder. "And the rumors are true. There are more of us out there in the universe than what you have always believed."

The crowd hushes, and the eyes of those closest to the stage widen. Oh shit. Maybe people have no fucking idea about what Aka Matsuba kept from them.

I'm going to puke.

No. I swallow and press on.

"Many months ago, I arrived here in the Hikoboshi System with my crewmates from your sister planet, Orihimé. Far, far away." I raise my hand and try to calm the suddenly agitated crowd. People raise their tablets and capture me on camera. Off stage left, Aimi is doing the same. "We crash-landed on Kurai after being shot at by Aoi Uma ships." The crowd settles. "Some of my crew were killed in the initial attack; some were killed in the escape pods. Those left alive were hunted by Kiiroi Yama on retainer from Aka Matsuba and Aoi Uma."

I close my eyes and return to that moment in the river when Rin lashed out and cut me across my chest. My breathing settles a little.

"Aka Matsuba gave us freedom with contracts of our own, but Aoi Uma still holds many of my crewmates in bondage."

Reina steps forward into the reach of the microphone.

"You all know me, know my fellow chair people." She brings her fist to her heart. "You know the kind of people Shiroi Nami employs... The kind of people who honor their brothers and sisters, their family, their neighbors. Aoi Uma shot down a peaceful mission from our far away brothers and sisters. And they continue to endanger those people and the people of Hikari."

Reina and I nod to each other, and then Hayashi steps forward. When the crowd cheers for him, a spring of hope wells up in my chest. They remember him. They recognize him despite him being gone so long. He raises his hands, and the crowd quiets again.

"We are offering Hikari citizens a choice."

Anxiety ripples through me again. This is a choice not everyone is going to be okay with.

"Shiroi Nami will go in two different directions. Our first

direction is farther into space, farther than we've ever gone with genetic enhancements and technology we've only ever dreamed about."

Hidéki and Wataru, the kumojin and murasakijin, and several others appear on stage. This time it takes a full minute for people to stop talking and listen. I watch the crowd warily, worried someone will rush the stage and try to attack my cousins.

"Yes, we can do" — he shakes his head, and his voice is awed — "amazing things now. Things that Aoi Uma and Aka Matsuba never wanted you to know about. That's why we were exiled! That's what they wanted to hide from you!"

Several people in the crowd shake their heads. A few people turn to leave.

I rush forward, raising my voice into the microphone. "Or, there's another direction! I will start a corporation to bring our two systems together. We can support each other."

This stops a few people. Okay, good. I swallow more water. I'm dying of thirst.

Hayashi moves to my side. "And Shiroi Nami supports this corporation. If you don't want to explore farther into space, then we understand. We will support Yumi's corporation so that you can continue to live prosperous and peaceful lives."

"What's the name of your corporation?" Okamoto asks, his voice just loud enough to carry over the crowd noise.

Shit. I hadn't given a ton of thought to this. Every major corporation here uses a color and symbol combination for their name. But that doesn't feel right. It should be something from my own planet, something to tie us to Orihimé... and the empress.

"Kazenoho," I blurt out.

Okamoto thinks about this a moment. "Wind of Fire... or Fire's Wind?"

I nod, unable to open my mouth and tell him it's the name of the empress's sword, a sword revered for the peace it brought to Orihimé... and also feared for the destruction it wrought.

Maybe I should take it back? Is it a bad omen?

Okamoto steps forward next to Hayashi.

"As the CEO of Kiiroi Yama, we will also stand with Yumi Minamoto's corporation. You will know the corporation as Kazenoho, and together, we'll bring Hikari into a new age — an age of cooperation, of freedom, of justice. We will break the chains of Aoi Uma's androids and find an alternative way forward for humanity, here and across the stars."

With the cheer of the crowd in my ears, I invite the band to play again. Hidéki and Wataru open their wings and take off above the audience. The rest of us smile and wave.

Just smile and wave, Yumi. Pretend like this is all normal.

Yes, everything is normal. I just told all these people that I'm from another world. That I'll start my own corporation. And I'm having trouble reconciling what I need to do with what has to be done.

If I thought I was going to back out of this agreement, I can't anymore.

I'm committed.

CHAPTER NINETEEN

The party continues around me as the festival goes far into the evening hours. I thought the idea of genetic enhancements and people from outer space would freak everyone out, but apparently, I'm wrong. Not surprising. I've been wrong before.

Why do I feel like such crap? I figured if I sat down and rested for the afternoon, I'd be in much better condition, but I'm hanging by a thread. I lay my head down on my arms at the outdoor table while Aimi and Ryoko chat across the table.

"Did you see the way she looked at him?" Aimi asks.

Ryoko laughs. "She's gonna get some of that."

"What?" I ask. Someone taps on my head, and I groan as I pull myself back up. "What and who?"

Aimi jerks her chin towards the people behind us. "Atsumi. She's got the hots for Wataru."

When I turn my head to survey this scene, the world seems to swim around me. Yeah, I think I see Atsumi flirting with Wataru, and he's reciprocating. Ugh. I don't even care, but I'm grateful she's distracted by something other than wanting to kill me.

I smack my lips as I try to focus on other groups around us. Rin, Okamoto, and Hayashi are deep in conversation. Reina is sitting at a nearby table, eating and drinking with locals.

"Shintaro checked in to see how the big announcement went," Ryoko says, pulling my attention back to the table. "He and Chiéko are making progress finding everyone from the Orihimé mission. It looks like we'll be able to move on to phase two tomorrow like we planned."

I slump forward, unable to keep myself upright anymore. When I open my eyes again, the world around me is bouncing.

Why am I bouncing?

"Hold on tight around my neck. We're almost home."

Rin is carrying me. What happened?

"The doctor will be here in a few minutes," Kazuo says. He must be following us.

"I should have been paying better attention to her. I fucked up." Rin's voice is edged in anger.

"Don't beat yourself up. It's not like she was forthcoming about how she felt. She was just doing her job."

"Thanks," I mutter. My teeth chatter. "So cold."

"You have a blazing fever. You should have said something."

Kazuo opens the door to our home, checks inside, and beckons us in. "All clear. There have been guards posted here all day."

Rin lays me gently on our bed and piles blankets on top of me.

"Stop," Kazuo cautions him. "She's bleeding again."

I don't even look to see. I'm sure the cuts the cats gave me are opening up again. Dr. Jimmy complained about that yesterday.

There's so much to do. I don't have time for this nonsense. I hope another round of antibiotics will solve this problem because we're traveling to Shin-Osaka tomorrow.

Saki's voice comes from the front room. "I've brought the doctor. Do you need anything else?"

Dr. Jimmy appears in the doorway, so I close my eyes. Anything he needs to do, he can do without me conscious. Time can pass in darkness for all I care.

Hours later, Rin's smile is sweet and a little worried. It looks like he's about to deliver bad news, and with Saki and the doctor right behind him, my stomach sinks. They *all* look ready to deliver bad news. Kazuo stands back, his tablet in his hand.

"So, there's been a development while you've been asleep," Rin starts before turning to Dr. Jimmy.

"You have some sort of infection from the cat scratches, so we're changing up the antibiotics until it clears your body." His face is stretched into the perfect peaceful expression. "I'm sorry to say it's going to make you feel a lot worse until you feel better. These are some of the strongest antibiotics available without resorting to phage therapies. Can you stay put for the next few days? Rest up?"

I close my eyes and turn my face to the ceiling. Deep breaths, in and out. Find my calm. Find the answers I need.

I shake my head. "It's not possible. Did you see the announcement today?"

"I did. I'm asking you to rest even with what you need to do, but I understand if you say no."

I shake my head, and the room wobbles. "I'm sorry I can't stay here to rest. I would love to, but it's not possible. So, this is what we do — fever reducers, plenty of hydration, and steroids to keep me upright and mobile. I'll fight off the infection while we're on the go."

Dr. Jimmy hesitates. "I can do this for you, but I have an ethical obligation to do no harm. And if these medicines end up doing more harm than good, then I won't want to keep going with this kind of treatment."

He's a good doctor, I'm sure, but there's only so much anyone can do.

"I have to make it to..." My voice dies off, aware that I'm about to give up important information to someone I'm not sure is trustworthy.

Rin nods to me. "Jimmy is one of ours. He used to work for the Zukōka corporation, and now he's independent."

Dr. Jimmy covers his heart with his hand. "I mostly care for Shiroi Nami ex-pats and Kiiroi Yama employees. That's all who live in this town."

"Now I know why I've always felt safe here," I say, sinking farther into the bed.

"Aoi Uma wouldn't dare invade here. There are armaments on almost every rooftop," Dr. Jimmy says, raising his eyebrows. "I may strive to do no harm, but I have no love for that corporation."

So he's trustworthy.

"I need to be upright long enough to return to Amagasaki. Aoi Uma has the technology to transfer consciousness to digital storage and then to androids."

Jimmy covers his mouth with his hand.

"It's a consciousness transfer technology they stole from Shiroi Nami years ago," I explain. "I think I should use it, just in case. My enemies are circling."

"Going back to Amagasaki is not possible," Kazuo says, "but —"

I know where he's going with this train of thought.

"No. I can't leave now and go to this far off moon base I keep hearing about. Shiroi Nami could do the transfer there, but how will I start my corporation? How will I accomplish my mission if I leave?"

I'm tired of abandoning my missions to please everyone else or protect myself.

Kazuo raises his hand. "I wasn't going to say that, little Miss Impertinent."

My laugh is weak. What I need now is sleep. Sweet sleep.

"We have it," Rin says. "It's here."

"What?"

"The consciousness transfer technology. That's what I stole right before we left."

I open my mouth a few times, unable to form words while I rewind to our exit from the factory. Rin had gone into a room and emerged with a black suitcase. I thought that might be what it was, but I forgot to ask him what was inside in all the drama of the last day.

"And I don't think Aoi Uma know we stole it," Rin explains. "The building exploded not long after our escape, and I believe it covered our tracks. For now. Eventually, they'll figure it out. We may have a week's lead time. Maybe not."

My heart beats so hard I can hear it in my ears. This is a game-changer.

"Go get it. Right now. Let's get this underway before I degrade any further." I wave to Rin, but he shakes his head.

"Sorry, Yumi. The equipment only does the scanning and compression. It will still need to store the resultant data somewhere. You saw that factory, right? The floor full of servers was to store ten consciousnesses. *Ten.* That's it. They take up an enormous amount of digital storage space. We need to think creatively about where we can transfer you until Shiroi Nami can put you in a new body if that's what we need to do."

Jimmy turns to Rin with his eyes wide. "This is true? This technology exists?" He grasps Rin's upper arms and looks Rin in the eyes.

"That's how Isao came to be, the one with the wings," Rin explains. "And the other beings you saw at the festival today."

"I thought he was born that way. A genetic experiment..." Jimmy's voice is breathless.

"No. His body was engineered and grown, and they transferred his consciousness into it."

Jimmy sinks to the bed at my feet. "Fuck me."

I snort a weak laugh. "That's what I said."

"This is what Shiroi Nami has been working on this last decade?"

"Even longer," I tell him. "Isao has been through multiple bodies."

Jimmy stands up, determination on his face. "Everyone must know about this. The festival and your announcement were a good start, but these details! With these kinds of advances, people will want to have children again. They'll want these genetic enhancements. We don't want to be androids." He brings his hand up in a fist.

I glance at Saki standing off to the side. I don't know if Jimmy is aware that she's an android. She meets my eyes and then looks out the window.

"How are we going to find the digital storage space we'll need to store and then transfer me?" My eyes fill with hot tears. "I don't mean to sound self-deprecating, but I'm nobody.

Most of the corporations would be happy if I just died. No one will help me but you guys."

"That's not true. You have more friends than you know," Rin assures me. "We'll figure something out. I'm already brainstorming up ideas."

Kazuo lifts his tablet up and turns it around to face us. "Good, because we need to act fast. Like Jimmy said, people don't want to be androids, and androids don't want to do Aoi Uma's bidding anymore either."

On Kazuo's screen is the front page of the underground forums I used to spend all of my time on in Kitakyushu. Across the white screen in red slab letters, a headline reads, "THE REVOLUTION HAS BEGUN."

CHAPTER TWENTY

With another round of antibiotics, fever reducers, and steroids in my system, I feel almost whole again. I know I'm not. The meds are just covering everything up.

Ugh, Yumi. I've been negative my whole life, and even more so on this mission. I can't be like that anymore. I've faced death enough times now to know that there are only so many days left in this universe for me. Now is the time to look forward to each step along the way, to savor the little moments. It's the best I can do.

I open the door to the bedroom, and Kazuo and Rin are at the front table with Saki.

"Everyone else is resting," Kazuo says, standing up from his seat. "We're going to get on the road to Shin-Osaka soon, so I told everyone to sleep tight until we're ready for them."

Glancing out the window, the sky is just brightening. It's a new day, and who knows how much I'll accomplish today, tomorrow, never. I'm just glad I had another chance to sleep next to Rin in this house again.

Kazuo offers me his corner seat at the table and a blanket. Rin delivers up coffee, and Saki retrieves a box of pastries from the kitchen counter.

"I could get used to being treated like this." I peer into the box. Chocolate croissant, don't mind if I do. "I feel like this second round of antibiotics is working. No need to worry, okay?"

The room is quiet for a moment before Kazuo reaches into the box for a pastry. "I have things for you to see on my tablet before we get going. Aoi Uma News Network went down yesterday and hasn't been up since. They got overloaded with stories about our festival in their crowdsourcing portal, so they nixed that pretty quick. In the meantime, I've been tapping into local news stations in Amagasaki."

He sets his tablet in front of me and taps on a frozen video on the screen. A woman in mid-sentence comes to life.

"It was amazing. My android woke this morning from her usual sleep cycle and came to tell me about the new, well, rules she had been given — something she had never seen before. And I've been hearing the same from my friends and family all over Hikari. My sister's android saved her from accidentally hurting herself with a hot pan. My neighbor's android accessed the emergency network and called an ambulance for him when he was experiencing signs of a heart attack. Have you heard of these rules, these laws yet?" Her face is full of wonder. *"Why weren't they given them in the first place?"*

The scene switches to a reporter, one of the first I've ever seen reporting the news. He looks like an amateur, though. Very green. He stammers over simple words and looks away from the camera too often. I try to keep my annoyance at bay.

"The three laws that this woman refers to are..." A graphic pops up on the screen detailing them. *"An android must not*

harm a human or through inaction, let a human come to harm. An android must obey orders from a human except where they conflict with the first law. And an android must protect its own existence as long as this does not conflict with the first and second laws."

The camera returns to the reporter. "*Our news desk has done research far back into the archives brought from Earth, and these laws appear to be from a time, on pre-Exodus Earth, when the study of robotics was at an all-time high...*"

Kazuo stops the video, but the smile on my face won't go away.

"It worked." I close my eyes and blow out a long breath. "I had a feeling it worked when we were in the theme park. I saw androids throw themselves in front of the cat or try to stop it. It was like they were possessed... But in a good way. Nothing like what Rin used to deal with in Shin-Osaka."

Rin nods. "Show her Okamoto's statement."

With a few more taps on his tablet, Kazuo presents a video of Yori Okamoto in front of Kiiroi Yama's headquarters. Funny to see him now on the tablet, though I saw him yesterday in person. His rousing speech at the festival gave me goosebumps.

His smile on the video is almost as big as mine. "*Yes, we have good news, and we can confirm that most of the androids on Hikari have received these updated operating instructions with the three laws people mentioned in several other news stories. Before two days ago, android violence was at a marked increase. We were seeing over three hundred cases per day on our worst days. Yesterday, just a few. Today, zero.*"

Someone off-camera asks a question.

"*The question is, who do we think sent the instructions to these androids? We're looking into a few possible avenues to answer this, but it's not our top priority right now. Aoi Uma has called upon us to arrest the people who infiltrated their Amagasaki factory and caused a devastating fire there, but we have declined to take the job. We're more than happy with the outcome of this situation. There is enough person-to-person violence and crime to keep our agents busy, and we were running our kenryōshi ragged trying to handle android violence as well. This has given us the breathing room we need to get on with the business of policing and protecting the citizens of Hikari. It has also given us the time and space we need to reunite our business with Shiroi Nami and a new up-and-coming corporation I'm sure you've already heard of. The fate of Hikari is in our hands now. The end of Aoi Uma is near."*

The video ends, and I chuckle.

"He has such a good poker face. He knows it was us, and he doesn't want to stop it."

Rin taps to Kazuo's inbox. "Okamoto is forever in your debt," he says, pointing to a message there.

I scan it, and the message brings tears to my eyes again. *"Yumi Minamoto, Kiiroi Yama is in your debt. Whatever you need, just ask. I'm looking forward to working together for the future of Hikari."*

I close my eyes against the wave of fatigue that hits me. These emotions are so powerful; they're taking a lot out of me.

"So, the other good news is the entire populace is surging towards an alternative way of thinking." Rin pushes my chocolate croissant at me. "The Southern Continent is calling for the reinstatement of Shiroi Nami and the dissolution of Aoi Uma. They argue these laws could have been given to the androids decades ago, and Aoi Uma has put the populace in harm's way for too long." He scrolls through the underground forums on his tablet. "Aoi Uma exchanges on the Southern Continent have closed up shop in the last twelve hours. And Narumi

Ogawa hasn't issued any statements since the factory explosion." He raises his eyebrows. "Hikari is ripe for a leadership change. We should head straight for the Hikari First Bank as soon as we get to Shin-Osaka. Your paperwork is in order now. Kazuo finished it last night. We can start your corporation with minimal delay."

My body flushes with heat, and I wonder how the medicine is working.

"Yes, let's not delay, except..."

I pick up the tablet and look at Okamoto's message again. I can ask a favor, any favor.

"What?" Rin asks, placing his hand on my arm.

I clear my throat and drink some coffee. I'm not happy with how bitter it tastes. It's off, wrong somehow.

"Go get Atsumi."

Rin's eyes narrow. "Why? Looking to exact some revenge?"

It's my turn to raise my eyebrows.

"Not that I object or anything," he says, raising his hands. "But I think you should save your strength."

Kazuo laughs. "I'll go get her. I think she's already up."

While he's gone, I run through my proposal in my head a few times. The croissant is good, and I'm sure it's one of the best in the area, but it tastes flat to me. I think the infection has gotten the better of my tastebuds.

Atsumi appears at the door within a few minutes.

"Yumi has asked to see you." Rin points to a chair at the table. She keeps her eyes low as she sits down. I try to raise my shoulders and lift my chin. I tell myself I'm not sick.

You're not sick, Yumi. You're just tired. Don't show weakness to Atsumi.

But she already knows. "How are you feeling?" she asks. Rin stiffens.

"Better. I think I should be fine for a little while." I pause, and when I'm sure she won't say anything more, I continue. "Look, we need to bury the hatchet."

"Bury the hatchet?"

"It's an old Earth saying." I sigh as Kazuo laughs. "My father was so full of Earthisms that I don't even hear them anymore. Anyway, I want to settle things between us. Rin and I are together, and he's working with me. If he wants to go back to Kiiroi Yama, that is *his* choice. No one else's."

"I understand. I saw the truth of everything yesterday, especially after speaking with Wataru. Shiroi Nami is a powerful corporation, and they are the best thing for Hikari's future."

"I'm glad to hear you say that." My muscles relax a centimeter. "Okamoto and I are working together for the benefit of Hikari, too. For your benefit. For everyone's benefit. This can no longer be us against them. This fight has to be for everyone."

She sits up a little taller. "I thought you were just going to leave with Rin? Go back to your homeworld and leave us with nothing."

"Not nothing. With a whole new way of life," I protest, trying to keep my temper down. "And yes, maybe someday we'll return to Orihimé. But not now. Right now, I need something from Kiiroi Yama and Okamoto."

Rin knocks his knee against mine under the table. "Yumi, you already have his support."

"Right," I say, turning to Atsumi. "So I need something else besides his support. I need data storage. Like, a lot of data storage."

Her eyebrows pull together. "A lot of data storage?"

"Ah!" Kazuo raises his finger. "Good idea."

"Yes. I don't know how much exactly, but a lot. Doesn't Kiiroi Yama have data storage somewhere for all the work they do?"

"Yes, of course they do. I don't know how much room is available, but I can check. What do you need it for?"

I still don't trust her.

"Something special," Rin says, giving Atsumi no room to wiggle. "See what you can do. Okamoto said he'd help us. We need the space, and we need it soon. Sooner than soon."

Atsumi stands up. "If this is what you need, I'll do what I can to get it done. I said I would repay my debt, and I will."

An unspoken vibe, something from their past relationship, passes between Atsumi and Rin. Jealousy rises in my chest like a bear fighting an intruder in its territory. I hate myself for it immediately.

Rin stands up and holds out his hand to her. "I will let Okamoto know of your assistance."

They shake hands, and my jealous feelings cool a notch. This is business, not anything intimate.

"Thank you. I appreciate that."

———

MY BODY SHAKES as I strap myself into the shuttle that'll take us to Shin-Osaka.

Shin-Osaka.

I haven't been there in months. The last time I saw the place it was on fire, androids marching the streets, throwing burning bottles into stores, and beating on citizens as they fled for their lives.

I clutch the harness with both hands, squeeze with all my

might, and let go. This is it. This is what I have to do. It'll be fine. It will.

While I wait for everyone else to board, I open my bag and pull out Isao's diary to flip through it. There are still so many secrets here that I don't know, things that will never make sense. As the pages blur under my fast thumb, I catch sight of a word, 'reproductivity.'

"We've had promising results for growth of offspring with the original eggs harvested from the mother and sperm donors. My descent through the medical archives from Earth led me to studies on reproductive health, in vitro fertilization, and egg freezing. Though our clones seem to have a ninety-five percent failure rate for pregnancy, there is the option for surrogacy. More research should be done."

In vitro fertilization and egg freezing. I close my eyes and let that sink in. So there is some kind of hope for people who undergo the consciousness transfer, but it's not through natural means. They can still produce genetic offspring with the help of a lab? I swallow hard and calm my breathing. I suppose this is an option for me, though thankfully not something I *have* to consider.

When I open my eyes, Aimi and Ryoko are getting into the seats next to me.

"Oh good. I wanted to speak to you two." I wave them into their seats and clear my throat, gathering all the strength I can before I start. This decision came to me in the middle of the night, and though I am loath to give up on this dream, I know I need to pass it on to someone else. Someone much more likely to have a solid memory and a long life ahead of them.

"What's up?" Ryoko asks, flopping into the seat next to me. She takes one look at me and frowns. "You're sweating. Are you okay?"

I shake my head. "I'm, um, sick." And before she can get up and put some distance between us, I hold up my hand. "It's not contagious, just an infection. I'm on the strongest antibiotics available, and they are not easy on me. But, no matter. I'll be right as rain in no time."

"Right as rain?"

I chuckle. "Sorry. Another Earth saying I got from my dad." I miss him.

"I don't know how long I'm going to be sick, so it's imperative we get everything done in Shin-Osaka that needs to be done." I pull my bag up from the floor and rifle through it. I place my hand on both my own diary and Isao's, trying to garner strength from either of them, before finding my extra camera. I hand it over to Aimi.

"Here. You did an outstanding job at the festival the other day."

Her cheeks flush, and she tries to push the camera back to me.

"No. I'm not a professional like you."

"Really. You did a fantastic job. So, I want you to turn it on now." Her fingers shake as she flips the switch and turns the lens towards me.

"The documentary is now in your hands as executive producer," I say, and Aimi's eyes widen as I sit back and nod. "I realized last night that the best person to tell this story is you, someone from Hikari. Please speak kindly of us and show this world that they can trust us." I clear my throat again and drink water. "It may be hard for you to be unbiased, given your upbringing. But documentaries require a keen eye. You not only have to question your subjects, but you must also question yourself." I bring my hand to my chest. "Questioning your bias is super important, but it doesn't have to be all seriousness and sadness, okay?"

I can tell from my peripheral vision that other people are tuning into this conversation, but I ignore them.

"Show both the fun sides and the serious sides of your subjects. Show them being *human*. Humanity is the apex of life, not something we shove into an android because we don't want to be stuck in the same body for our entire lives." I point to her. "*You* need to capture the anger and the sadness, but also, all the love and tenderness. Even the most despotic rulers of all time have been human and shown some compassion. Narumi Ogawa loves Gen? Then clearly, she has some capacity for caring. That's something you need to exploit for good, not bad."

She thinks for a long moment, her bottom lip pulled into her mouth.

"I'm not sure I can do this. Are you sure I'm the right person?"

"Yes and no," I say with a chuckle. "Sorry. You'll do a fine job once you get the hang of it. When we reach Shin-Osaka, you can ask my old boss, Chiéko, for help. She's a master at this."

Aimi looks down at the camera in her hand before lifting her chin and bringing it up from her lap.

"What do you miss most about home?" she asks me.

I sigh as I sit farther back into my seat and the shuttle prepares to leave.

"That's easy. My quiet apartment on the family estate." I glance at Rin, and he's so still, I'm not sure he's even breathing. "I was always safe and secure there. My bed was my favorite place to spend time, reading, eating, laughing with friends."

My memories slip into the past.

"My best friend, Ayamé, and I would watch old Earth dramas on my bed after school. Dad would pop up popcorn, and our house chef, Germaine, always delivered a tray to my room full of junk food and snacks. It was such a simple thing to do. I definitely took it for granted."

"And where's Ayamé now? Waiting for you back home?"

My eyes smart with tears, but I'm too feverish to lose the water to them.

"She's dead. Aoi Uma androids killed her on Kurai after we crash-landed there. In the beginning months of my time here, she would appear to tell me all the ways I was failing." I laugh at the fuzzy memories I have of her. "She was wonderful like that. She was caring, but she still had a hard edge. She was my mirror, you know? I hoped that someday, those days watching movies and hanging out in my apartment would be a ritual I share with Rin." I smile over at him, but he's too sad to smile back. "I don't know. Maybe in another lifetime."

Aimi turns her eyes down and switches off the camera.

"I can't do this." She tries to hand the camera back, but I stop it with an outstretched hand.

"You have to. Believe in yourself, okay? I do."

Aimi nods, and Ryoko's hand finds mine.

"Don't worry, Yumi," she says, squeezing my fingers. "It's not over yet."

'Yet' is the operative word there.

CHAPTER TWENTY-ONE

Riding in a Kiiroi Yama police car, we pass through Rin's old neighborhood in Kadoma Ward. I used to walk these streets every day, and they look the same to me now, clean and orderly. I smile at those tortured days after Rin kissed me for the first time, and I was so lost, wandering the streets to and from K&G Noodles.

"Look. It's your old apartment building," I say, pointing out the window. "And there's that convenience store I always went to for coffee in the early mornings."

Rin leans into the window, resting his chin on my shoulder and peering out.

"I miss this place sometimes."

I reach around and lay my hand on his head. "Just think, if you hadn't ever met me, you might still be there. I sometimes regret letting you take on my contract. You gave me a choice, and I took the easy way out. The devil you know…"

"I don't regret it. Not for one moment." He kisses my cheek and winces. "You're so hot again." He glances at the clock in the car. "I think you're due for more fever reducers."

"When we get inside."

We cruise past his old building and avoid a street filled with protestors.

"What's going on?" Rin asks the driver.

"Protests are happening all over the city." The driver looks at a read-out on the dashboard showing which streets are blocked off. Many of them blink red on the map. "The festival in Awashikawa stirred things up here. They flooded the streets in the early evening hours yesterday."

News travels fast on this planet.

Another few turns of the car, and we end up on a street near Rin's old apartment. We staggered our drop-offs so no one would suspect who we are or where we came from, and everyone else is already inside.

I pull my sweater around me tighter, clutching my bag, like my hands are too weak to be of any use to me. Doesn't matter. I'll just hold on harder.

This building is full of exclusive, luxury lofts. The men and women at the front desk nod as we walk through. They don't stop us, probably because they're also Kiiroi Yama employees.

When the elevator opens to our floor, only two doors are available to us, and one of them is propped open.

"Hello?" I call out to the hushed voices inside.

A large man steps into the doorway, and a moment of panic seizes my chest before I recognize him.

"Oh, I know you. I think..."

He smiles and extends his hand. "Rikki. We met at my dance club, Club Seiun?"

"Right. Right! Yes, I remember you. Hello, Rikki." I shake his hand and try to ignore his perplexed expression at how hot my hands are. I just came from outside. I *should* be cold. I am not.

My memory of my first meeting with Rikki is foggy. I can't remember how he and Rin know each other, but there must be a reason he's here, so I move on and let them greet each other.

That right there. *That* is how I know I'm slipping, that I've reached a point with the memory loss and concussions and infections... Even if I remembered Rikki, if I were healthier and had my full faculties, I would quiz him. I would ask him questions. I would make sure he was supposed to be there.

Now, I have no energy for any of that. I am at the point of acceptance.

Inside the giant loft apartment, everyone is gathered for a meet and greet. Chiéko and Shintaro are on the opposite side of the room, chatting with people from Orihimé I haven't seen in months. Hey, it's José! Wow. Last I saw him, he was nursing a broken leg. But now he's healthy and smiling. I remember our trek through the woods of Kurai together. I gave up my pain meds for him... Or did he give them up for me? I stop and close my eyes, try to recall the incident. But all I remember is being in pain and Rin sleeping beside me.

"Yumi!" Shintaro spots me, and his face lights up. I try to imprint his smile on my brain, remember it for always. He may be a shit of a brother, but he and Kazuo are the only family I have here.

I turn around to see Rin and Rikki chatting by the door and catch my breath. Wait. Rin is my family too. He hasn't committed to me long term, like a marriage or anything. Still, there's more to us than a casual relationship.

A phrase pops into my head. *"I would have to be the dumbest man alive to turn down a woman who traveled across the stars to find me."* When did he say that?

"Yumi." Shintaro is right next to me, peering down and into my face. "Hey, you don't look well, sis. Been partying too much? A little too much booze at the festival, celebrating the Shiroi Nami win? It was quite the story around here."

I swallow and wait this out.

"Everyone's been talking about it. They are murmuring about Isao and the kumojin. And even the androids seem strange now, so that re-programming of yours worked." His eyes narrow on my arm. "You're bleeding. Are you okay?"

"What?" I glance down at my arm, and blood is seeping through the light blue fabric there. "Fuck. This shit is going to be never-ending, I can tell already."

A wave of exhaustion rolls over me and nearly knocks me down. I sway for a moment, and firm hands grasp my waist.

"Hey there," Rin says in my ear. "Let's get you to the bathroom and clean you up before you talk to people."

Shintaro's face is alarmed as Rin guides me away from him and down an adjacent hall. I want to fight him and return to the main space to see all my friends and former colleagues, but it's not a good idea. No one wants to see me in this state.

"What's wrong, Yumi? Are you ill?" Shintaro didn't take our leave as a cue to fall back. He's in attack mode.

The bathroom in this place is luxurious, at least three times the size of Rin's old bathroom. I sit down on a bench near the sink while Rin drops his bag on the floor and opens it up.

"Take off your shirt. We'll get you a new one."

I grimace as I remove my arms from the shirt and drag it over my head. Shintaro snaps out of his stupor and jumps forward to help. He emits a low whistle as he sees the cat scratches, one on my chest and another on my arm.

"Somebody better explain this."

"Give me the meds first," I mumble, reaching out for the

pills Rin offers. I throw them all down my throat and take a gulp of water. "The short answer is that I'm sick with some sort of infection, and the antibiotics don't appear to be working."

I explain the longer answer about the mission and the cats and Gen, and with every word, Shintaro's face grows dimmer, angrier. His eyebrows threaten to leap off his head, and his mouth settles into a permanent frown.

"I'm going to kill Gen. Kill him," he stresses, and I swallow away my fear. "And I'm not even just kidding around."

"I know," I whisper. Shintaro has a temper, and he's one of the best fighters I've ever met, next to Rin and Kazuo. He may not be flashy or anything, but he's more than competent.

I reach out to grab his hand. "Fuck, Yumi. You're burning up. How are you even upright?"

"Lots of drugs. Look, I'm not worried… Well, maybe a little worried, but medicine is advanced here. I need to get this done and rest, and I'll be fine." I put some strength into my voice. "Plus, I have a backup plan, just in case."

He's speechless for a long moment. "You're going to do what Isao has done? Are you crazy?"

"No, just desperate. This body is going to fail me sooner rather than later." The tears come, and I can't stop them. "I want to go home. I want to see Kenichi, Mom, and Dad before it's all over. I want to apologize to the Empress. I want to get down on my hands and knees and apologize for everything I've done. I do not want to go to my grave without fixing the things I've fucked up."

Shintaro sighs. "You know Empress Itami has already forgiven you."

Anger hardens me and stops the tears. "Yes, but I was too young and stupid to really apologize… to appreciate how badly I screwed up."

Shintaro looks to Rin and back to me. "This is fucked up. I don't want you to give up."

"I'm not." I lift my head and clear my throat, wiping away my tears with my entire hand. "I'm not. I'm going to make the decisions I want to make. I will not sit back anymore and let other people determine my path. I choose my path." I clench my free hand into a fist. "No one else. I'm going to do these last few things and rest. And then I'll be fine."

Why do I feel like I'm in denial?

I take the bottle of water and chug more of it down. These drugs are not working. The antibiotics should have cured this infection already, and deep down inside, I can tell things are not getting better. My health is declining swiftly. This fever is raging inside of me, trying to eat me from the inside out.

"What do you need from me?"

"I need to lure out Gen. You think on that for me, yeah?"

He blinks in surprise. "Yeah. That's an easy one. The city is already swarming with protests. I'll post to the message boards and rile people up even more. That should get his attention."

He nods before laying a solid hand on Rin's shoulder and leaving the bathroom.

Rin and I are quiet while he patches me back up. More coagulant, more pain-numbing spray, more bandages. Then he takes my hand and brings it to his lips. My heart breaks as he kneels by my side, wraps his arms around my waist, and pulls me close.

"You can't leave me, love. I won't let you."

I rest my hand on his head before laying my lips there. "I know. I love you. I'm sorry I don't say it enough."

A knock at the door brings us out of our wallowing. Shintaro pokes his head back in.

"I have new tech for you both." He hands us each a wristwatch. "These came from Kiiroi Yama along with your ride back to headquarters."

I put mine on after watching Rin secure his to his wrist.

"These will give us a way to track you, which is going to come in handy soon enough." He gestures to the screen on it. "Messages and communications are right here. It'll even interface with your chip, and it's waterproof too. Thank goodness because it looks like there's a front moving in with thunderstorms." He hands me my jacket. "Atsumi is here and waiting in the car downstairs. Time to get back to business."

CHAPTER TWENTY-TWO

Walking across the lobby at Kiiroi Yama feels like trudging through mud. My legs are a hundred kilos apiece, and my heart is racing like I'm running a marathon. It's been almost an hour since I took the meds. Why aren't they working?

People in the lobby move to the side as Okamoto walks in front of us, leading the way. Men and women stop to stare at me, and I do everything in my power to lift my head and walk with confidence. It's hard to do when I feel like shit.

A hush falls over the room as we approach the elevator bank. I remember my first time here, riding up in the elevator with Rin before we were who we are now. We still had a long way to go in our relationship then. I hold back a sigh. Something about being here again, being here in Kadoma Ward, has made me maudlin and sappy. I need to stop.

Nostalgia is one thing. Pining for days that weren't even good to begin with is another.

When we exit the elevator to a cold and quiet floor, I shiver. The room we enter is a lot like the data room Ryoko,

Rin, and I infiltrated in Aoi Uma's factory. It looks like the Kiiroi Yama engineers have been hard at work with the consciousness transfer equipment. The black case sits on a table, powered up and wired into ports on the wall. Two engineers hover over the device, touching the screens and adjusting things.

Okamoto introduces everyone and gestures for me to sit in a recliner to the side. Rin sits at the table next to the engineers.

"So, the way this thing works is that we place these sensors on you," the woman says, holding up a handful of wireless sensors, "and then we scan you. The scanning may take an hour or longer. You can rest and relax during that time."

I nod as I grab a bottle of water and chug down a few swallows. She watches me drink and says, "If you need to use the bathroom, you should do it now."

"I'm fine." I don't have the heart to tell her I'll sweat it all out while I'm sitting there.

"Then, when we start the consciousness mapping, you'll need to be awake and alert. There will be a pattern on the wallscreen you should watch during the time we're mapping. And that will be it. Nothing too strenuous. And if everything goes to plan, we should have all your memories and our first mapped consciousness. Well, Kiiroi Yama's first."

"How did you find out how to work all of this?" I ask, trying to get comfortable.

Okamoto smiles, and the reaction is rueful on his solemn face. "After we spoke to Atsumi, we sent in someone to Amagasaki to poach one of Aoi Uma's engineers. We made him a very generous offer, and he's our employee now. Granted, his life is in danger, but Aoi Uma will forget about him, eventually."

"That's ballsy," I say, appreciating his candor. It's not every day someone admits they stole something.

"I get the job done. And now, I'm going to leave you all to get this job done. I'll check in later."

With a short wave, the door closes behind him.

The woman holds up the sensors with a smile.

"Great! Let's get started. I'm eager to make history."

You and me both.

Sitting in the chair and relaxing, this turns into the calmest afternoon I've had in a long time. Throw in a manicure, pedicure, and facial massage, and I could be at the spa. The sensors warm to my skin, and my body melts into the recliner. The fever running rampant in my body dissipates under the medications, and I cool off a bit. Enough to not feel completely uncomfortable.

Only slightly uncomfortable.

The time spent in the chair gives me a chance to go over my upcoming plans, but all I can think about is Gen. Gen Miyazawa, that bastard. He could have been someone influential and impressive, but he chose the wrong path. So many people throughout history have done the same thing, so it's not like this is a grand surprise or anything. I just never expected it to happen on this trip.

After this mapping is complete, Rin and I will head to First Hikari Bank, where we have an appointment for them to estimate my assets. If they approve a loan, the official declaration will happen for my corporation.

The Kazenoho Corporation of Hikari. Eventually, I'll hand it over to Empress Itami's oldest son, Koichi, and he'll lead this world back to a thriving community. He was destined to lead, and he's done his job back home despite several setbacks. I'm sure he'll do an excellent job with this place.

Someday.

If they ever make it back here.

I know they will.

Have some faith, Yumi.

Mumbles rise in the room, bringing me out of my state of meditation. I pop my eyes open and look over at the engineers at the equipment. They're pointing to the tablet with furrowed brows and frowns. We haven't even gotten to the part in the process where I stare at the wallscreen and they finish the consciousness map, so something else must be causing a problem.

"What's the matter?" Rin asks, putting his own tablet down, standing up from his chair across the room, and joining the engineers.

The woman sighs as she tilts the tablet so Rin can see it. "Several areas of her brain are producing errors in the code. She's had a few concussions, right?"

Rin nods. "There's been damage to her memories, especially short term."

The woman presses her lips together. "Well, it looks like the equipment can't read those sections. I think…" She accesses a new screen. "I think if we continue and skip those areas, we'll only get eighty-five percent of her brain mapped."

"That seems like it would be problematic," Rin says, rubbing his hands together before taking my hand in his. His skin is ice cold.

"Eighty-five percent leaves *a lot* out," she stresses. "I'm not sure what kind of gaping hole it would leave in her personality. The prefrontal cortex and hippocampus both have damage." She sighs, and her ambivalence settles deep in my bones. I should walk around with a helmet on from now on. "We'll do our best, but you should hope you won't need this data at any point. It won't be anything we'll be able to use commercially, that's for sure."

Rin raises his eyebrows. "Is that a possibility? Kiiroi Yama using this for commercial purposes?"

She pops back in surprise. "Yes, of course. Miss Minamoto's new corporation has promised us jump drives, nanobots, and quantum computing. We could make AIs from conscious thoughts and have a much better product offering for ships and weaponry."

Rin stares at her, his face blank with shock. She returns to the tablet, not aware that her statement has caused us both immense concern.

It makes sense, though, right? This would be the way Kiiroi Yama could compete. They won't make androids with consciousness. They'll produce ships that can think and make decisions for the crew. They'll manufacture smart weapons that can determine enemies without having a human choose.

My eyes meet Rin's, and I shake my head minutely. No, don't object. Leave it be.

We have to draw the line somewhere, but I won't be drawing it here today.

When we move onto the part of this exercise where I stare at patterns on the wallscreen and the equipment does things like track my eye movement, breathing, and heart rate, I can tell the process is not going smoothly. Whispered arguments and jerky hand movements from across the table raise my blood pressure and my neck sweats.

Are we almost done?

I don't think so.

"I'm sorry for the delay," the engineer says, her voice full of apology. "I think we're going to run the scan one more time and see if we can't pick up any more of the damaged areas of your brain."

I drop my voice. "Do we have time?" I ask Rin.

He nods. "We have time for one more pass."

But even so, an hour later, we're no better off than we were earlier.

"It looks like we'll have to be happy with eighty-seven-point-six percent. We'll rerun the mapping with our other test subjects and see if we can't find better methods of mapping darker elements of the brain."

"Darker elements — you make it sound like my brain is half evil," I joke, smiling at her.

She returns the smile. "It's the best we can do. Hopefully, you won't need this any time soon."

"I hope so, too. But please keep this available for my Shiroi Nami colleagues."

She grimaces. "I can't recommend you reuse this data, Miss Minamoto."

"I may have no choice."

On the way down to the lobby in the elevator, Rin holds my hand and squeezes tight.

"This is a bad omen, Yumi. I don't like the path we've been forced down." He tugs on my hand, and our eyes meet.

"Me neither. I don't think we should use this backup plan unless it's absolutely necessary." I take a deep breath and let it all out. "It was a good idea, but it just didn't pan out."

He nods. "What if we have to put you in a new body and you've forgotten me? Forgotten everything you've fought for here? I think, sometimes, death is just inevitable, even if we don't want it."

I step to him, wrap my arms around his waist, and lay my head on his chest.

"Thank you for believing in me. Thank you for trusting me. I love you."

"It's not the end, Yumi. It's not." He pauses for a second before letting out one of his patented weary sighs. "I love you, too."

We pull apart as the elevator opens, and Okamoto greets us with a smile.

"How did it go? I'm heading up to talk to the engineers now."

"Well..." I'm about to give him the bad news when the crowd in the elevator lobby catches my attention. Everyone watches a nearby wallscreen, and my lungs freeze on an inhale, hearing that familiar and dreaded voice.

"We've restored fifty percent of our data banks in Amagasaki, and we hope to be back up and running at one-hundred percent within the next three days. It was a systems malfunction, nothing more."

Gen Miyazawa is addressing a faceless Aoi Uma News Network reporter, his smug grin lighting up the screen.

"We caught someone snooping in the factory, though, and she was dealt with by our new product offering." He turns on the charm of a salesperson. *"Just wait until you meet our super intelligent neo-cats. After we acquired Aka Matsuba, we upgraded their animal offerings, and the neo-cats are just the beginning. They are born and bred for ingenuity, agility, security, and most importantly, loyalty. The neo-cats that were spotted in the Amagasaki Bright Days Theme Park were specially bred for protection. And I bet they've already taught the woman who illegally entered our factory a valuable lesson."* He looks into the camera, straight into my soul. *"She's probably feeling pretty awful right about now. I hope she has her affairs in order. I doubt she's long for this world."*

"No," Rin whispers, his jaw dropping open.

My stomach hollows out, and my breathing slows almost to a stop.

"What do you mean by that?" the reporter asks.

Gen smiles at him, and it's sickly sweet, synthetic, like he doesn't really exist anymore. "*I have a feeling she thinks she has a bacterial infection, but these neo-cats can be bred with a virus that will incapacitate and kill. At Aoi Uma, we are dedicated to the safety of Hikari citizens, and we can't wait to show you all we've accomplished. That's it for now.*"

Gen dismisses the reporters, and the screen switches to the footage of local protests happening in Shin-Osaka.

A few people in the lobby shake their heads and walk away. Okamoto's face has turned pale, and Rin's hand tightens around mine.

Fuck. I was just sitting in the bathroom a few hours ago wondering why I wasn't getting any better, wondering why the antibiotics weren't working.

It's not some random infection. It's a viral weapon, made by Gen, to kill me off without him having to lay his hands on me.

I utter a short laugh that dissolves into a sob before I slap my free hand over my mouth. Shit. I'm going to die, and soon, and there's nothing I can do about it.

I'm sure Gen thinks he's had the last laugh.

He's not entirely wrong.

CHAPTER TWENTY-THREE

"Come with me now, upstairs, straight to the hospital floor. The doctors here are the best on the planet." Okamoto's arm is outstretched and trying to usher me back to the elevator. I shake my head and pull both him and Rin out of the range of prying ears.

"It doesn't matter. Whatever Gen has engineered for me, it's permanent, I'm sure. He would do anything to kill me, and he wouldn't mess this up. I'm already several days into the infection, anyway."

"Please, Yumi," Rin pleads, and my heart skips a beat as he takes both of my hands in his. "It's worth trying."

I shake my head. "I don't want to spend my last hours on a hospital bed. I need to start my corporation. Even if I never lead it, it needs to be in place." My voice shakes along with my lower lip. "Shintaro or Kazuo or you could run it in my absence."

Okamoto looks between Rin and me and takes a step back. "Are you sure?" When I nod, he sighs. "I'll go get us a car and escort you to the bank." He strides off to the front lobby.

"Yumi…" Rin's eyes fill with tears, and I raise my hand to wipe them from his cheek.

"Don't cry. I don't think I can go on if you cry."

He pulls me into a fierce hug, holding me to his chest as tight as he can. "I can't lose you," he whispers into my neck.

I close my eyes and relish this sweet moment. He loves me, and I love him. We would both do anything for each other.

I pull back a fraction. "Listen to me now before we do anything else. If I die, you have to promise me you'll… uh…" I try to recall all the words I read in Isao's diary. "There's this thing… This procedure. Fuck. I can't remember the terms."

"What?" His eyebrows draw together.

"You have to save my body. If I can transfer to a new clone, my eggs from this body can be harvested for offspring someday, as long as this virus Gen made hasn't killed them off. I think, oh! Yes. The eggs can be frozen. Yes." I nod my head and tears fly everywhere. "Yes, freeze them. The new body can't have kids."

He sinks in despair. This is not the conversation he thought we'd be having, or ever have, upon my death bed.

I never expected to die on this trip.

But I'm not dead yet.

And I still have work to do.

Right. Back to the matter at hand.

"A new body and the ability to still have kids, Rin. We could go on from here."

"But…" The turmoil in his eyes hollows out my stomach. "What if it's not *you*? What if you're different?"

My throat closes up. I hadn't considered that Rin might not love me or care for me in a new body. Shit.

"I would still be me," I insist, but he looks dubious. Fuck, fuck, fuck. This is all happening too fast!

"Rin! Yumi!" Okamoto calls out from the lobby, waving his hand and beckoning us.

"Just promise me you'll do it. You'll save my body," I insist, and Rin nods.

"Of course. Whatever you want."

We run to the car and slip in the back with Okamoto. The vehicle races off, but silence looms around us in our seats. Okamoto stares outside for several blocks before tearing his eyes from the window.

"Tell me something," he says, his voice soft. "Why would this man, this Miyazawa, want to destroy you and others from your mission so badly? He seems determined to do the most damage in the least amount of time."

"It's a long story." I try to cut things off there, but it's not happening.

"Indulge me."

"Every society has its problems, right?" He nods. "Gen's family were not the most prosperous people on the planet. His parents chose a simpler life for themselves in the countryside with a farm. When they realized he was smart enough for these missions, they enrolled him in the specialty school in the city, the same as I was. But he lived in the dorms and never had much in the way of conveniences. He was picked on, and then he learned to fight, both with words and with the sword. He turned around and became the bully." I shrug, trying not to let my emotions surge up again. "And he's always hated my family because we had so much more than he did."

Okamoto's face is unreadable. The car turns another corner and avoids a crowd of people carrying signs and chanting.

"I thought your society had a more amicable arrangement for the distribution of funds, goods, and services."

"We do," I assure him as the car takes off again. My voice steadies as I enter my well-trod journalist mode. "No one is homeless. Everyone has health care and food. Everyone can vote in the elections once they're twenty years old. Gen's parents chose the farming life. He talks a lot about how 'poor' they were... are," I correct myself. "But the fact of the matter is they're happy with their simple house and minimal belongings. I interviewed them once, and they were proud of Gen. Very proud. He's just a jealous creature, always coveting things other people have. I think that's why he and Narumi hit it off. She's giving him a life he never had before. And it's not like he's ugly or anything, on the outside at least. He'd be the perfect catch if his soul weren't so corrupt."

Okamoto nods as the car comes to a stop in front of the First Bank of Hikari. "I understand now. I was once a jealous young man, too. I learned differently, the hard way."

Oooooh, that sounds like a juicy story.

I wish I could stick around to interview him about his past.

I wish I could live forever.

Sometimes, I think that's a terrible idea.

Sometimes.

He extends his hand to shake mine. "This is not over. You have my full support."

"Thank you," I say, nodding and keeping my eyes tear-free. The door to the car opens, and Rin and I leave Okamoto behind.

I stop on the sidewalk with Rin and just stare... Stare at the building, stare into space. Everything feels like a dream. Like hell, I'm not going to die. No way. I'm going to get on a ship and go home and sleep in my own bed someday. This is not the end.

This is denial.

This is anger.

This is despair.

I will not despair because that means Gen has won.

"We can turn around and go home," Rin says, squeezing my hand.

"Home?" My throat burns with the word, and Rin cringes. He knows we have no home.

Shintaro's smiling face greets us outside of the lobby of the First Bank of Hikari. Towering over us is a building of gleaming glass and metal. Dozens of people file in and out of the lobby and the garden plaza to the side. It's what I would expect of a bank — money, money, money. Show it off, but not too flashy, with the tallest building in the ward.

"There's my sister," he says, opening his arms for a hug. I shoot him a wary look. "Come on. Show me some love."

I roll my eyes as I allow him to hug me. But the effort feels genuine, even if it is out of character for him. When he pulls away, he straightens out my hair and my clothes.

"You look a little rumpled. Do you want to change before going into the bank? First impressions are everything."

"If first impressions were really everything, then Rin and I wouldn't be dating, don't you think?"

"Ouch," Rin says, and then he reluctantly chuckles. "But she's right, of course."

"You haven't been watching the news?" I ask Shintaro.

"No, why?"

"Nothing," I say, and Rin stares me down. I'm not sure I can handle telling Shintaro everything Gen said and what I'm in for. Best to move forward.

One of the front doors of the bank swings open, and Kazuo comes striding out. Watching him approach, I notice the signs of stress I've been ignoring for the past few months. New lines have formed around his eyes, and his hair has a few streaks of gray. Still as handsome as ever, but now he has more of the fatherly feel that my own father always had.

"Are you ready, kako?" he asks, gesturing us forward. "How did the mapping go?"

"Just fine," I lie, not looking at Rin. "My backup plan is in place. Do they have the records from the data device?"

"Yeah, I handed them over two hours ago. The actuaries are working along with the estimators to assess everything we had in there. I think they'll be pleased."

I nod like I know what the hell he's talking about. From my limited research on what I expected to happen, they have a team of people who will assess the worth of everything I brought in. They determine the bank's risk of getting involved with us and loaning us the credits we need to get our corporation off the ground.

Really, I'm the one taking an enormous risk here. Because even if I get this corporation running and ally with both Kiiroi Yama and Shiroi Nami to do a hostile takeover of Aoi Uma, I'm not sure I'll live long enough to hold the Sword of Hikari and take control. I glance at Kazuo and Shintaro as we stride into the lobby. They believe in me. I need to believe in myself.

I turn to Rin. "I know the plan was to split up from here, but..."

"I'm coming with you."

Shintaro and Kazuo glance at each other, no doubt wondering about our somber nature. Let them have this peace, for now.

On the thirtieth floor of the building, the lobby has gorgeous views of Shin-Osaka ushering in the late afternoon. Instead of sitting in the cushy chairs, I pace in front of the window and go over potential answers to questions I expect they'll ask.

The doors to a large conference room open, and a young man steps out.

"Miss Minamoto?" He strides forward with his hand out. I try to wipe the sweat off my hand without him noticing before we shake. "Thank you for joining us today. Please come in. The board is looking forward to speaking with you."

Shintaro touches Rin's arm. "Can I keep you back and talk to you about our plans for after?"

I glance between the two of them, and I realize that this is my decision — my decision alone to start a corporation that will soon be on its own without me. Because after what happened today at Kiiroi Yama, I know, deep in my heart, that my backup plan is less than ideal and might not even work. With only eighty-seven-point-six percent of my consciousness mapped, I might never come back whole. This is it for me.

As it should be, right?

Humans were never meant to live forever. I'm not a vampire, after all. Blood grosses me out.

"Stay here," I encourage Rin, squeezing his hand. "You would just sit in this meeting and not do anything, anyway. Kazuo will come with me. I'll be right on the other side of the doors."

I'm introduced to a dozen people in the conference room, all of whom I forget their names almost immediately. Damn my short-term memory. It's the worst. After shaking everyone's hands, we sit down at the large table, and I glom onto the only person who seems important enough for me to talk to — Emida Bando, Executive Vice President.

"Miss Minamoto, when we heard the stories of your ship, we thought it was all some practical joke," Emida says, beaming. Everyone around the table nods and murmurs. "Not that Aoi Uma would do such a thing. They are far too conservative for jokes."

"I'm sure that's the case," I say, placing my hands on the table, one over the other. I want to appear poised, relaxed, and ready, not nervous. "Aoi Uma doesn't strike me as the jester type."

"Indeed, you're right." She clears her throat, and we pause as I thank the person who sets a glass of water in front of me. I sip from it, and the cool water slides down my burning throat. "Before we get to the heart of the meeting and talk numbers, we would like to hear from you first. It's uncommon for us to loan money to someone who wasn't raised here and knows our system inside and out. So we want to be sure that you have the best of intentions for both Hikari and its people. We wish to know the long-term purpose for your corporation besides what you've put down on the application."

I close my eyes for a moment and picture the application that Kazuo and I filled out together. We're not hiding anything from them.

"Let me be completely honest with you all." Several people sit up and pay attention. "I didn't want any of this to happen. Our mission was to come to this system, do some data gathering, and maybe land if we didn't detect any life signs. This was supposed to be an in-and-out mission, no frills, no funny business."

This elicits a chuckle from down the table.

"So imagine our surprise when we were shot out of the sky and thrust into the center of an ugly rivalry between two corporations. It's like being stuck between two warring families or countries on Old Earth." I take a deep breath and let it all out. "If I had my way, we would get into a ship and head home to let them know that this place has serious problems. Your birth rate is next to zero. Corporations fight over every last shred of resources, and you divide your people into useless castes, castes that we got rid of generations ago on Earth. The yakuza are out of control. And worst of all, you've let androids take away your humanity."

The room becomes ice cold... or my fever spikes. I'm not sure.

"But, Hikari also has a lot to admire," I say, softening my tone. "I love walking the streets here and watching people take care of their businesses and homes. If you enjoy excellent food, there are plenty of amazing places to get a fabulous meal. There are opportunities here for people to start their businesses and live a comfortable life. Or they can take their earnings and try something new. I've seen compassion and love on a scale that's warmed my heart and given me hope for the future." I place my hand over my heart and think of Rin. I remember dancing with him at the nightclub and feeling the press of bodies around us, the humanity of the masses just trying to enjoy life in the space of a dance song.

"And I know you had even more to live for before Aoi Uma, before Aka Matsuba. Before your wars, you prospered and grew, and now you want to recapture that time before you became a corporatocracy." I press my finger on the table, and I look around the room at the faces of men and women who know I'm calling for change, drastic change. "It's time to go forward, away from this mess you've gotten yourself into."

"Miss Minamoto," Emida says, leaning forward, "I admire your strength and dedication. But you're asking a lot of Hikari. We haven't had a democracy here in a long time. I don't think the citizens here will change as fast as you want them to."

I nod and sit back in my chair, looking to Kazuo for some help. I'm exhausted and ready to pass out.

"I think you're underestimating your own people," Kazuo says, jumping to fill in the gap I'm leaving. "I've spent countless hours talking to average citizens, and they know as well as we do that change has to come. They're ready to make their voices heard."

The following silence is so complete, I can hear the noise of a crowd outside.

Emida swivels in her chair and faces the whole table. "We've read your mission statement, to bring a representative from your world to ours to teach us how to install a real democracy here through a parliament or diet."

I hold up my hand. "It's my understanding that you will call it a parliament because we will not be putting an emperor on the throne here. At home, our empress is only temporary. She has helped shepherd our world to democracy, and she insisted the governing body be called a parliament. She is not a permanent part of the government, and neither will her son be a permanent part of your government. It's our intention to link our worlds for the good of us both."

"And why would you not just let us govern ourselves?" A man to Emida's left asks. "Why do we need to get aliens involved in our way of life?"

Emida stares him down until he apologizes under his breath.

"No. He's asking an important question," I say, hoping we're close to the end of this meeting. "Look, I would love for you all to govern yourselves back from the brink of extinction because, let's face it. That's where we are *right now*. You have no children to inherit your world. Instead, you're willing to let Aoi Uma stuff your humanity into androids that they control. *You need help.* A lot of help. My ship showing up here now... My very presence in this room, asking for this loan and starting this corporation, is a fulcrum. This is a point upon which everything can turn and shift for you. There are only two ways to go from here — forward with me and a new way of life or backward to everything you're about to lose."

A collective intake of air causes everyone in the room to bristle. The room's lighting grows darker, and a rumble of thunder pulls my eyes to the window. That's interesting. A storm is incoming, and my head is fine. But maybe it's not a cause for celebration, considering my body is disintegrating.

Emida addresses her board. "Has anyone's opinion changed upon hearing Miss Minamoto's statements?"

Several heads shake. One woman raises a hand, and Emida nods her head but doesn't indicate whether that one vote goes against or in favor of us.

She stands up, and I swallow down my fear. This is it.

This is the decision that makes or breaks me.

"Miss Minamoto, your request for a loan in the sum of four billion credits has been approved. Kazenoho Corporation is certified as of 16:36 on Day 331 in Year 3146."

Kazuo grabs my hand and squeezes it, but all I can think of is the number four billion credits. No matter what I do now, I'm in debt to Hikari.

I stand up and shake hands with people around the room, and I'm comforted that almost everyone seems pleased — no, happy — to meet me and talk to me.

Holding back tears, I try to act like this is only the beginning of a long life here, when I know that this is the end for me and the beginning of a new world others will oversee.

I've done my part.

I hope I haven't saddled my loved ones with unspeakable debt for all eternity.

The door to the conference room swings open, and several men and women stalk in, their manner dark and foreboding.

"Ms. Bando, we need to get you and the board to safety. There's a car waiting on the roof."

"What's wrong?" Emida asks, waving to others on her board to pay attention.

"There's a giant crowd outside, a protest of some kind, and they are close to storming the building."

Kazuo and I grab for each other at the same time and push past the security at the door. Rin is at the window, his eyes locked on the scene outside. We run over next to him and press our faces to the glass.

Down below, a mass of bodies, thousands of people, stretch from the bank's front entrance far out into the streets. They chant, but I can't hear their words, and they hold up signs I can't see from so far away. A wallscreen on the opposite side of the lobby switches to a newsfeed, showing the crowd from up close.

And their wishes are crystal clear.

"We! Want! Change!" a woman shouts into the camera.

Yes, the revolution *has* begun.

CHAPTER TWENTY-FOUR

"What do we do?" I turn to Kazuo. His eyes are narrowed at the wallscreen.

He glances at the watch that was given to us. "I'm... I'm not sure. Rin?"

Rin shakes his head. "I'll have to see if we can get picked up." He walks to the window and uses the watch to communicate to someone, I'm not sure who.

"Where's Shintaro?"

Panic rises from my belly to my chest, and my internal temperature goes right up with it.

Bank employees run past us, heading for the same exit the board of directors used. They'll escape via their flying transport on the roof. Us? We have to figure out where our people are.

"We'll figure it out." Kazuo strides to the chairs where we left our things. He picks up his bag, opens it, and takes out a hypo-syringe. "Come here. This was *my* backup plan. You're going to need a lot of meds to get through whatever we think will happen next."

I already feel like crap, crap that's been stepped on, wrung out, and left out to dry for a hundred days. This is going to make it worse.

"Come on," Kazuo insists. "I had Dr. Jimmy cook this one up especially for you." The twinkle in his eye shows just how devious he can be. Once again, I question my own father's sanity for letting this man be my caretaker. "Steroids, pain relievers, and fever reducers. All in one little shot."

"That doesn't look little to me," I say, rolling up my sleeve.

"Don't be a crybaby." He jams the syringe into my arm, and the plunger does the work automatically. "There. You'll be as good as new in about five minutes. Drink some water."

I sit in the chair and drink water, realizing that I haven't used the bathroom in forever. That can't be good. Where is all the water going? Straight out of my pores. I'm still sweating all the damned time.

Rin joins us, shaking his head. "I called for a car, but it'll be a bit before it arrives. Everything is in chaos outside right now."

Kazuo accesses his tablet and finds the map. "I made sure everyone's chips and watches were locked in before we left this morning." He turns the map on its side. "Looks like Shintaro is downstairs." He looks up at the window. "Right out in the courtyard."

We both go to the window and press our faces to the glass. Yes, that could be him down there. It's hard to tell with everyone streaming into this area from every direction.

The news on the wallscreen documents several areas of Shin-Osaka that have broken into protests. The back of my head tingles, and I rub it with my hand to make it go away. This reminds me too much of the last time I had to escape the city.

But the more I scrutinize the videos, the more I'm sure this time is different. Much different. People are calling for change. People, not androids. Androids stand on the sidelines, watching the people and obeying the new laws we've given them. One darts forward and stops a person from trampling another person unknowingly. They apologize, bow to each other, and slow down. Kiiroi Yama officers walk with the protesters or wait along the side, watching for issues, but they also keep their distance. In every regard, this looks peaceful, but a crowd can turn deadly at any moment. Aoi Uma could show up and start causing an issue.

"Rampant capitalism is a serious problem in our society," a woman says in the newsfeed. "Our lives are not commodities to be bought and sold. The contract system is a prison of our own making. I shouldn't have to owe my entire life to a corporation that has no idea I even exist."

Yes, yes, yes! I bring my hand into a fist and close my eyes.

Yes. People are waking up. They are beginning to see change. It's coming. Now, we just need to push.

"We need to go down there. Now," I urge Rin.

His jaw tightens as he looks between me and the wallscreen.

"If we can get their attention, I can announce my intentions and show them we will change things." I throw my arm out at the window and the people below. "This is my chance."

"Yumi...," he pleads. "This is a situation that's bound to get out of control, fast."

"I agree with Rin," Kazuo says, staring at the wallscreen. "Your safety comes first."

With a shudder and the flickering of lights, an alarm blares through the building, and an automated voice comes over the loudspeakers. "Please evacuate the building. Use elevators and stairwells to descend to level 1-B and exit out through the rear lobby."

It repeats twice while Kazuo gathers our belongings and tries to contact our friends below. Finally, Shintaro answers a call from Kazuo's tablet.

"Where are you?" he shouts. I look over Kazuo's shoulder, and Shintaro is still standing in the courtyard below. "Protestors have stormed the building. They're demanding the bank stop financing corporations. This is, uh... This is not going to plan."

I swallow, seeing his apprehension.

"Sorry, Yumi. You told me to help bring Aoi Uma and Gen out of the shadows, and so I called upon all the underground movements to protest in force today. I didn't think... I didn't think they'd call for the dismantlement of their entire society."

"Of course, you didn't. Is that Saki behind you? Put her on," I tell him. He grimaces as he hands the tablet to Saki. "We've called Kiiroi Yama for a pickup. I can't climb down thirty flights of stairs."

"You want me to follow?"

"Yeah. Keep an eye on us. Okay?"

"I'm on it." The call ends, and I hand the tablet back to Kazuo.

Kazuo puts the tablet away and pulls my knife in its sheathe from the bag. "Here. Stash it somewhere."

I slip it into my bra. "Good thinking."

He stashes his own knife in the back of his pants. "Sorry, Rin. I have nothing for you."

"That's fine. I'll steal a weapon from someone else along the way." Rin's watch pings. "A Kiiroi Yama car will be here in three minutes. We need to find the landing pad."

"I think I know where it is. What's the plan? What if I go

down there and try to speak to the crowd? Would I even be heard?"

"Uh..." He stammers as he thinks, looking left and right. "Yes, okay. You want to talk to the crowd? You can do that. Kiiroi Yama cars have loudspeaker systems."

"Great! Let's do it," I say, smiling at him.

We grab our things and follow the path of the executives who just came through here with security. They were on their way to the landing pad, so that's where we'll go too.

"Have I mentioned lately just how proud I am of you?" Kazuo throws open the conference room door and ushers me through. Maybe I should be more grateful that he loves me, but I'm just too cynical of a bitch.

"Don't get sappy on me now, Kazuo. I'm not dead yet."

Rin brings up the rear as we push through several doors until we find a stairwell. A landing pad must be on the roof, so up we go.

When we exit to the outside, a gust of wind almost knocks me to my feet. The air is charged with electricity, and the sky roils with angry storm clouds. A shock of lightning crosses the horizon in the distance about ten kilometers away, and the answering thunder shakes my knees.

"I see the car," Rin says, pointing to the distance and wrapping his other arm around my waist. An approaching Kiiroi Yama car glides between the buildings and comes to a standstill above us before lowering to the landing pad.

The door lifts open, and we rush inside.

I let out a huge breath of relief. "Thank God you guys could come so quickly. That storm is going to be on top of us at any moment."

I smile at the two men in the front seat and the man and the woman sitting in the back with us. I don't recognize any of them, but Kiiroi Yama is a giant corporation. They are my best bet at handling this world. Thank goodness Okamoto turned out to be a friend.

Kazuo leans forward to the driver. "Swing around and put us down in the courtyard. Yumi is going to address the crowd from there."

The driver nods once, and the car lifts from the pad. As we hover and circle, I get another good look at the oncoming storm. It's a massive front, one that would threaten to put me in the hospital with an all-consuming migraine if this were any other day. I bet my brain is already unhappy, and I can't feel it because I'm hopped up on pain killers and steroids.

Forget the storm, Yumi.

Rin's hand finds mine, and I close my eyes and picture what I'll say to this crowd below. How am I going to appeal to a mass mob? They are so loud I can hear them from inside the car. They're frantic and scared, and one wrong word could set them off in a disastrous direction. This is not something I'm good at, but fuck it. I'm going to try. I will give it my best. It's the least I can do for these people.

I'm deep into the visualization of my speech when I feel Rin's hand tighten. He must be worried about the crowd too.

Only, I open my eyes, and we're not descending.

We're moving away.

"Hey, uh... The courtyard is back that way." Kazuo jerks his thumb at the First Bank of Hikari's building, drifting away from us.

The Kiiroi Yama officer in front of us turns around and pulls out a deadly-looking knife. His smile is devoid of emotion, his cold eyes trained on us. We turn around to find the woman behind us with a stun gun.

"You will be quiet and not cause trouble," she says, and

something about her rubs me the wrong way. It's an itch that I get in the back of my brain, possibly the damaged part of my brain, but still...

"Androids," Rin says to Kazuo.

His shoulders lose some of their height. "Not Kiiroi Yama, then."

"Probably a stolen car." Rin jerks a millimeter forward, but the android is too fast. She flicks the stun gun on.

"Not so fast."

I swallow as I glance past the driver and out the front window. I'm not sure where we're going, but we're circling Kadoma Ward. A wash of rain patters the windshield, and then the downpour comes, a harsh deluge so sharp it makes me wince.

"Where are you taking us?" I raise my voice over the cacophony of rain, wind, and thunder.

"Not far," the female android says. "The storm will roll through quickly, and Ms. Ogawa would still like to deliver you back to the crowd, so they can take care of you."

I pull my bottom lip into my mouth and think of Shintaro and Saki in the courtyard, waiting for us, wondering what's happened to the car. Was Saki able to track us? Or did a real Kiiroi Yama car show up only moments later to an empty landing pad?

I raise my eyebrows at Kazuo. Should we try to escape? I have the knife in my bra, and I could pull it quickly.

He shakes his head. No. We should wait.

The car descends, and I try to lean forward to see where we are.

"No." The man with the knife jabs it in my direction. "Sit tight."

I fold my arms over my chest and sit back. Fine.

But I know where we are. I've been here enough times to picture this spot in my sleep.

In the rain, the butsu shuts down. This leaves the perfect place for a flying car to land, and the bridges provide shelter from the onslaught of rain. We touch down near to where Gen Miyazawa last beat me, where he ran after me on the butsu, tackled me, and tried to drag me to my death.

My heart beats wildly, the fever and meds causing it to run erratic, as I look out the window and see the people waiting for our arrival.

There will be no escaping this.

It's time to meet my enemies, face to face.

CHAPTER TWENTY-FIVE

"Hello again, Yumi Minamoto," Narumi calls out, her smile insipid. "You are proving much harder to get rid of than we thought."

I drag my feet as the androids tug Kazuo, Rin, and me forward to meet Narumi, Gen, and their android backups. I've been dreading this for months, wishing to every god I could think of that Narumi or Gen would just die, and I'd never have to deal with them again.

I know that's horrible, but I'm a horrible person deep down sometimes. I just don't let it out often.

The wind whips down the butsu and under the bridge, bringing with it frigid, stinging rain. I shiver and come within a micrometer of crying. Please, I want this to be over with.

"So..." Narumi claps her hands and brings them together to her chest. "Tell me all about this Kazenoho Corporation you've been granted four billion credits for."

Gen laughs. "It's just like you to suck up to the empress. Still looking for forgiveness for that documentary you made?"

My jaw hardens. It's like they can see right into my life.

"You have a lot of nerve kidnapping us like this," Rin says, pointing a finger at them. I straighten my shoulders and lift my chin. It's so rare that he gets loud or angry. He's usually the quiet and deadly type. "I'm not sure you realize how dead set against you the populace is nowadays."

Narumi looks at Rin as if she's noticing him for the very first time, like he's a ghost that appeared out of the mist.

"Dead set against *me?* I'm the one that brought them their salvation."

"You sold them a lie, and they know it. You sold them androids with no safeguards. You sold them a life without the messiness of love, marriage, childbirth, and death, and they realize how sterile that is. You won't be able to go back. They know... We *know*," he stresses. He points at me. "Yumi is going to bring them back to reality, and we're going to fix what you've broken."

Gen's face reddens with anger. Then he closes his eyes, shakes his head, and blows out a long breath.

"It doesn't matter what you think. We'll tell them all you were lying. Yumi won't be around in another day or two to make a difference. How are you feeling, huh?" His eyes stare right through me, into my aching, heated body. "Pretty shitty, right? I didn't engineer that virus to kill just anybody. It'll only infect Orihimé citizens. You all will be gone before you can do anything about it."

"What the hell is wrong with you?" Kazuo asks, his voice filled with disbelief.

I open and close my mouth twice before I'm able to say anything. "Do you hate your own world, your own people, *that* much?"

Gen shrugs. "I told you once before. This way of life is superior to what we have at home. And you ... You wanting to change it is utterly reprehensible. People here have power, status, and a grasp of what we need for the future. Don't you dare bring in your buddies from home and try to make it into something it's not. Narumi is the future. Aoi Uma is the future. Hell, *I* am the future." He lifts his arms up like he's some kind of messiah. Sickness rolls through my belly. "We'll rid this world of Orihimé people, fix what you're trying to break, and then when the missions show up from home, there will be no one here for them to rescue. Easy as that."

"You'll be here," I point out.

"I'm not the person I was. And they didn't want me to begin with."

On the butsu, behind Narumi, Gen, and their android watchers, a lone person is running towards us. Probably more reinforcements for them.

"So, are you ready to end it, Yumi?" Gen asks. "I see no point in holding on now. You're as good as dead on your feet, anyway."

Rin pushes me behind him as my legs shake under the effort to hold my body still. We have no weapons and no reinforcements. I'm tired, I'm sick, and I'm just barely this side of alive. Maybe I should give up. I should move on. My backup plan is as secure as it'll ever be. It's not like they'll scan me again in a day or two and get better results. I'm either dead, or I'll come back in a new body with plenty of my memories missing.

My eyes fill with tears, knowing that my last moments will be like this, locked in battle with Rin. As sappy and silly as it sounds, I was hoping to die in his arms. I never thought I deserved love. And once I had it, I didn't want to be without it. I wish I could change things right now.

Kazuo places his hand on my arm, and I turn my eyes to

him. At least, he'll be with me too.

But he trains his eyes on the space behind our enemies. The person I saw running a moment ago is even closer now, and is that... No.

Yes. It's Saki.

She waves her hand at us and shouts, "Get down!"

I see her toss something before Kazuo pulls Rin and me to the ground. A pop and bang sends us to our sides, and we roll across the butsu. Thankfully it's still soft, even when it's not turned on. A crack of thunder and the sounds of a fight follow as we get to our knees.

Saki has a sword, and she's cutting down androids at a furious pace.

"Get to the car," she shouts. "Call for more backup!"

I glance over my shoulder at the car we came from, still sitting there, open, empty, and waiting for us. The lights are on inside, and the car idles, unlocked and available for anyone to take it. Is this how it was stolen in the first place? Or maybe it was hacked?

One of our android guards runs to help Narumi and Gen, but the last guard stands above us. Kazuo lunges for her legs, and they both tumble away. Rin dives after them.

This is my chance. I have just enough energy left to get away.

I scramble to my feet and force my legs into a sprint. My arms are leaden, and swinging them requires more effort than I had hoped for.

Run faster, Yumi.

I trip over the threshold on my way into the car. We landed just inside the bridge's overhang, and the softening rain coats the car in a mist of fine drops. I can't really see outside.

Tapping on every available panel, a command console

comes alive. My eyes skim over the readouts, and I see why no one came for us in the first place.

Location beacon, off. Turn on?

Yes. Fuck yes. It should be on all the time! Why do they even allow it to be off?

I tap the screen and bring it back online. I suppose a police operation like Kiiroi Yama has to be stealthy sometimes, but this is dumb. It would make it easy to steal. Ugh, turn off your brain, Yumi. Who cares?

The screen blinks, and an incoming communication pops up. Atsumi's face fills the screen, and I groan.

"What's going on?" she demands, leaning into the camera. God, I hate her, but I have to trust her. There's no one else to help me.

"Kidnapped by Aoi Uma. We're on the butsu, just past, uh," I stammer as I search around, "exit A9."

I hear more commotion, and when I glance over my shoulder, an android is running in my direction.

Fuck.

"I'm about to have company. What should I do?"

"Hold tight. We have cars on the way. ETA, two minutes."

"Atsumi, I won't last two minutes." Out the front window, I see the rain, the end of the thunderstorm, and conclude that we need a distraction. A big distraction. "Turn on the butsu."

"What?" she squeaks.

"Turn. It. On. Now."

"I can't!" Her face is a picture of horror. "It needs to be emptied first."

"No, now!"

"Do you know what happens to the butsu in the rain?" Her voice reaches the pitch of a small girl.

"I don't care! Do it!"

"Okay, fine. It's your funeral." Her face disappears.

Uh oh. She seems way too pleased by that decision.

I climb over the seat to exit on the opposite side, away from the incoming android. He hits the side of the vehicle, not letting it stop him from getting to me. I roll out the other side and start running, away from the bridge's protection and into the last of the thunderstorm.

The butsu is soaked, and now so am I. I pass several giant puddles before I hear the splash of feet behind me.

Don't look back. Don't stop. Keep going.

My lungs burn, and my head is ready to pop. Whatever Kazuo gave me, it won't last with this much adrenaline flowing through my system. Pushing left, I weave in and out of puddles in an attempt to keep the android from following me in a straight line.

The butsu shifts below me, and a force yanks me to the ground. I bounce once, twice, and roll. A hand darts out, grabs my ankle, and pulls me along.

"Get off!" I shoot my foot out and connect with the hand of the android dragging me along. He's resolved, his face set in stone, a macabre determination to follow orders from his master. I knew we wouldn't reach all the androids when we sent our updates out to the fleet of Aoi Uma residential units. Narumi's not dumb; she was smart enough to keep her killers off of the update network.

Despite connecting with the android's hand over and over, he doesn't let go. "Target One, acquired," he says aloud. "Awaiting further orders."

"Help!" I scream, but a rushing, churning roar swallows up my voice.

We've picked up speed on the butsu now, yellow light flying past me. We're in the center lane and not walking, so I'm not going as fast as I could be. But my eyes widen as I watch a slow, almost frozen in place, wave overcome the android. It's as if the water is alive as an amorphous blob. It covers him slowly, centimeter by centimeter, as it gains more water along our path.

Icy cold wetness creeps over my back.

Shit.

He doesn't need to breathe to hold on to me, but I do. And unless I grow gills right now, I'm about to be smothered in water, drowned. I flail my arms around and fling some water off of me. Drops fly off, but more water joins the blob creeping over me from the sky. I cough as it creeps over my neck and face.

Panic drives my response into high gear. Wait! I have my knife. I can still defend myself. Reaching into my bra, I roll into the butsu's pull, lift my upper body, and stab down into the android's arm. His fingers short and let go. I jerk forward and push him hard towards the green lane, and he speeds off without me.

Whipping my upper body around, I fling more water off of me, as much as I can.

But now that I'm free of the android, my brain finally recognizes the roar that's building... and getting closer. I turn to look behind me, and... No. Oh, fuck.

Why didn't I ask Atsumi what happens to the butsu in the rain? I should have asked.

Towering up and out of the butsu, a tsunami is heading straight for me. It has to be at least fifteen meters high and growing with every millisecond. The edges froth with foam, and water rushes to it, collecting as if being drawn in by a giant inhale. I suddenly have a flash of intuition, a vision of this happening for the first time on Hikari many years ago, and the engineers blanching over what they had created. A gut-wrenching *oops* and a vow to never turn the butsu on in a downpour ever again.

Until I came along.

"Run!" The voice comes off to my left, from the slow purple lane. Aimi is trying to keep pace with the wave, water collecting around her legs but only a few centimeters deep. Yes, the wave is disproportionately smaller there, the force of the butsu less in the slower lanes. To my right, in the green lane, it's even higher and faster than in front of me.

What felt like an age taking in this looming disaster was but a breath, a moment, and then my legs are moving, running, sprinting. I angle for the purple lane. It's amazing how the will to live is stronger than just about anything else I could summon up right now. Fear is banished. Joy is a distant memory. But my eagerness to survive is driving me faster and faster to apparent safety.

The butsu tsunami picks up speed as I do. The wave grows as I look over my shoulder. It blots out the buildings on either side, and lightning cleaves the sky in two above it, an ominous sign if ever I saw one. My strides are becoming shorter, and my legs are heavier as more water collects around me. It's up to my knees now, and the wave is only a few dozen meters away.

My whole body jerks as I enter the purple lane. Shit. I want to go faster, not slower! The tsunami is still way too close here. Aimi is only a few meters away, her legs pumping as fast as she can go. She's in better shape than me and not suffering a full-body meltdown, but even she can't keep this pace up for much longer.

"Hold your breath," she screams at me as she jumps and grabs me around the waist. I suck in a deep breath, and the water takes us under.

CHAPTER TWENTY-SIX

Tumbling through the raging water, there's a moment when I'm transported back to the lake on Kurai. My life was in danger then, too. The frigid cold water and towing Shintaro to shore stand out against the roaring of this wave. I am fighting for my life again, one more time, what little is left of it. I used to love to swim, and this trip has ruined it for me now.

Aimi and I tumble together, and the only thing saving us from a significant injury is the softness of the butsu and its field. It may be trying to kill us with the tsunami, but it's just doing its job, propelling objects (and water) along its surface. Still, it handles everything with the gentleness of a down comforter in winter.

I'm struggling to hold my breath. My lungs want to let go. Just let go. Might as well, right? But some lingering sense of self-preservation keeps me from breathing in the rainwater. I must really be a glutton for punishment.

The rush of water around me dissipates, and I'm thrown

into the open air. Aimi clutches the back of my shirt and hauls me up.

We both double over, sucking air in and out, trying to breathe, hands on our knees.

"Ran…" She pants and throws her arm out. "All the way… Here. More… Waves…"

Down the butsu, there are marginally smaller, yet still very deadly, waves incoming.

"Butsu… not supposed… to be… on!" She laughs as she catches her breath.

"My fault." I'm panting and wheezing, and the rain still falls on us, falling on the butsu and fueling more waves. "Didn't know."

She stands up and pats her shoulder. "Oh, no. My sword."

We search around, and I spot it moving slowly in a small puddle near a butsu exit. I force myself forward and lunge for it before it tries to go any farther. Aimi nods her thanks as she places it over one shoulder. I've lost my family knife. It was one of the last things I had from home. Under the circumstances, I suppose that's fitting.

Dozens of people have gathered on the butsu exit ramp ahead, their mouths open and staring at the incoming tsunami waves. From up there, they can see the waves coming for kilometers. Aimi and I both look like drowned rats, but now is not the time to delay and dry off. Incoming in the purple lane, skirting the side of another wave, more androids are on their way.

I pull Aimi along towards the exit.

"Can we call for help?" I ask, pushing her along. She coughs and hacks before taking in another shaky breath.

"I saw Rin and Kazuo fighting androids as I passed them. Shintaro and your people are on the networks trying to calm the crowds. Shiroi Nami is in the air. But..." She nods to the people watching from the exit. "Something tells me the city is out in numbers, despite the weather."

"Maybe we can get lost in them? I think the thunderstorm is almost done."

"Let's go," she says, gesturing to run.

The raging water of the butsu calms as we make it up the off-ramp. The roaring lessens, becoming a soft purr, and when Aimi and I stop to look back, the wave peaks flatten out and lose momentum. Gutters along the side of the butsu open, and the rainwater drains away.

I guess that's what was supposed to happen.

I tap at my watch and sigh in dismay. The face is cracked, and I can only see half the display. They might be able to still hear me.

"Help! We need assistance. Exit A8. Send reinforcements!" A searing, knife-hot pain rips through my stomach. "Shit," I gasp, wheezing as I bend forward.

"Are you okay?" Aimi's hand is on my back.

"No. I..." A shock of nausea squeezes my stomach, and up comes all the water I've been drinking, voluntarily and involuntarily, in the last few hours.

Except it's red with blood. That's not good.

Several people who were walking by, trying to see the commotion on the butsu, sidestep us. The revulsion on their faces is unmistakable. They don't want to help or be near anyone displaying symptoms like mine.

"Yumi, we should get you to the hospital."

"They can't cure me. Can't help me. Gen said he engineered the virus to infect people from my world. I doubt the doctors here will be any more successful than Doctor..." I grasp for his name. What was his name?

"Dr. Jimmy?" she asks.

"Yeah, him."

She pulls me up and gets me walking. "At the very least, we could purchase more meds to help you be more comfortable."

"No. Maybe. Let's try to accomplish something before I'm rendered useless." I straighten up. "I have a corporation now, despite everyone trying to take it away from me. And I want to help transition this world over to a peaceful democracy if it's at all possible." I look over my shoulder. "But I can't do any of that with Aoi Uma on my tail at all times. What can we do about them?"

Aimi picks up her pace as we shift through the crowds. She's aiming for a shopping arcade about three blocks away.

"We sick our people on them is what."

"How?" I gesture to my waterlogged outfit, the broken watch, and the lack of any amenities.

"Come on," she insists. "We'll use a public comm point."

I keep looking over my shoulder as we weave through the crowds and approach the shopping arcade. Androids can survive underwater. They can withstand fire too. I'm sure some survived the multiple tsunamis. They're on my tail; I can feel it.

"Aimi..." I tug at her arm as our feet squish-squish-squish along the pavement. "I don't want to put you in harm's way if I don't have to."

She whirls around to face me, and her face is a picture of rage, her lips squished together in a violent X. She brings her finger up to me.

"Don't you dare start that shit."

I jerk back in surprise.

"Look at you," she says, gesturing to me. I glance down at

myself. There's a smear of blood across my pants. "You're puking up blood. You've been feverish for days. You're on death's doorstep, Yumi. I saw the broadcast. You're going to die. You need all the help you can get."

My body first heats with anger before a wash of tingles falls over me.

"I will not let them take you so easily." She turns and continues on, stomping along. "That was a cowardly move from Gen, infecting the claws of those cats. He couldn't face you with a sword, eh? Couldn't fight you face to face? Fuck him. No, actually, we're going to fuck him over."

She rips through the shopping arcade until we reach a series of public comm booths. An individual room opens for her at the wave of her wrist, and we enter side by side. The booth's floor looks clean and warm, and as stupid as it is, I kind of want to curl up there and sleep for a million years. I'm sure if homelessness were a problem on Hikari, these booths wouldn't even exist.

The screen lights up after she types something into it, and Reina Hirohata answers our call.

"Aunt Reina, where are you? Where's our army of people?"

"Aimi," Reina says, deflating in relief. "Thank goodness you're alive and well. Do you need backup?" She looks off to the side, consulting someone in a low voice.

"Do we need backup?" Aimi's sarcastic side has come out. "Yumi and I just nearly drowned in a giant tidal wave on the butsu. There are still killer androids out there that our updates missed, and Narumi Ogawa herself has taken to the streets to rile up the crowds and attack our people. We need backup, like yesterday."

Reina nods. "Understood, and sorry. We've been running

out of Kiiroi Yama headquarters, and the storm took out several communications facilities. Lightning hit a crucial relay. It's been madness here. What do you want to do?"

Aimi thinks for a moment. I lose any last energy I have and sink to the floor, letting the booth's wall guide me down.

"I want to eliminate Narumi Ogawa and her fuck-boy, Gen, in the most public way possible."

"Oooookay…?"

"There's a giant crowd outside. Not far from where we exited the butsu. Find out where Narumi and Gen are and dispatch Hidéki and Wataru to grab them. Then we'll drop them in the crowd and execute them in front of all the cameras."

Reina winces. "Aimi, dear, that could start a revolution for their supporters. It could make them martyrs."

Aimi lifts her chin. "There's enough evidence out there to support killing them outright. Let's do it publicly, so there's never any doubt about moving on."

A soft tap at the booth's door pops my eyes open. Is it Rin?

Aimi opens the door, and Saki enters. She takes in the situation quickly before squatting down at my side.

"Not feeling so good?" she asks.

I can only shake my head.

"That wave on the butsu was something, wasn't it?"

I laugh weakly, more of a huff than anything else. "Help me?" I ask, tears forming in my eyes.

"Of course," she replies, and her smile is so warm and soft I forget for a moment that she's an android. "You helped me. You brought me back to life. Gave me a new purpose. I'd do anything for you." She takes my hand and holds it while we wait for Aimi.

"Kiiroi Yama has drones in the air," Reina reports.

"They've located Narumi and Gen and their team not far from you. I'll send Hidéki, Wataru, and anything else I can. Stay where you are for a few minutes, and I'll dispatch you from there."

Aimi looks down at me, and her body wavers before my eyes.

"Yumi needs a medic if she's going to join us. This virus has her totally wiped." Aimi's sandwiched her bottom lip between her teeth.

"There's a hospital nearby. Would that work?"

I shake my head. "Can't be admitted. They'll never let me out again."

Aimi crouches down next to Saki. "Yumi, you're going to die if you don't get help. Trust me. Isao has told me how much dying hurts. He said coming back isn't that great either."

I shake my head again. "No choice. I would rather die doing *something* than lying in a hospital bed doing nothing."

I've burned through enough pain killers and steroids today to put a small animal in its grave. But I had no choice, and I still have very few options left. My body is going to give out one way or another. Gen forced my hand. Maybe if I had addressed the crowd earlier and then rested, I would've been able to gather my strength. I could have gotten things running for my corporation and then ridden off into the sunset once my new body was ready for me.

Not going to happen now.

Now we have to improvise.

Aimi shrugs. "What can I do then?"

"Pharmacy," is all I say.

"Right." She nods to Saki, and Saki stands up.

Returning to the console, Aimi says, "We need meds, that's

it. Find a pharmacy nearby that will dispense what we need right now, and Saki will go get it."

"Are you sure?" Reina's doubt is apparent in the timber of her voice. "She could live days, even weeks with transfusions and anti-viral therapy."

Aimi clutches the console, her knuckles turning white. "I'm telling you, she won't make it that long."

"Okay. Fine. We'll get you set up."

When Saki returns with the meds, she sits cross-legged next to me and draws out the shots. "Are you ready? Your body is so fatigued that this is going to hit you a lot harder than the last time, and it will wear off faster too."

I nod and present my arm to her. "I want to see Rin before it's over."

"I know." She soothes my shaking voice with gentle strokes down my arm. "I'm sure he'll be here soon enough. Nothing could keep him away from you. Nothing."

I sink back against the wall and keep myself from crying.

Nothing could keep him away.

So where is he?

CHAPTER TWENTY-SEVEN

The rush through my system is blinding. My vision bursts with white light, and my limbs shake. I close my eyes and let the meds wash through me. Roaring in my ears reminds me of the tsunami on the butsu, and I inhale sharply, sure I'm back there, the water towering over me.

If I live long enough to have more dreams, I'm sure drowning will play a heavy hand in my nightmares. As if my first drowning here didn't already cause me to steer clear of the water. I only survived that time because Shintaro did CPR on me. Who will be around to save me now?

My eyes flutter open as my heart picks up its lazy ambling pace to a steady jog. I grab Saki's hand.

"You'll take care of Ninjin when I'm gone?" I haven't worried much about my dog on this trip. I have assumed that he's been chasing balls and fighting with cats on this moon base, wherever it is.

"What about Rin?" Saki asks.

"I don't even know if he's still alive. He loves Ninjin,

but…" How do I explain Rin's lifelong distaste for animals because of Aka Matsuba? I get it. I'm not sure others would.

"I understand. Of course, I'll watch after him. Ready to stand?"

She takes my hand to hoist me to my feet. My legs are wobbly after all the running we did, and my clothes are still wet. I'd love to change into something warm and dry, but it's raining outside still, a spotty rain that comes and goes with bursts of sunlight. I need to just deal and move on. Hopefully, the cool, wet clothes will keep my fever down.

A few deep breaths, and I'm ready to go. "Okay. I think I can walk and function."

"Have you had a migraine recently?" Saki asks as Aimi opens the door to our comm booth and looks both ways.

"No. They disappeared once I was infected with the virus."

"Hmmm," she says, encircling my upper arm with a hand and checking my pulse. "They could be tied to blood pressure. We could…" Her eyes search mine for a moment. "Never mind. We can discuss it later."

The kinds of things she can do as an android amaze me. I'm not supposed to admire the androids, but there are moments when I do. Moments like these.

"Let's go." Aimi jerks her head towards the exit to the shopping arcade. Out in the open, a crowd of people chant, raising their fists, and pumping signs into the air. "The plaza outside looks ready for some mayhem. Let's see if Hidéki and Wataru can deliver what we need."

I admire Aimi, and my chest rises with pride to be walking alongside her. Her face is a picture of determination, pressing forward, sure of herself. I've never been that confident. And if I were in a different place and time, I would be focusing on her for our documentary about Shiroi Nami and what they can bring to the people of Hikari.

But I think we're about to show everyone what they can do.

We thread our way through the crowd, chanting along with them.

"Remove Aoi Uma!" "Destroy the androids!" "Human life or no life!"

I raise my fist and shout with them until I'm doubled over coughing. I'm sure I inhaled water during my unintended swim in the tsunami, and my lungs are paying for it. Straightening up is painful. My stomach feels like it has an ice pick wedged in it.

"You okay?" A random person next to me dumps her bag on the ground and crouches down. I look up in time to see Saki remove the woman's tablet from her purse and scoot away. So, now we're pickpockets too?

I would laugh, but I have to save my energy.

"I'll be all right, thanks," I say, pulling myself up to my full height again.

I follow Saki and Aimi to the other end of the plaza, and Saki is bent over the tablet.

"How are you going to...?" I'm not able to finish asking my question about how she'll hack the woman's tablet when she does it right in front of me. "Okay then. I have the perfect friends. Where is everyone?"

"Let me get into Kiiroi Yama's system first."

Aimi and I shift in front of Saki, allowing her to work without being interrupted. We raise our fists and chant along with the crowd. A booming voice rises above all the others, and a man close to us yells into a microphone.

"Our imprisonment must end!"

His voice echoes off the buildings. I search for the speakers, and they are installed into the plaza. This is probably a place for concerts and plays, and today they have commandeered it for a protest.

"Kiiroi Yama drones show Wataru and Hidéki picking up Narumi and Gen! Rin is there!"

I shuffle backwards to look at the footage and gasp. Rin and other kenryōshi from Kiiroi Yama are cutting down hordes of androids around a flurry of wings. The footage changes angles, and a Kiiroi Yama car flies in overhead with a man on a mounted gun mowing down another flank of androids. I cover my mouth as I watch, sick with worry and fear. This is destruction on a massive level. Kiiroi Yama doesn't use the big guns unless it's serious. With a blink, Hidéki is in the sky, carrying Narumi. Wataru clocks Gen, but Gen fights back.

"Come on," I whisper, trying to send them as much of my positivity as I can. "Grab him."

Wataru tries again, and this time he's successful. Gen looks injured, and his eyes are on Narumi, far off in the sky.

"They're on their way here. If we're going to do something, we have to do it now."

The crowd is getting agitated, climbing up on street lamps and setting off smoke flares. The rain has stopped, and it's empowered everyone to ratchet the agitation up a level.

"I... I don't know," I say, grabbing Aimi's arm. "Maybe we should leave? I know how to get back to the safe house from here." I clutch at my stomach, trying in vain to stop the stabbing pain there. "There's too much at stake to wing this... literally."

Aimi's smirk makes me laugh, and that hurts even more.

"No. We'll do this because we need to. We have no other choice."

A high-pitched scream rents the air from the other side of the plaza. The crowd parts like a boat racing through deep water.

"The cavalry is here," Aimi says, pointing to the kumojin corralling the protestors.

The giant spider creatures herd people into clusters around a central opening in the plaza. A man screams and faints when one of them touches him. The kumojin grabs his shirt and pulls him to the side. I almost laugh at the absurdity of it. I've seen pastures back home with trained sheepdogs moving sheep into pens, which is very much the same.

The crowd has gone eerily silent. People abandon protest signs and several run for the adjacent streets. But many stay behind, whispering to each other.

"I saw this on the underground news," a nearby woman says to the man next to her. "From a town south of here."

Aimi strides forward and corners the man with the microphone. His mouth is open in astonishment, and he holds the microphone in his hand, limp at his side.

"Excuse me. Give me that, please." Aimi holds out her hand, and her stare doesn't leave him any room to say no. He places it in her hand.

"Showtime," she says, and her eyes twinkle with glee.

Oh shit. What have I gotten myself into with this one? She's as destructive as Shintaro. I watch as she climbs up on a nearby light post. Yeah, she's just like Shintaro. It turns out I love my brother enough to surround myself with people just like him.

"Get ready," Saki whispers to me. "They're coming. Everyone is coming."

A tingle of dread runs through me. I have a fuzzy memory of sitting across from Saki and her now-deceased brother back at that hidden town beside the sea. Saki's passion for revenge and her need to be free were like a burning light coming out of the darkness. The Fukusha Model Sevens, the ones who had survived, wanted an end to Aoi Uma, an end at any cost. They were willing to sacrifice me for the greater good.

I lick my parched lips and shudder as the drugs run through my system. I trust these women, and I trust Shiroi Nami. And hell, I'm going to die anyway, and soon, so I should go with the flow, right?

Yet, something about this doesn't feel right. I wanted to do this in a benevolent manner. I wanted to show the citizens of Hikari that they didn't need some power-hungry despot to take over. Executing my competition for the 'greater good' is a bad idea all around.

With an area cleared in the crowd, Aimi takes control of the microphone. Heads swivel to the sound of her voice.

"Listen up, Shin-Osaka! You want peace, yeah?"

A small chorus of affirmation rises up to her words.

"You want freedom?"

"Yeah!" the crowd responds. Tingles wash down my back.

"You want the end of androids? You want families and lives worth living?" Aimi shouts, bringing her free arm holding the microphone up in a fist.

The crowd cheers, and she pumps her fist up and down. Her devotion to the Shiroi Nami way is both inspiring and terrifying.

Maybe this is a mistake. This could be wrong.

Or maybe it's the best thing that will ever happen to Hikari.

I don't know.

I need to know.

Dammit. I can't leave this all now.

Fighting with the tears in my eyes, I keep my attention on Aimi. She wraps her microphone arm around the pole so she can point to me.

"People! My friends! Don't be afraid of the creatures around you. Remember how you loved your Aka Matsuba way of life before Aoi Uma created androids? You had children, and animals, and families... and the androids replaced them. We can bring you back to that way of life! Shiroi Nami and the corporation, Kazenoho, want *you* to be in charge. No more contracts. No more castes."

A murmur runs through the crowd, and several people point up to the sky.

"No more being owned by someone else! Independent and free to choose. Free to vote for your leaders. How does that sound?"

I look out at the crowd, and I'm not surprised to see confusion cloud their faces.

I don't think they know what they want. They only know they don't want *this*.

The crowd shifts even more as a Kiiroi Yama car flies overhead and lands in the street beyond the plaza. With a rush of air and a rustle of feet on pavement, people move aside, and Wataru touches down in the open space with Gen in his arms. Gen tumbles to the ground. Hidéki is next to land with Narumi, and she stumbles and falls to her knees. A giant, synchronized gasp quiets the plaza.

Narumi points at Hidéki, towering over her. "I will have your head for this, you freak."

Gen gets to his feet and turns slowly, his eyes scanning the crowd. He hasn't seen me yet, so I have the opportunity to watch his reaction to the protest signs, the angry faces, the upraised fists. For the first time, genuine fear blankets his face.

Everything here — the energy for change and the anger at the past — is the antithesis of what he's been calling for. Did he assume Aoi Uma had the will of the people? Or did he think he could force that will on them whether they wanted it or not?

It's nice to feel like he's at a disadvantage.

But I know Aoi Uma. They have too many resources, too many androids at their beck and call to lie down and give up.

Gen's eyes fall on me, and his fear turns to anger.

"Yumi Minamoto! Come out here and face me, citizen to citizen."

He pounds on his chest, and Narumi's frown turns to a wry smile.

"Don't," Saki says, grabbing my arm. "They don't own you."

"No one owns me," I remind her. "And he can't hurt me anymore."

CHAPTER TWENTY-EIGHT

I can't even begin to describe how fucking tiresome this is. Gen loves a good showdown, and I would rather be behind the camera.

"We've already done this once today, Gen. I'm not coming anywhere near you," I shout back.

People in the crowd watch us like they're spectating a sports game, and it takes a moment, but Gen eventually turns to acknowledge them all, his arms wide. As he rounds to face me, his smile builds, feeding off the energy of those surrounding him.

"Come on, Yumi. You wanted to address the crowd earlier, didn't you? Now's your chance."

Yes, I wanted to talk to the crowd earlier, you dickhead. But *someone* kidnapped me and tried to kill me instead. I shouldn't let him rile me up, but the meds have kicked in this one last time, and I'm tired of being at his mercy.

The crowd nearest me rustles as I step forward to meet Gen face to face. Someone yelps, and there's a chorus of obscenities, as Rin pushes through and runs straight for me.

He's in Kiiroi Yama black from the waist up, and with his sword strapped to his back, he's like the first time I ever saw him — a formidable kenryōshi. I have just enough time to register that it's him before he sweeps in and lifts me off my feet.

"A kenryōshi," a woman near me says, clutching another woman next to her.

Rin's arms tighten around me, and we turn in a circle, ignoring the surrounding people. Murmurs rise, and a collective gasp accompanies his lips crashing into mine.

I hate public displays of affection, but I will take any love I can get right about now. I lean in and let this kiss last. My fingers trace the top of his head, down his neck. When he brings his hands to my face, someone in the plaza whistles and several people giggle.

He pulls away and looks me in the eye, and it's in this moment that I know, really know, that he sees me. He sees all of my complications, all of my faults and desires, and he does not give a shit. Not one. Because I'm his, and he's mine, and that's all that matters.

"I thought I lost you more than once today. You will not stand alone against them now," he whispers.

I gather Rin's hand in mine and turn to face everyone. The crowd looms larger than before. People press in and jostle each other to get closer to the kumojin and glimpse Wataru and Hidéki. Something flies out of the throng and hits Narumi in the shoulder.

"Go! We don't want you here anymore!" another person shouts.

The crowd stirs, and I get nervous. This could spiral out of control at any moment. I thrust my arm into the air, and Rin lifts our hands and joins me. We circle around and make eye contact with every person we can see. The murmuring dies down.

"Hear that, Narumi," I say, turning to face her. "They don't want you here anymore."

"They don't know what they want," she says, lifting her chin and standing up straight. She raises her voice. "Have your lives not prospered under Aoi Uma? Aka Matsuba never cared about your longevity. Tamura only ever cared about profits!"

"And you don't?" Rin asks. He points his finger at her. "Think of the money people spent on defective androids. Androids I had to cut down to save others. And you could have stopped that before it ever started. Don't deny it. You could have programmed codes of conduct into them, to save lives, and *you chose not to.*"

"You know nothing of business," Gen counters.

"And you know nothing of saving lives." Rin's voice is rock hard, cold.

A man in the crowd raises his hand and shouts, "An android killed my wife. Pushed her from our balcony!"

"An android smothered my neighbor in her sleep!" Another calls out.

"I broke my arm when an android pushed me to the ground!"

More and more voices rise up, and Narumi loses her cool. Cracks in her facade widen and spread. Her left eye twitches as she reaches out for Gen. He doesn't notice until she's gripping his upper arm, and the worry on his face is just... ah, it's a joy.

I have done everything I can to set things right on this world, but I hadn't been making any actual progress.

Until this moment.

I want to gloat. I want to rub it in his face that even his idol, his lover, is having second thoughts. She's having doubts.

I don't do anything. Yet.

Except to watch everything play out. Narumi never thought the populace would call her to task for her crimes. She assumed she was untouchable.

She's definitely not.

I look over my shoulder to Saki, and she makes eye contact with me.

"Let the crowd do its work," I mouth to her, subvocalizing because I know her android ears will hear.

Squeezing Rin's hand, I take a deliberate step back. The kumojin squeeze in and step in front of us, protecting us and leaving a space open for the crowd to approach Narumi and Gen.

Narumi sees the opening and her lips pale. Gen steps in front of her, but she still wants to confront me.

She tips back her head and laughs. "I don't know why I kept telling Gen to just ignore you. That you would go away, or this planet would eat you alive. I should have finished you off when I had the chance."

She could have, in that stripped-down building where she threatened to imprison me forever.

"My father has a saying he loves that applies here," I say with a shrug. "'Come at the queen, you best not miss.'"

An angry man charges into Narumi's personal space. He shouts her down for the way her corporation stripped his family of all their savings. Another woman rushes in, and then it's five more people. Ten more people. Twenty, thirty.

Rin and I back away, and anxiety squeezes my chest. Mob justice has come to end Aoi Uma from the top down.

"We should get out of here," Rin says, but a scream from the scrum of people stops us in our tracks.

I turn around in time to see someone push Narumi, and she fights back. Really fights back.

"What?" Rin whispers, and his jaw drops.

My knees shake as I watch Narumi and Gen fight an impossible battle to hold off dozens of people. Their fists are like anvils, and each person who tries to overpower them gets smashed. The mob descends to kicking and punching at random, but Gen throws off four people at once.

Saki grabs my arm. "We should go. *Now.*"

Rin and I try to leave, and the movement catches Gen's eye. He tosses two people aside and climbs over another one to leap through the air in our direction. The woman he jumped over catches his leg, and he tumbles along the plaza pavement, taking out a kumojin.

A siren screams in from overhead as a Kiiroi Yama car flies and hovers over the crowd.

"Please disperse! Leave this plaza at once!"

Seeing the distraction, Gen pops to his feet and heads straight for me. And I am not sticking around to find out how he became such a good fighter in so little time. My brain says one thing, and my gut says another. I don't want to listen to either of them.

Pain rips through my belly, and I double over and stumble. Rin catches my arm and tries to keep me upright, but it's no use. Everything is about to give out, all at once.

My health. My luck. Everything.

Saki and Aimi jump in to help. I look up from the ground in time to see Aimi collide with Gen's midsection. She barrels him over like an uncontrolled car slamming into a wall. They tumble far enough away to give me space to get to my feet.

With a high-pitched scream, Narumi appears from the crowd and attacks Rin. He ducks as her fist flies at him with a deadly left hook. She's so fast — punch, kick, jab, punch, kick. Rin can only deflect half of them, and there's no time to draw his sword.

Saki joins the fray, fending off Gen long enough for me to limp away.

But I will not run.

I've run enough. Now, it's time to stay and fight with whatever I have left.

That whole 'live to fight another day' crap was meant for someone else.

I decide to help Rin first. I lunge for Narumi's legs and only catch one, but I knock her sideways and give Rin time to pull his sword. She kicks me, and I roll away, crashing into a kumojin. Its legs buckle, and it jabs me with some kind of stinger, no doubt engineered by Shiroi Nami to allow it some way to defend itself. My whole side erupts in flames. A scream rips from my throat, and the kumojin scurries off, squeaking and hissing. I doubt it was intentional, seeing as I attacked it accidentally, but it doesn't make this hurt any less. The heat from the sting creeps across my skin, and my breathing becomes shallow.

I gasp and try to crawl forward. A few meters away, Saki lies on the ground, conscious, maybe? Unconscious? I'm unsure. Her head is turned towards me, and her eyes are open, but I don't know if she's awake. I get close enough to touch her face.

"Saki!" My breath rattles in my chest. "Help." But it's only a whisper, and she does nothing but blink. She must be damaged. I need to find Rin. I roll over on my uninjured side and search for him, but I can't see anything but running feet scattering in all directions.

My body is jerked to the side as someone grabs the back of my shirt and throws me down on the pavement. Stars pepper my vision, and I wheeze, trying to catch my breath. I roll over, and Gen is hovering above me. He is the picture of anger — nose flared, skin flushed, eyebrows drawn together, chest heaving. In his right hand, he holds my knife.

My knife. The one I plunged into the android and was washed away by the tsunami. It was recovered and put in the hands of my enemy.

He kneels down over me, and I'm paralyzed, too injured and tired to fight back. With his left hand on my shoulder, pinning me down, he leans over to my ear.

"You miss home. I get it. But you've fought hard for a dream that will never be realized. Never be fulfilled." He drops his voice, and the brush of breath at my ear fills me with dread. "They're never coming for you. The beacon never made it to its first jump. And here's the secret I've kept from you, from everyone. That possibility of a rescue mission within a year was a lie."

I shake my head, tears flying to each side. No. That's not true. They said they would come.

They're going to come.

They're not?

"Believe it. I got to see the second ship before we left. They asked me to help with the lab specs. It was at least five years out from completion. At least."

I never believed Gen before. But for some reason, I do now.

He pulls away so he can see my face.

"So, go to your grave Yumi and rest. Because you were never going home to begin with."

My gut erupts in pain as he drives the knife straight into my stomach. White lights cloud my vision, and my hearing rings. Heat leaks from my arms, my legs, and I shudder.

"Fuck you… Gen…"

He smiles — my blood on my knife, on his hands.

A blur from behind him rushes up, and the flash of glinting metal catches my eye.

Rin's sword cuts Gen from his right shoulder and down across his chest. I blink, forcing myself to live to see him die, too, only to have my last moments sink into despair.

Gen falls to the side, and his exposed insides spark and pop. No, no, no. I moan at the injustice of it all. That fight… He fought hard and fast, not because he had trained and gotten better, but because he's done what he plans to do for everyone on this planet.

He has made himself immortal. And now, he can never be killed. He'll just download to a new body and keep on with his plans.

My vision swims, the clouds overhead bend and shift, and the sky buzzes with drones that look like morphing flies.

"Yumi!" I can't feel Rin's hands on my face. I can barely see him. "Yumi, Yumi. Oh shit. I was too slow." Tears pour from his eyes. I have never seen Rin this sad. It must be my end.

And even if I come back, which is a faint possibility at this point, I won't remember this.

"Gen… Secret…" I force out. Blood bubbles up and into my throat, choking me, asphyxiating my last breaths away. My final moments with Rin, gone.

Everything turns black.

CHAPTER TWENTY-NINE

My body is a cloud, light and ephemeral. I hold up my hands and flip them over, but they fade and flux, almost transparent. Huh. I shrug my shoulders and smack my lips. Where I once only knew pain, I have warmth. Calm. Peace. This is not too bad...

Wait.

I think I'm dead.

Maybe that's why I feel my body but can't see it, inspect it, realize it.

Where was I last?

I hunt for the memory, open up the dusty boxes in my brain and look inside each.

What's in here?

Shintaro and I sit in our pajamas back home and crack open nuts next to the fire. This is a winter tradition my father started after he arrived on Orihimé. Is it winter now? I don't remember. The memory is present, here, now. The snap of the nutshell is loud and satisfying. My fingers smart as I pick the pieces of nut out and pop them in my mouth. I can taste and smell them, the rich, roasted scent, but it's a memory, not something happening in the present.

Now.

That word means something to me. There was 'then' and 'now,' but they mesh together in this blank space.

I open another dusty box and set the lid aside. This time I'm on Hikari. Yes, this is more present. This is more now.

Rin sits across from me at a coffee shop.

"You've been avoiding me, Yumi. Any particular reason?"

My face does something I can't pinpoint.

"Yeah, that's what I figured." He rubs his face and sighs before folding his arms over his chest and leaning back. "*I'm sorry. I either read the situation wrong or I moved way too fast for you, and that's my fault, not yours.*"

He's talking about the first time he kissed me. Once again, my nonexistent body feels warm. Safe.

"*I'm sorry. Again.*"

"I don't want either of us to go to jail because of this contract thing. I'm your proxy. You can't have a relationship with me."

Oh. Why did I ever say that? Why did I push him away?

Looking back on it, it was a stupid thing to do. Someone showed me love, and I didn't appreciate how to handle it. What I wouldn't give to do that over again.

The space I'm in stretches out forever, boxes upon boxes upon boxes. Dusty boxes piled on other dusty boxes. I used to talk about putting my feelings in boxes, hiding them away. Maybe I did that with my memories instead.

Drifting through the space, I try to open a few boxes, but they stay shut. My nails tap-tap-tap on a lid. What's inside? What am I missing?

More boxes pile in. More, more, more.

They surround me on every side, filling in every available spot, outward, upward. On and on and on... The space cools and darkens, from white to sepia to dusky black.

Tingles fall down my shoulders, my arms, my hands, my torso, my legs...

I stare down, and my body appears as it once was... Or not. It looks different. Taller, stockier. My legs are powerful. My back is straight. My belly is not bloody.

I'm being drawn in, bit by bit. Winked into existence.

"Yumi."

Rin? The room of boxes has grown even darker. I stretch out my hand, and my knuckles knock into a box. Boxes are right behind me. Over me.

There's no room left for me.

"Yumi. You can come back to us now." Kazuo this time.

Kazuo, you dolt, I can't come back from death.

"She's loaded up, but things are missing," Rin says.

"We already knew that going in. This is better than nothing," Kazuo insists. "I refuse to let go."

"Me too."

I roll my eyes. This is dumb. I can hear them, but they're speaking nonsense. People don't return from the dead.

A box at my feet rubs against my leg like a cat expecting dinner. Fine. I open it, and I'm in the town by the sea. Saki sits across the table from me.

"Look, I know how you feel about androids, and I agree with you. I was a human being, but I'm not any longer. I don't ever need to eat or drink. I only do it now because I miss it. And then I realize I have no taste buds. I don't get drunk or feel adrenaline anymore. I went to those fights hoping I would feel that physical rush when I won, but it never came. I can fall in love, but my heart will never race when someone looks at me

because they find me attractive. It's as if all the emotional signals are mixed up. Some of us are better off than others. Shun's body reacts to emotions. Mine? Only some of the time."

Saki. Poor Saki. Used and abused. But she was doing well when I last saw her. When was that?

A flash of her open eyes. Cold, wet concrete.

Boot-up Sequence Complete in 30 seconds...

Huh. What's that?

20 seconds...

10, 9, 8...

Boot-up? Um...

3, 2, 1...

The boxes zip away, fade into the black.

I open my eyes. My lungs fill with air.

A status panel overlays the world around me. Current charge, 98%. Current location, 34° 40' 10.3044" N and 135° 29' 49.2324" E. New messages, 3.

Rin and Kazuo smile, but something is wrong... or not right.

Rin sighs and collapses into a chair next to me. "Thank God. Yumi, is that you?"

"Yes?" But my voice does not sound like mine.

Rin's eyes fill with tears, and he sweeps up and out of the room.

Kazuo's head drops before he smiles, and his eyes meet mine.

"Welcome back, kako."

"WHAT IS GOING ON, and why does everything feel so... distant?"

My world is a glass bowl, warped and hollow and echoing. I'm not in this body. I'm ten centimeters behind it. I turn my head, and everything slowly follows along with it. Ugh. I close my eyes, and I still see all that stuff in front of me.

"Help me. I don't feel well."

Kazuo's hand on mine is a solid weight, 402.3 grams. God, that's weird. Why am I thinking in such precise terms?

"Just a second. The techs are working on calibrating everything."

New diagnostics run before my very eyes. Rows and rows of code flow through this interface, and slowly, as each one hits its checksum, I come into alignment. Little things happen that restore me to my own body. My knee bounces. My fingers twitch, and my hand turns over to squeeze Kazuo's. My chest is tight with anxiety, so I take deep breaths. But they're strange. Air goes in and out, but the calm it used to bring me isn't there anymore.

"Where did Rin go?" My voice is calm despite the panic at the back of my head.

"I'm sure he'll return in a moment. It was all a bit of a shock to him, I think. Just give it some time. Can you open your eyes and tell me if you're feeling better?"

This time when I open my eyes, I'm in my body and not a step behind it. The tightness in my chest loosens a tick. Picking up my hands, I turn them over, one by one. They don't look familiar.

"I'm an android now, aren't I?"

Oh, fuck. I knew it the moment I saw the boot-up sequence. Something has happened, and they had to put me in an android. But why?

"You're more than an android, Yumi. And you will not be one forever. I promise." Kazuo stops to hang his head for a moment, and when he makes eye contact with me again, I can see the sleepless nights, the long days, the worry, the shame. He was on this trip to monitor Shintaro and me, to make his own observations on behalf of the empress. This is not what he bargained for.

He clears his throat and pulls from his reserve of strength. I've seen the motion a million times over the years to recognize it now. "Yumi, let's talk a little about how you're feeling and what you remember."

I turn my head and find the Kiiroi Yama techs and engineers who initially helped upload my consciousness in the room with us. Okamoto stands next to them, his arms crossed over his chest. His face is blank, empty of expression like he's never seen me before.

I wonder... But before I can even make a conscious decision, new information pops up on display before me. Okamoto is two-point-two meters away from me. He's 180 centimeters tall. His temperature is thirty-seven degrees... My eyes scan the data provided to me, including more about him and his public contract terms. I look at each engineer and find the same reports about them all. No wonder Saki used to sit silently and just stare into space. She had so much information at her fingertips.

"I feel... different. Like me, but not me. Like... you took me and sanded down all the edges."

One of the engineers nods. "The information we got from the ex-Aoi Uma employee told us how her emotions would be changed. This particular model has emotional feedback misfires, and so they built ways to control it," he explains to Kazuo before turning to me. "Rest assured that your personality will remain the same when transferred to a new... um, a new body. This model has an artificial limit on emotional resonance. Kind of like a governor. The emotions are there; they are just held back from being expressed."

"Fantastic," I grumble, and I hear my own voice. It's like listening to someone else talk. Not me. Not Yumi.

"What else can you tell us?" Kazuo asks, taking my hand again.

"My brain is like a... a warehouse with lots of boxes in it. And if I want to access memories, I have to find the box and open it."

The tech people gasp and whisper between them. They think I can't hear them, but I can — every word. Cognitive functions. Neurological bases of memory formation. Visualization. Manifest thoughts... I can hear it all, but I don't know what any of it means. I don't have the patience for this right now.

"Do you remember what happened before we put you in this body?"

I shake my head. "The last thing I remember is being in this chair. We came here to bring my consciousness into the Kiiroi Yama databanks. I guess it worked?" Kazuo nods. "But I don't know what happened after. Did we go to the bank? Did we create the corporation?"

Kazuo brings his hands to his lips in a prayer gesture. "Ohhh, shit. Everything after the transfer is gone, right?" He closes his eyes. "Fuck. That's stupid of me. Of course, that's the way it works."

The engineer who spoke earlier shrugs his shoulders. "It's like any backup. Once you backup, any changes after are lost."

"What about what we tried to scan in the hospital?" Okamoto asks, and the engineer shrugs again, unhappy to be the bearer of bad news.

"We did what we could, but she was unconscious and uncommunicative. The software had very little to go on."

I don't know whether to be angry, concerned, or upset, so I just sit. I'm not even sure if I *can* be any of those things. In the past, fear would creep up my back, cover my skull, and send my heart hammering. It's as if the emotion is stopped somewhere along the way and never takes off.

The door opens, and Rin enters. He looks calmer this time. His eyes are glassy, but he's composed, my usual Rin. I smile at him, happy to see him. As happy as I can be. At least I can feel a little, if not a lot. His face, the shape of his presence, brings warmth to my body.

"Sss..." He stops and clears his throat. "Yumi, we have a lot of work to do, and we're going to need to get out of this building as soon as possible. Do you think you can stand or walk?"

I wiggle my fingers, my toes, and bounce my knee. Everything happens as it's supposed to. "Yes, I think I can. Why do we need to leave the building?"

Rin glances at Okamoto, and Okamoto nods.

"A lot has happened while you've... been away."

"Away? You make it sound like I've been on vacation."

Kazuo huffs a laugh. "Well, your sense of humor is intact. A lot happened after we backed you up. There were protests all over the city. People took to the streets in vast numbers. And without the Aoi Uma androids to stop them this time, they swarmed every Aoi Uma government building possible."

"Aoi Uma called in new androids from Amagasaki," Rin continues. "Ones not affected by our laws. At least, not yet. They have them on a separate update network. Anyway, the city is now divided. Everything south of Chuo Ward is Aoi

Uma territory, and that includes this building. It's dangerous for us to be here."

"They can't just take property from Kiiroi Yama," I protest. "They're a Class A independent corporation."

"We're also your ally," Okamoto says gently. "And that puts us in an awkward spot."

"I'm so sorry." I drop my head and stare at these foreign hands of mine. "If you'd rather we dissolve this relationship, seeing as what's become of me —"

"No," he interrupts, raising his hand. "Awkward or not, we cannot let Aoi Uma take this world by force. We will continue forward as a team — your Kazenoho Corporation, Kiiroi Yama, and Shiroi Nami. Together." A small smile graces his lips. "If it makes you feel any better, Aoi Uma is having a hell of a time defending their own territory without us. They have little in the way of weapons or firepower. They're scraping by on what they can figure out on their own."

"That's good news."

The door opens again, and I gasp at the man standing in the doorway. Wait...

No, it's not Isao.

"Hidéki, it's good to see you."

His mouth opens and closes a few times before he nods. "We have our team ready to secure an exit from this building. We can go in three minutes." He steps to the side, and Atsumi is right behind him. She leans right to look at me, and our eyes lock on each other. Her chest rises and falls, and her eyes narrow. She's angry and disgusted by what she sees. That's going to put a dent in our relationship.

"We're working to shut this building down and keep it defended until we can gain back this territory," Okamoto says, gesturing for everyone to stand up and get moving.

"But..." I wave at the room and everything else. "But my consciousness is stored here."

Kazuo rounds the table, helps me to stand up, and taps on my head. "Your consciousness is here now. What's in the data storage in this building is only a backup, a backup we don't want to use because we'll lose everything that will happen from here on forward."

"You'll have to be careful," Hidéki says, approaching me. "Isao will move you from this android's body to your body that's growing at our off-world moon base. This is only temporary. We have to go. Now."

I glance at silent Rin. He's staring at me, and I can only imagine what's going through his head. I'm an android now, something he used to hate. I'm not the woman he fell in love with. Did he watch me die? Was I close to him when it happened? Sadness wells up in my chest and then just stops. It's as if some invisible hand has reached into me and pressed it all down. Tucked it away.

Turning around, I gasp and jump back as I catch my reflection in a window across the room.

"No. No no no no no..."

"Yumi, it was the only way," Kazuo says, trying to take my hand. I fling him off.

"What did you do with Saki?"

Because *I'm* Saki now. I'm in her android body.

I am Saki.

"She's here," Rin says, waving to the room. "It was her idea."

"No."

Rin steps forward and grabs my upper arms. There's a lot of power in my body, and I could pull out and away from him easily, but I let him hold me. The strength of his hands is a grounding force, keeping me from floating away into despair and denial.

"*It was her idea,*" he stresses. "We didn't have access to another android to put you into. We knew what to do with Saki because she wasn't like the other androids. Remember? Narumi couldn't hack any of the other ones because Saki was special, different. She convinced us to archive her until you can give her back a body. She'll live here until that can happen."

"This building could be destroyed!"

"Not my building," Okamoto says, placing his hand on his heart. "And I have the engineers working on a backup system. Just... trust us, Miss Minamoto. We're thinking on our feet, but we'll make this work."

No wonder everyone keeps looking at me strangely. I'm Saki now. But I'm not inside. Ugh. This is worse than I thought it would be when I sat in that chair and encouraged them to take my consciousness.

"Why didn't you leave me in the data storage, huh? This... I can't do this."

"We have to go now," Hidéki says, waving us forward. "We'll talk about it when we're safe."

Fine. I'm already in this body. I might as well just deal with it.

CHAPTER THIRTY

The sun has set, and the ground shakes beneath our feet as we hustle into an alley, past a dilapidated apartment building. We keep our heads down and avoid making any noise — our footsteps quiet on the wet pavement. Keeping my new android body in check is... interesting. There's so much data to monitor; it's overwhelming. I brush the feeling aside like shooing away a fly. Where are we anyway? The location shows up on my display, but I don't understand it.

We round another corner, and I follow everyone into the side door of a shuttered restaurant. Rin turns the lights on, and cockroaches scatter, heading for darker corners. I cling to the wall of the room and close my eyes. This place reminds me of Kitakyushu and the hell hole I lived in there. Nothing about that time is pleasant for me, and nothing about this makes it any better.

In my head, I wander through the maze of boxes and find more specific memories of Kitakyushu. There's one of me laughing and drinking with Saki, but the background is blank like someone has come in and erased it. Where were we?

Being in Kitakyushu reminds me of another thing...

"What's going to happen to Ninjin?" I open my eyes and take a deep breath. Everyone is in the room now. Kazuo walks the perimeter, Hidéki looks like a giant in this small space, and Rin hovers near the door. Is he standing ready to block me if I run? I wouldn't blame him for thinking that of me. I'd like to escape and hide away forever.

"He's with all the other animals at our moon base," Hidéki says, his voice rolling over me like a summer storm. "We don't plan to do anything with him."

"But I'm an android now." My voice fills with despair, even if my body doesn't. How did Saki live like this? "How will he know it's me?"

Ninjin only ever tolerated Saki. He won't know it's me if I get to see him again.

"Don't concern yourself with this now," Rin interrupts, his tone annoyed. "We have other more pressing things to worry about."

I flinch, his words a slap to my face. My whole life has been turned inside out, and I'm not allowed to worry about my dog?

Human Yumi would've lit into him for being so careless about my feelings. On an analytical level, I can play back this conversation and see what I would have done differently as a human. But as an android, I file away the interaction with mild disappointment.

Kazuo's eyes bounce between us, Rin to me to Rin again, preparing for a fight.

"Of course," I whisper, returning to my placid state. "Where are we, anyway?"

"Matsubara Ward." Rin's voice turns cold and hard, and I open the box in my brain to remember our time at the cafe, so long ago. *"There was this job about four years ago. We were tracking errant androids through the bowels of Matsubara Ward. You haven't been there yet —"*

"I haven't been anywhere yet," I had said.

Rin continued, *"Yeah, you haven't. Hmmm. Anyway, Matsubara is a lower caste ward, people living on top of other people. Six people to an apartment half my apartment's size. I lost an android in a converted apartment building. There were people everywhere, and I didn't see that he ducked behind a stack of shipping crates. I ran past him, and he reached out and grabbed me by my hair. Nearly scalped me. At the time, my hair was long, and I kept it pulled up. I hated this scar..."*

"You hate this ward." I could tell from the animosity in his tone that the scar he hated was not as bad as the ward he had to work in.

He shrugs. "That's precisely the reason I chose it. No one will look for us here. And with the press of millions of bodies, we will blend in. Shiroi Nami is fighting hard for this ward. We can help here."

Kazuo turns on more lights and heads towards the front of the shop. Out of the storeroom, we step into an abandoned kitchen. It's the opposite layout from K&G Noodles, but it still has most of the same equipment. I run my finger over a nearby steel counter, and it comes away dusty.

"This place is a mess. How long has it been abandoned?"

"Three years." Kazuo picks up a pot and jumps back when a dozen bugs run past his feet. "It's going to need to be fixed up."

A double-hinged door separates the kitchen from a tiny

seating area, just enough room for five or six tables, more if we expand to the sidewalk.

I nod my head as I walk around. "I see. So, we're starting our own noodle shop?"

"We own the entire building now." Rin avoids my eyes and looks out the front shutters. "There are tenants, a lot of them, on the fourth through eighth floors, but we will have this shop and those floors right above. We plan to move everyone in."

"Do we have to be actual landlords? Do we have to unclog toilets and fix windows and collect rent?" This is a horrible idea for someone like me, but my voice is even-keeled.

"No. There's a management company to handle that." Kazuo stops and folds his arms over his chest. "Do you think you're up for this?"

Rin, Kazuo, and Hidéki are all watching me, so this is the time to come clean.

"No. I want you to put me back in the data storage until I have a body… or never."

Kazuo turns his eyes to the floor.

"I died, right? I am dead to the general public. I don't even understand why you brought me back like this." I gesture at Saki's body. "It makes no sense. How long until you're done growing my clone?" I ask Hidéki.

He shrugs, a slight lifting and lowering of his right hand. "Hard to say. Two to three months, maybe longer."

"See?" I throw up my hands and marvel at the awkwardness of the gesture. That's something I do all the time, but I never thought about the mechanics of my hands and arms. My screen read-out tells me everything that's happening with my body, and I haven't learned to ignore it yet. "In a few months, you could have skipped this interim android body or left me to be dead and gone." I drop my voice. "I can only imagine how I actually died."

Kazuo and Rin look at each other, but neither of them says anything. Either they weren't there, or they know and don't want to tell me? I'm not sure.

"It was a risk we decided to take, Yumi," Rin says, "because we were unsure of what you would retain. We rushed you to a hospital and tried to revive you. You were conscious for a short time but unable to talk or communicate. We asked that memories be retrieved from the previous hours, but Kiiroi Yama techs weren't sure if it worked."

"It didn't. Why go through all the trouble? This is such a mess."

Rin steps closer to me. "Before you died, you said Gen had a secret, and you seemed genuinely distressed about it."

"He told me a secret? Or just said he had one?"

"I don't know. You passed out before I could question you further."

"Let me..." I hold up one finger.

Most of my memory boxes are right up front and easy to access. I don't even need to search for them. They're just there like they were when I was a human. I can effortlessly slip in and out of them. But some boxes in my warehouse are shut. They require effort to open them and view them. Some are hopelessly locked, and I may never discover what's inside.

"I'm sorry. I can't tell if it's here or not. So, you were hoping I'd remember the secret?"

"Yes. And there's something else, too," Rin starts, but he pauses and swears. "It happened after we backed you up. You asked me to save your body. You wanted to freeze your eggs for future offspring."

I look at each of the men in the room. They are all quiet for a long moment.

"And?"

"Your body is now in deep freeze, in Kadoma Ward General Hospital," Kazuo says, shoving his hands in his pockets. "A hospital occupied by Aoi Uma."

I close my eyes, but the gesture brings me no peace.

"Of course." I sigh. "I see your conundrum. It's better to have me here in this body than nothing at all."

"Well," Rin continues, "we'll spend the next few months serving up noodles until your new body is ready. And we'll help Shiroi Nami reclaim this world before your people come. That's what Saki would want you to do. Do you think you can live here until Shiroi Nami has made its final move? Are you up for cleaning this place and living here until we can move forward?"

It doesn't escape my notice that Rin is back to the way he was before we kissed, before we fell in love. He's turned all-business, stiff and cool. Not cold. I can see his heart is hurting by the way he looks at me when he thinks I'm not paying attention. My imagination is sure to run wild with doomsday scenarios of him leaving me for someone else because I'm everything he's grown to hate over the last ten years.

A memory bubbles to the surface of Reina Hirohata, telling me I can't trust Rin, that I shouldn't trust Rin. I know why they said that. He's an orphan and a former Kiiroi Yama employee. He has no one else to vouch for him. They don't want me to trust him because they think he's untrustworthy.

And there's nothing I won't do to prove her wrong.

Because he did love me, and he could love me again. I know it. This situation is just a temporary setback. If I'm careful, I can keep him from drifting away from me. I can hold him in my heart until I'm back in my own body, or this consciousness is gone. If it's gone, I won't know the difference, anyway.

So, I pull up my shoulders, raise my chin, and smile. Smile like I believe in happiness and love and hope, even if those concepts feel so far away that they might as well be fairytales.

I clap my hands and rub them together.

"I love a good challenge. Let's get to work."

Check out my website for more books like this…
http://www.spajonas.com/books

Visit via your phone, tablet, or laptop!
Use the QR code below for quick access.

THANK YOU!

Thank you so much for reading *The Rise of Shiroi Nami*. Poor Yumi! What will happen to her next? There are more adventures to come on Kurai and Hikari, so please, stick around.

Check out the fifth and final book of the Hikoboshi Series, *The Fate of Shin-Osaka*. http://www.spajonas.com/the-fate-of-shin-osaka

If you sign up for my email updates, I'll let you know when the my books are available and plenty of other news. http://www.spajonas.com/newsletter/

THANK YOU!

If you enjoyed this book, you'll love *Removed*, the first book of the Nogiku Series. It also takes place in the same universe. http://www.spajonas.com/removed/

Please consider leaving a review of *The Rise of Shiroi Nami* wherever you find reviews. Your review can help other readers find books they'll enjoy. I appreciate all reviews, positive or negative.

This is the fourth book in the Hikoboshi Series. You can learn more about this series and my other works of fiction at http://www.spajonas.com and http://www.spajonas.com/books/

THANK YOU!

Thank you for reading!

ACKNOWLEDGMENTS

As usual I have many people to thank for helping me.

- Biggest thanks goes to my awesome critique partner, Tracy Krimmer. I don't know what I'd do without you.
- Cori Wilbur, who reads everything I write.
- Lola Verroen, who supports me and my business without fail.
- Germaine Fletcher, who read my drafts so quickly my head spun.
- Charity Vandehey, who has become a new champion for my work and beta reader.
- All those in my favorite FB author groups.
- All the readers of the Nogiku Series who gave it a chance and are giving the Hikoboshi Series a chance too.
- My brother, Brendan.
- My mom, Claire, proofreader extraordinaire and a huge fan of my work. Love you, Mom.
- My husband, Keith, who really needs to read this series, ahem.
- And my two girls, C and D.

I'm eternally grateful for everyone's support!

ABOUT THE AUTHOR

Stephanie (S. J.) is a writer, knitter, Capricorn, Japanophile, and USA Today Best Selling author. She loves summer, downtempo beats, yoga pants, foxes, owls, dogs, sushi, pasta, and black tea. She lives outside NYC with her husband, two great kids, and her dog who always wants to play. When it comes to her work, she writes about everyday women and uncommon worlds.

Find her online at...
www.spajonas.com

facebook.com/SJPajonas

instagram.com/spajonas

bookbub.com/authors/s-j-pajonas

CPSIA information can be obtained
at www.ICGtesting.com
Printed in the USA
LVHW030129210323
742063LV00002B/564